Prai

My Big F

An Oprah's Book Club K

"This zesty page-turner will hook readers with romance and energy while addressing a woefully ignored subject."
—*Kirkus Reviews*

"Jamie is a strong, interesting character who grows over the course of the novel, recognizing her own contradictions. This is a powerful story for readers of any weight." —*SLJ*

"Thought-provoking and, frequently, vigorous."
—*Publishers Weekly*

"Jamie's character is so well drawn that readers will feel her misery. . . . The story is so well written that Jamie's agony is poignant to anyone, regardless of where one falls on the weight scale." —*VOYA*

"Writing from experience, Vaught explores the challenges of being branded different." —*New York Daily News*

"This painfully humorous novel is worth every penny."
—*St. Louis Post-Dispatch*

"Jamie will remain in the hearts and minds of readers long after the last page is turned. . . . *Big Fat Manifesto* is a winner!"
—*Teenreads.com*

My Big Fat Manifesto

BOOKS BY SUSAN VAUGHT

STORMWITCH

TRIGGER

MY BIG FAT MANIFESTO

EXPOSED

OATHBREAKER
WITH J B REDMOND

PART ONE: ASSASSIN'S APPRENTICE

PART TWO: A PRINCE AMONG KILLERS

My Big Fat Manifesto

Susan Vaught

BLOOMSBURY

NEW YORK BERLIN LONDON

Published by Bloomsbury U.S.A. Children's Books
175 Fifth Avenue, New York, New York 10010

The Library of Congress has cataloged the hardcover edition as follows:
Vaught, Susan.
Big fat manifesto / by Susan R. Vaught.—1st U.S. ed.
p.   cm.
Summary: Overweight, self-assured high school senior Jamie Carcaterra writes
in the school newspaper about her own attitude to being fat, her boyfriend's
bariatric surgery, and her struggles to be taken seriously in a very thin world.
ISBN-13: 978-1-59990-206-7 • ISBN-10: 1-59990-206-0 (hardcover)
[1. Overweight persons—Fiction. 2. Self-confidence—Fiction.
3. Interpersonal relations—Fiction. 4. Prejudices—Fiction. 5. High schools—Fiction.
6. Schools—Fiction.] I. Title.
PZ7.V4673Big2008   [Fic]—dc22   2007023550

ISBN-13: 978-1-59990-362-0 • ISBN-10: 1-59990-362-8 (paperback)

Typeset by Westchester Book Composition
Printed in the U.S.A. by Quebecor World Fairfield
3 5 7 9 10 8 6 4 2

All papers used by Bloomsbury U.S.A. are natural, recyclable products
made from wood grown in well-managed forests. The manufacturing processes
conform to the environmental regulations of the country of origin.

For Erin,
who helped set me free

When I wake up in the afternoon,
Which it pleases me to do,
Don't nobody bring me no bad news.

"Don't Nobody Bring Me No Bad News"
from *The Wiz*

BACK TO SCHOOL SPECIAL EDITION

for publication Wednesday, August 8

Fat Girl Walking

JAMIE D. CARCATERRA

I am so sick of reading books and articles about fat girls written by skinny women. Or worse yet, skinny guys. Tell me, what in the name of all that's creamy and chocolate do skinny guys know about being a fat girl?

The fat girl never gets to be the main character. She never gets to talk, really talk, about her life and her feelings and her dreams. Nobody wants to publish books about fat girls, by fat girls, or for fat girls, except maybe diet books. No way.

We're not even supposed to mention the word *fat* in print, because we might get accused of supporting "overweightness" and contributing to the ongoing public health crisis in this country [insert hysterical gasp here], or because we might cause an eating disorder.

To heck with all of that.

I'm a fat girl!

And I'm not just any fat girl. I'm *the* Fat Girl, baby. I'm a senior, and I by God do own the world this year, so put that on ice and gulp it down. I'm *The Wire*'s new feature—the Fat Girl Manifesto. I'm large. I'm loud. Go big or go home!

Let me shoot down a few myths right now, before you even set up a stereotype:

Myth Number One. Speak gently to poor Fat Girl. She can't help her terrible disability. Okay, bullshit. I'm not chubby. I'm not chunky. I'm not hormonally challenged or endocrine-disordered. I do not prefer platitudes like "large" or "plus sized," or clinical words like *obese*.

I'm fat, fat, fat. If the word makes you uncomfortable, that's your problem. Go to www.naafa.org and get a *real* education. Yeah, that's right. The National Association to Advance Fat Acceptance. *F-A-T*. That's the word. Get used to it. Get over it. I have to. Every single day of my life.

Myth Number Two. Poor Fat Girl needs to be educated about her problem. Even more caca, this time on toast. I'm not clueless about nutrition and exercise or waiting for that wonderful aha moment to motivate me to "lose weight." I know how to eat. I know how to exercise.

Guess what? I'm still fat, and blond, with so-so skin and big feet, just like my mom, my dad, and most of my relatives. We're the Fat Family. Or the Blond Bombers. Maybe the Psoriasis Clan? Oh, wait. The Bigfeet. Actually, we're the Carcaterras, and we don't apologize for taking up two seats on airplanes. Well, my mom does, but she apologizes for everything, so don't take that too seriously.

Myth Number Three. Poor Fat Girl laughs to hide her tears. More and more poop just piling up in the corner. I'm not a jolly round person. I'm a peevish, sarcastic, smart, dramatic round person. I'm larger than life. I've had roles in Garwood's stage productions all four years of high school. I'm playing Evillene in *The Wiz* this year, and the role sooo suits me. I helped start our cable channel that my friend Frederica—Freddie—Acosta anchors now. I'm *The Wire*'s feature editor. When Fat Girl laughs, it's because something's funny. Usually something *I* said.

Myth Number Four. Poor lonely Fat Girl can't get a date. Big blare from the bullshit sensor. My boyfriend's name is Burke Westin, he's a starting tackle on our championship football team, and we clear the floor at every dance.

Being fat isn't always like those sappy

after-school specials and snot-rag sob books. Not every fat person is twisted up about how their outsides don't match their insides.

Myth Number Five. All poor Fat Girl wants to do is lose weight. So not true. Fat Girl has a to-do list almost as big as her beautiful body. It goes something like this: Don't wonk the math section this next (and last) time you take the ACT, keep Burke happy, meet one thousand senior-related deadlines, play practice, and, oh yeah, the biggest one of all—finish college and scholarship applications.

Now we can get to the point. Why am I printing my manifesto in the school newspaper?

Pop quiz! No, don't panic. It's multiple choice:

A. I'm running for homecoming queen.
B. I want you to testify for me when I go postal on some stick-figure supermodel or that freak pedaling his exercise machines on late-night infomercials.
C. I want the world to get a clue about life as a Fat Girl, from a Fat Girl's perspective.
D. I want to win the National Feature Award, for "outstanding journalism

4

promoting the public well-being," a scholarship to the journalism program of my choice. My family doesn't have much dough, so that's the *only* way I'm taking the big ride to higher education. Otherwise it's work a job and take a few classes at a time. I want the scholarship!

E. All of the above.

F. None of the above.

G. Don't you wish you knew.

H. Hint: It's not A.

I. Hint, hint: It might be B. Depends on the night—and the supermodel.

J. Hint, hint, hint: C's a really good bet. But then again, so is D. In fact, D's major.

I'll give you reports on what Fat Girl has been up to, and I'll answer the questions you send to fatgirlscholarship@gmail.com. Write to Fat Girl and send her to college!

Come on. You know you want to do it.

CHAPTER
ONE

I have two must-achieve-or-die goals this year.

The first do-or-die is probably the easiest: Write the best Fat Girl feature series ever, expose the politics and social injustices of being a fat female in today's world, and win the National Feature Award to ensure my collegiate funding.

The second do-or-die, related to the first, is earning admission to Northwestern University. I would, of course, accept the University of North Carolina–Chapel Hill or one of the other amazing journalism/mass com programs in the country, but I'd rather be at Northwestern. As for the entrance application, Fat Girl plans to win them over, freak them out, or both. No matter what, I'll bring my fatness to the table as an issue, instead of as an auto-reject stamped across my application.

A third task, not a do-or-die, and probably the hardest, is surviving the absurd number of deadlines pitched at my head, all because I'm a senior.

For openers, there are deadlines for class papers and

assignments, deadlines for ordering our special senior edition yearbook, deadlines registering for the last-gasp ACT, deadlines for registering for the way-past-last-gasp ACT, deadlines for signing up for homecoming committees, deadlines set by those homecoming committees, deadlines for buying homecoming game and dance tickets, deadlines for filing intent to graduate, deadlines for ordering graduation invitations, deadlines for cap and gown measurements, deadlines for ordering class rings, deadlines for Senior Shoot, deadlines for senior pics, deadlines for early college applications, and deadlines for regular college applications.

And all of those deadlines happen *before friggin' Christmas*.

It's insane. But I'm a senior. Insanity must become my mantra.

Never mind the whole grades-still-count-until-Christmas thing.

Or the fact that my advanced biology and calculus grades are so not in the bag.

English IV and theater I could do in my sleep, and the rest is journalism. Piece of Fat Girl cake there, except for the midnight cram-the-paper-together sessions, then speeding it one hour south across the state line to get it printed at a cut-rate little print shop.

I'll be getting to do the paper run again this year, since I didn't make editor-in-chief. Nope. Of course not. The good-looking guy got that role. Heath Montel. His family's known for being old-money rich. His mother's on the school board, and he's always been immune to the standards the rest of us have to meet. Oh, and he's not fat.

Neither is our journalism sponsor. No real surprises there. I think Ms. Dax really just likes to watch Heath bend over the drafting tables.

As people go, though, Heath's not so bad, even for a rich, handsome type. He's just … a little weird. Kind of a loner. And I've done the paper with him so long it's like working with my own shadow. At least I snagged feature editor, which looks reasonably good on my NC–Chapel Hill application and gives me a full-bore shot at the NFA.

Know what Heath said about my first Fat Girl feature?

Good work, Jamie. But maybe you shouldn't have started so strong. That'll be hard to top.

No, seriously. He said that.

All he needed was a cigar, tweed pants, and suspenders, and Heath would have looked just like some 1950s version of Perry White from the *Superman* comics.

Okay, he's more than a little weird. He's hugely weird.

Editor–in–chief might be swelling Heath's pretty head, too, but I absolutely do not have time to worry about him, or about the fan mail and hate mail and question mail beginning to pour in after Fat Girl's first big rant. I barely have time to check on my best friends Freddie and NoNo, breathe, pee between classes, and stick to the senior obligations schedule I lovingly drafted for Burke and me.

. . .

"Burke!" I shove my way down Building Two's crowded hall at my lunch period, keeping my eyes fixed on the broad shoulders and thick dreads marking Burke at his locker.

Did he just flinch?

Oh, not good.

I slow down. Two scrawny freshmen bounce off my right arm, glance at me stricken with total fear, and flee into the crowd before I can grab either of them by their braided brown hair.

"Burke?" A little closer now, and he's definitely flinching. *Damn* it. What's wrong? Did he fail another earth science quiz? Because if he did, his average will suck and he won't be eligible to play next Friday and . . .

It seems like half the two thousand students at Garwood High are trying to cram into Building Two's hall, all at the same time. Wall-to-wall backpacks, blue jeans, chattering, hollering, hair gel, and sweat. Somebody has on bubblegum lip gloss, too. Gag. Bubblegum lip gloss would be illegal if I ran the world.

When I reach Burke, he turns to face me, but he only looks at me for two seconds before he hangs his head.

Big trouble.

His dark eyes, they usually sparkle. Today, they look like flat black plates.

I put my hand on his arm and squeeze. "What's wrong?"

He says nothing.

"Burke?" I scoot closer and try to look up at him.

This makes him grin, but the grin slides away. I have to push up on my toes to give him a kiss on his smooth, sexy cheek. Can't do more in the hallway, even though I'm Fat Girl, and I'm a senior. Our school's liberalism doesn't extend to sucking face in public. Garwood has a zero tolerance policy on all things sex, sexual, or even remotely physical between males and females. The way the ban's written, though, two lesbians or two gay guys could go at it naked and, technically, they wouldn't be breaking any rules at all. Nobody's tried that yet, but I've been offering to pay Freddie to give it a go.

"Come *on*." I bump Burke with my belly, glance around for teachers, then snuggle up to him. His arm drapes around my shoulder, and I love how heavy and possessive it feels. "It can't be *that* bad." Then, yelling over the squealing, screeching, teeming masses, "Right? Tell me it's not that bad."

"I'm grounded," Burke yells back.

Every single muscle in my body goes tight.

I didn't hear that. Can't be. Not possible.

Before I can say anything, Burke hangs his big head all over again, then bangs it against his already dented red locker.

I stare at him, feeling something like inferno mixed with ice storm. "No. Way."

"Sorry, Jamie." Burke bangs his head on his locker again as I shove some half-sized chick back toward her giggly girlie friends. "I got home too late Sunday night. The parental units imploded. I'm busted for at least a week. Maybe two, since I called one of my sisters a witch for telling on me, and Mom heard it."

Standing on my tiptoes again, this time to avoid the surging crowd, I wave my neatly printed, *perfectly* crafted senior obligations schedule in front of his face. "We have to shop for clothes for the Senior Shoot. And get our research cards done for midterm papers. And work on college applications. If we wait two weeks to get started, everything will snowball. We'll be screwed!"

Burke gives his locker a rest and me another grin, the kind that usually makes me smile back and forget why I want to kill him. "Don't go all Evillene on me. Sorry to bring the bad news, baby, but you'll have to do it without me. Take NoNo. At least you'll have fun—and maybe you can use it for your newspaper thing."

"Get real. I'm not clothes–shopping with Nora Nosten-fast. Never mind the whole vegan–animal–product-obsession thing. She's a size two, for Chrissake. And she's way busy getting ready for her next protest rally." I fry Burke with the you're–a–big–ox stare. "Besides, they don't make stores that sell both our sizes."

"Yeah. Exactly. It has shock value." He fastens the lock on his dented locker. The bell rings and he says, "Take Freddie, too, and some cameras and recorders. It'll be epic." He grins again, and I feel a little thawing in my icy glare. "You're so gonna win the NFA, Jamie. This'll put you over the top."

All right.

Fine.

I let out a breath, and let go of the Evillene persona. Evillene's the jazzed–up wicked witch in *The Wiz*, the character I'm playing in this fall's production. We tried out last year and rehearsals started a month before school. She and I have *way* too much in common sometimes.

And Burke the big ox does have a point.

Just going into a store with NoNo might be serious Fat Girl fodder, if she has time, and if I can get her to agree to the hidden camera and recorders so we can immortalize the reactions of the salesclerks. That's no sure thing, however. NoNo gets way seriously freaky about cloak-and-dagger stuff. NoNo gets way seriously freaky about many, many things, especially animal products. But she's a lock for early decision acceptance at two Ivy League schools come December, so what the hell does she *really* have to worry about?

Burke grabs my hand, then plows us through the rest of the people trying to beat second bell to class. He doesn't hesitate to bash people out of our way, and what with all the screaming from idiots flying in every direction, most underclass fools take a hint and make room.

He drags me all the way down Building Two's corridor—against the crowd flow, no less—until we get to the entrance of the journalism suite. Just inside the door, he pulls me aside and lays a big one on me, right on the lips, right against school policy.

I don't wear bubblegum lip gloss. Mine's vanilla. Big-girl flavor, for the big girl and her very big boy.

"You taste good," he whispers in my ear, over the catcalls and whistles ringing from the hallway.

Burke smells like sandalwood and oil and leather and everything guys are made of, and for two seconds, he makes the world completely go away. Sometimes I wish I was smaller, just so Burke could hold me closer. I feel shielded when he touches me. Safe and comfortable and absolutely relaxed.

When he lets me go, I give his ear a brush with my fingertips, because I know he likes that. He salutes me, wishes me luck with Freddie and NoNo, then takes off to his class before second bell can ring.

I watch him charge down the hall until he's out of sight, smiling like a giant goofball.

Okay, so I can't stay mad at Burke even though I know he is stranding me on the shopping trip from hell, because that's what any shopping trip with NoNo will be. I could go with my family, of course, but throwing myself from the Building Two roof has more appeal.

So NoNo it is. And if I beg Freddie, she'll come, too, even if her ulterior motive is to grab a major school cable-news piece, and watch NoNo wig out and drool all over a major high-end store.

.   .   .

The cafeteria seems more crowded and hotter than usual, but that's probably because I'm worried NoNo won't cooperate. We're sitting at a back table near the door, in the section the seniors stake out and defend vigorously, and nobody's too close to us. I think they can tell we're tense, and when Freddie, NoNo, and I get agitated, people scatter.

"Does Hotchix sell animal products?" NoNo jabs at her homemade trail mix of nuts, cranberries, and something purple and kind of square and squishy-looking. I have no idea what the purple square squishy stuff is and don't want to ask. I probably can't pronounce it anyway.

NoNo's muscles tense, making her skinny arms look that much skinnier, poking out of her Greenpeace T-shirt. "If they sell animal products, I don't want to cross their threshold. This cafeteria is compromise enough for one lifetime."

13

Freddie, in a green designer dress that costs more than everything in *my* closet, lets out a groan loud enough to be heard over the lunch clamor. "Hotchix is probably full of leather and fur—but that's why you *want* to go in. We'll get 'em three ways from Sunday, on everything you can think of, in print and on the cable news." She manages a bite of cafeteria mac-and-cheese without getting a smidge on her dress. A skill, truly. One I don't have.

I'm not eating. I haven't eaten in front of people since fifth grade, when I got tired of the staring, even from the teachers. When I was younger, I used to throw fits and scream, or cry and try to explain that even though I was fat, I still had to eat a meal here and there. Then, slowly, I got to where I just didn't feel hungry if other people were around to watch.

"Please, NoNo?" I give her my best-friend gaze. "We need your body type to make the point, and we'll totally back you up on the animal-products angle."

NoNo chases around some of the purple squishy things with her fork. She glances up at me with those wide green puppy eyes, and her cheeks flush pink underneath her big brown freckles. Her red hair is shorter than most of the dykes Freddie knows, because she's donated it again, this time for cancer-kid wigs, I think.

"All right. I'll do it." She shivers. "But no animal products touch my skin."

I grin.

Freddie grins bigger. I can already see the wheels spinning in Freddie's newswoman brain, about how to play this, and play it big. She'll have some major ideas.

14

I foresee hidden cameras.

Social discomfort.

Sociopolitical commentary.

Animal products and by-products.

Yeah.

I wonder if NoNo is still taking pills for her nerves.

By the time we finish this little exposé shopping trip, NoNo will need some kind of medication. That much I know for certain.

. . .

By the time Freddie drops me off at home after play practice and newspaper stuff, it's nearly midnight, and my folks are already asleep. Mom's left me a sweet little note about not working too hard, and she's left me a plate, too.

I rip off the foil. Beans with greens and cornbread, and mac-and-cheese way better than anything the school could make. "Poor man's feast," my dad calls this meal. It's his favorite.

And I'm totally starving from not eating all day long. Just the sight of the food makes my stomach ache and rumble, and I eat it way too fast…everything on the plate and left over in plastic containers in the fridge, too—not that there's much, because my dad polishes off a lot, trust me.

I finish with five or six cookies. Just a few, even though I want the whole bag.

I'm trying.

I really am trying, though I'm not totally sure why.

It never really matters.

REGULAR FEATURE

for publication Friday, August 10

Fat Girl Pornographing

JAMIE D. CARCATERRA

That got your attention, didn't it?

Quit being a pervert.

I'm not talking about the oh-so-illegal-at-this-school sex thang. I'm talking about the third definition of pornography, according to the *American Heritage Dictionary of the English Language,* Fourth Edition: Lurid or sensational material.

Yeah, that definition. The one that gets lost in all the body parts and grunting sounds, especially in perverted minds like yours. Mind out of the gutter now? Good.

I think we all agree that dirty pictures, whatever the degree of dirtiness, probably qualify as lurid and sensational. Next down the ladder we have scenes of gory death like in stalk-and-slash movies or "real life" accident footage. There is definitely something wrong in a society where sex flicks get trashed as illegal, but snuff flicks make billions at mainstream movie theaters.

Then we have the more insidious—that's sinister, subtle, or menacing for all you can't-read-above-fifth-grade-level types. Like pictures of bloody streets and dead gang members and hysterical relatives screaming and waving their hands. That's lurid, and definitely sensational. Usually, newscasters say something about racial violence or poverty or God knows what, but behind them, blood and pain stain the television screen.

My friend NoNo and I think shots of Holocaust victims can be pornographic. Shock value. Exploitative. It depends on how they're used—to commemorate and honor the dead is one thing, but to do that "Face of Death" thing, that makes me totally sick. Ditto photos of civil rights workers who didn't survive. What they did matters, sure, but so often these pictures are pornography, used without regard for relatives, friends, or other people who might be devastated by the images.

So far, I think we might be agreeing on what constitutes pornography, in that third definition way. Now, I'll probably piss you off.

Let's talk about the endless television

news reports about obesity, featuring big jiggly bellies and fat waggling butts walking down the street. Fat bellies just strolling along, like they have some right to be in the world. They never show faces or eyes or mouths or opinions or thoughts. Nope. Just the bellies and butts, with a sound bite about what the obesity epidemic is doing to our nation or our health-care system or whatever they're hyped up about that day.

And worse—a whole new level of worse—health broadcasts showing fat people eating. Shoveling in those high-fat foods. Or shots of half-ton people flopping around in their beds or getting hauled to the hospital on slings and hoists usually used to lift whales for transport.

Why isn't this pornography?

Simple answer: It is.

It's designed to maximize the horror and disgust felt by people less fat than the bellies and butts. It's designed to make you say, "Jesus God, how can they *do* that to themselves?"

I'll tell you what it really is, though. It's spectacle. It's lurid. It's way past sensational.

It's pornography.

If the evening news wants a jiggling belly shot, hey, I'll go volunteer—but I'll get my say in the process. Tattooed across my swaggling giant butt will be the phrase: GET A FRIGGIN' CLUE.

Across my belly, you'll read: I'M STILL A PERSON.

Surprise. Did you know that? Does that matter to most viewers? Does it matter to you?

It doesn't matter to the pornographers.

Stop the exploitation.

Stop *all* pornography.

CHAPTER
TWO

Freddie, NoNo, and I stare at the glitzy storefront window of Hotchix on Wednesday afternoon, at exactly 4:30 PM. It'll make for a tight deadline given the paper goes to press Thursday, but play practice usually goes short on Wednesdays and I've got my homework in reasonable shape. We've already spoken to all relevant adult obstacles. No worries, though. We have the blessings of Principal Edmonds (*Yeah, stick it to the man—I mean, the woman—whatever—stick it to somebody*), Ms. Dax (*Bold journalism, girls*), our parents (*Don't you dare get arrested*), and his editorialness Heath Montel (*I like it. It's got ba—uh . . .*).

Freddie supplied the word *ovaries*, by the way, with an appropriate you-are-such-a-caveman glare.

Hotchix is *the* store, of course.

One thousand square feet of haute couture, teen-style. All the best girls get their hot threads from Hotchix, but I have never seen a Hotchix model who has any body fat.

The three of us gaze into the window of glamour as

the rattle-tattle thunder of the south end of Garwood Supermall washes up and back like a psychotic tide. All the
noise echoes the waves crashing in my brain.

NoNo looks like her brain went on holiday last week,
but NoNo often looks like that. It's deceptive. As for Freddie, well, her brain's probably busy picking out escape
routes for when NoNo finds animal products and starts
screaming and throwing things. Freddie's been best friends
with NoNo and Burke since they were little kids. I met
them all six years ago, when my family moved to Garwood.

Since NoNo's in such a wad, Freddie keeps peeking
over the top of her sparkly sunglasses and fiddling with
the jewel-studded earpieces. Any second now she'll dislodge the wires to the voice-activated MP3 recorder Heath
hot-wired into her prized shades—forget about the tiny
wireless cam crowning the V-neck of her purple lace and
muslin dress. With her silky black hair piled into a perfect
princess up-do, Freddie looks more like a fashion-runway
escapee (from a country with body-fat requirements for
their models, because honey, Freddie's got hips) than a co-
conspirator, but she's the biggest activist I know. Other
than me, of course. And NoNo. Buuu-uuut, NoNo's
"causes" run a little different from the mainstream—or are
at least more extreme.

I'm wearing my usual, a size 4X loose-fitting shirt with
a blue skirt. It's way easy to hide cameras and mics all
over me, though Heath thought my curly blond hair was
probably the best place to tuck wires.

You have the thickest hair, he had told me while he
worked with his big hands behind my ears.

21

That had made NoNo snicker, and made Freddie kick NoNo, at which point NoNo said a few words NoNo doesn't normally say. Freddie can do that to a person.

As for NoNo, she's in her usual attire, too. Bright blue hemp jeans and a dye-free colorgrown red striped T-shirt reminding me of that kid in the *Where's Waldo?* books, only lots less vivid. We had a hell of a time finding anywhere to hide anything electronic on NoNo, but she agreed to wear a bulky hemp necklace and carry a bag, after we proved it wasn't leather or any other product derived from animals or animal testing, and made in a country that does not use child labor.

We argue again for a few seconds about who should go in first and decide on Freddie, since she's sort of middle ground. Too big in the hips for a lot of Hotchix stuff, but not totally off their snubby little planet. Then we wait until the store's empty except for the saleswomen.

Freddie erases her usual serious, intelligent expression, the one that she uses when she's Ms. News Anchor on the Garwood High cable station, and walks into Hotchix.

NoNo and I watch as fashion hell swallows Freddie whole.

My breath catches in my chest—the group of clerks look like they might turn rabid and eat her.

Don't panic.

Have you lost your mind?

Probably.

I check the button on my recorder, then NoNo and I watch Freddie rifle through the racks and hold up a few items. The cluster of saleswomen glance one from the other. I see a sneer or two, and one whispers to the lady next to her. That lady takes about a minute to head over to Freddie.

That's NoNo's cue. Strands of her very short red hair stick to her pale, freckled forehead as I give her the go-on thumb jerk.

NoNo blinks. Swallows hard. "They have *so* many animal-based products in that store, Jamie," she whispers, like anyone but me could hear her over the dull roar of the mall.

"Nothing will bite you, I swear to God." I resist the urge to shove her forward. "We're *exposing* them, remember? Just think of how you can use all the animal stuff in your column."

Of course she writes for *Green Revolution*, the city's underground conspiracy rag, circulation twenty. Maybe twenty-five. But NoNo seems to take strength from this idea. She straightens to her full height, almost five feet ten inches, and heads into Hotchix.

She doesn't even get to a clothes rack before all three remaining saleswomen move to engage her. The one who reaches her first looks close to our age, but I figure her for midtwenties. All of them look about that old. Hotchix probably has hiring profiles, screening for girls with a youthful, thin, chic appearance.

NoNo's victorious clerk is busy yanking things off hangers and out of stacks and loading them into NoNo's scrawny arms while the other four saleswomen wander back toward the registers.

It's my turn now, baby.

Get ready, Hotchix. Here I come.

Over the threshold and through the door.

The aroma hits me first. Leather and cotton, with undertones of cedar. It smells new inside Hotchix. And young. And, as much as I hate to admit it, *good*. Didn't expect that, but okay. I can take it. Should have figured on some unknowns, since I don't go in stores like Hotchix very often, even to shop with NoNo or Freddie.

In real life, I'm relegated to Diana's and the West End, and lately, as I've gotten a little larger, just to Diana's. Diana's smells like old-lady perfume, and they sell lots of lime green and bright purple stuff for "mature, shapely" women, which I've never quite figured out. I don't fancy myself as a giant grape. Do older fat women cherish looking like grapes? My grandmother made my blue skirt. At least she gets the whole no-grapes-please thing.

NoNo's high-pitched voice lifts over the top-ten soundtrack blasting through the store as she asks if the jacket the clerk just loaded on to her try-on stack is real leather. Freddie's head turns, calculating the location of the exits. She locks eyes with me for a few seconds, then goes back to picking out an outfit or two with her bored saleswoman.

The clerk with NoNo assures NoNo it's faux leather and keeps piling on options.

Of the two available salesclerks in Hotchix, neither of them comes toward me. They study me, though, and I catch each expression on camera. Surprise, annoyance, then eye-rolling. Mild disgust, followed by a head-to-toe check of my body, and more obvious disgust. They stop looking at me and start talking to each other.

I catch bits and pieces of what they say.

... *Not sure why* she's *here.*

Can't be to shop . . .

Bet her boyfriend can't wait to get some of that . . .

Maybe buying a gift. You go.

No friggin' way. You.

This I'm ready for. I've heard it more than once. Lots, in fact. Which is why I shop at Diana's, where the clothes make me look like a grape.

The women at the register give me a few more snide expressions, then ignore me. Seems like the bigger I get, the more invisible I become. Another fifty pounds, and I'll be an outright ghost.

Freddie and NoNo, who are not ghosts, head toward the fitting rooms with their sales associates in tow. While they're gone, I go through three racks, all full-price stuff, and two different tables of shirts.

No one says a word to me.

The clothes *are* hot, damn it. Especially the stuff with tassels and bangles and wild designs. So much attitude. My taste, no question. It bugs me I can't wear any of the colorful, fresh things I touch, that the gods of clothes making don't mass-produce stuff for Fat Girls. We're what, three in ten now, stats-wise? But stores like Hotchix would rather ignore us thirty-percenters. Guess our money doesn't spend as well as Freddie's or NoNo's.

Still nothing from the clerks, except snickers if I handle something especially small.

After about ten minutes, like we planned, I wave at the counter huggers. "Hello? Excuse me? I'd like some assistance."

My two victims glance at each other. I swear if I hadn't been watching, they would have drawn straws or done rock-paper-scissors. The nearest clerk moves from behind the counter, but I think she got pushed, judging by the way she stumbles. By the time she gets to me, though, she's smiling and chirpy and sales-y and trying oh-so-hard not to rake my large body up and down, up and down, with her big blue eyes—and probably working twice as hard not to roll them halfway back in her head. With her spiky blond hair and the way her cheeks and lips puff out, she reminds me of a blowfish. Her nametag says *Pepper*.

Now it's me working not to roll my eyes. "I'm hunting for something in white with blue highlights," I tell Pepper the Blowfish as I gesture to my top region, the biggest part of me if you don't count the hips. "To match my skirt."

My smile would rival any beauty pageant contestant's, especially as Pepper the Blowfish goes crimson around the gills. "We—um, in this store, our biggest size is thirteen. *Junior* thirteen."

"Okay," I say as brightly as I can. "Give me the largest shirt you've got, and I'll try that."

We can drop the Pepper. She's all Blowfish now, and she hesitates. "We don't have anything that will fit you. Why don't you try—"

"Diana's?" I keep the brightness. "No thanks. Diana's is

for old ladies." I gesture to my face. "I'm large, but I'm not old. I'd rather try here and take my chances."

"We don't have anything you can wear," Blowfish insists, this time more slowly, and a little loud, like I might have a mental problem.

The woman at the register stares now.

"Why don't you let me be the judge?" I ask Blowfish. "Just find me a shirt to match my skirt."

She puffs out her cheeks, and I swear the spikes on her head get a little taller. When she turns her back on me and stalks over to the rack, the other saleswoman laughs outright.

Blowfish storms back over with a size 13 white short-sleeve number with the *best* blue wave pattern sweeping from shoulder to waist. When she holds it out to me, she frowns. "This is it, the largest in the store. If this doesn't work, nothing will."

I keep smiling as I take it from her and head to the fitting rooms.

From behind me she calls, "You break or tear or stretch—you buy."

The other clerk laughs again.

I hear something about me finding a tent store. How original. Don't they ever come up with new insults?

Blowfish doesn't follow me.

From her dressing room, NoNo says, "I really think *cabretta* might mean animal. I'm not sure I'm completely comfortable putting this against my skin."

Both clerks in the fitting room set about reassuring NoNo—lying wherever necessary—about what she's trying on. They tell her how *marvelously* everything fits her, and encourage her to try more. Some of the ensembles. What about shoes? Necklaces to match?

Freddie's slipping by the wayside, probably since she has big hips. She shrugs at me and traipses back into her fitting room to retrieve her actual clothes. I wonder if the clerks even notice that Freddie's own outfit probably cost more than two-thirds of what Hotchix has for sale.

Me, I'm something past invisible now. I drift into a dressing room, close the door, and hang the beautiful shirt. Three mirrors show off my size from various angles. Even though I know I'm large, it digs at me, especially since I don't really fit in the fitting room. I bump walls as I turn, position the cameras to miss anything they shouldn't see, and work on taking off my clothes.

I hate undressing in fitting rooms. I know most are monitored by cameras I *can't* position or, worse yet, actual people. If somebody's on the other side of those mirrors, they're stereotyping and laughing at me—about how I'm deluding myself, about how I have no idea how big I really am or I'd "do something about it."

I think about what I had for breakfast. Boiled egg, grapefruit, toast with just a little bit of butter. My stomach growls, since I won't eat again until I get home. I wanted lots more at breakfast, but I refrained. Not that refraining matters. I might lose five pounds, but I gain them back just as fast, plus a few. Five pounds means nothing at all.

Damn, I'm hungry.

I'm stripped down to bra and skirt now, staring at the gorgeous shirt. My own smell fills the dressing room. A little vanilla from my shampoo and conditioner and body spray, but mostly it's sweat and kind of a sweet but not too nice scent, like dough. I don't sweat a ton, but enough that by afternoon I'm noticeable if you get too close to the pits or other areas. It's a real problem when I'm in costume for plays at school—my dressing counter is full of sprays and creams to reduce the moisture and smell.

Nothing much works.

Even skinny people sweat, the director tells me. But I'm not stupid, and I don't look away from the truth. I stink worse because of my size. And in the dressing room mirrors, the smell takes on an almost visible shape, coating my rolls and folds. Burke calls them curves, like my parents, and my friends too.

But in these mirrors...

Like I said, I don't look away from the truth.

I'm here for the story. Don't forget the story.

I actually worry about wounding the beautiful shirt, but I take it off its hanger and pull it over my head. I even manage to get my arms in, though I stretch the fabric as far as it'll go. I can't even begin to pull it down over my boobs, much less my belly. The color's perfect for the skirt, but I'll never see that amazing matching blue pattern on *my* body.

For a few seconds, I just breathe and sweat and wait for the red to leave my cheeks. I guess I'm red because I'm hot and breathing hard and maybe embarrassed. The camera doesn't need to see that. I lift up my bag, pull out the little wireless lens, and make sure I get my stuffed-sausage

SUSAN VAUGHT

arms. I get the strangle-neck, and the fact the shirt won't come down over the rest of my upper body.

"These are my choices," I whisper for the microphones, in case Freddie wants to use it on her cable show. "Diana's and the giant human grape look, or clothes that fit like this. In a store where I should be able to buy something right for my age. This is my life, in a white-and-blue-sausage, strangle-neck nutshell."

Then I put down the camera, take the shirt off, hang it back up, and brush it back into shape as best I can. It takes me a minute to get my clothes back on, to get my wires and mikes and cam repositioned to walk out, and another minute to realize I'm crying.

God, but I despise trying on clothes, even in this store, where I knew what would happen.

Get a grip.

It's not your fault the fashion world uses plastic dolls for design models.

Get . . . a . . . grip.

I sniff, which sets off Freddie, who must have been lurking close enough to hear me. I never sniff, so she knows what that means. She reaches over the door, feels around, and snatches the shirt. The hanger clatters against the door.

"Excuse me," she says to somebody I can't see, since I'm still in the dressing room. Then louder, "Hey, chica. Listen up, if you can quit slobbering over stick-child there for a minute. Yeah, you. Do you have this in a larger size?"

This wasn't in the plan. Not in the script. We're done.

30

We should just be leaving now. But Freddie's getting louder.

"No? Well, why not? Don't you realize thirty percent of the girls in this town—probably more—can't buy your stupid clothes?"

I snatch my things, bang out of the dressing room, and try to grab Freddie's shoulder, but it's too late. She's gone red in the face, and with Freddie, that's *not* because she's hot or breathing hard or embarrassed.

"What?" Freddie yells at the collection of saleswomen now clogging the fitting room hallway, Blowfish front and center. "Jamie's supposed to shop at that old lady place, right? Not bother you and your precious little small-people store. Well, here's a clue. Life's a bitch, and so are you!"

And then, as if to bring the wrath of heaven down on Hotchix, Freddie shouts, "*Cabretta* is most definitely meat. You've got sheepskin touching your bod, NoNo."

NoNo's brain-vibrating scream makes the saleswomen cover their ears.

"No! No! No! No!" She keeps screaming and starts pitching stuff over the dressing room wall like she's got spiders crawling all over her and the clothes and the dressing room, too.

"No! No!"

Then she runs out in her bra and panties, freckles flaring, knobby knees knocking. She starts mumbling, and I'm not sure what she's doing, but I think she might be praying. Only the clot of saleswomen in the door keep NoNo from charging into the supermall half-naked.

"You lied to me!" she screeches at the clerks, who back away, I figure to call security. NoNo throws the "faux" leather jacket. It snags on Blowfish's hair. "No! No! Filthy, animal-killing liar, liar, liars!"

It takes us a few minutes, but we get NoNo dressed, drag her out of Hotchix before anyone in uniforms (or white coats) shows up, and exit the Garwood Supermall.

Freddie's still fuming as we strap NoNo into the front seat of Freddie's old Toyota, determine that she has no nerve pills, and decide to tell her mom to take her right back to that shrink she used to see for her phobias and panic attacks.

"Those women were so obnoxious to you, Jamie." Freddie opens the back door for me, and I crawl in and use the seatbelt extender she got me a long time ago to fasten myself in place. "I mean, they were bad enough with me, but what they said, how they looked, how they acted—Goddess, I knew it would happen, but I wanted to kill them *all!*" She yanks off her designer shades and checks the mic wires, then plucks the little cam off her shirt. "Hope this stuff registered. They are so gonna pay. I'm making this story one, leadoff."

Before I can answer, she pins her eyes on me in the rearview mirror. "You okay, right?"

"Yeah," I say, making my voice as loud and boomy as possible, even though for some reason I still want to cry, and I definitely want to crush the little cam that got all those pics of me in that pretty, pretty shirt with that delicate little pattern that I will never be able to wear. Not that it would be delicate on me anyhow.

But the world needs to see. I have to make them understand. And I have to win that damned scholarship.

As NoNo finally settles and starts sucking down her leftover decaf soy frappuccino (we never let NoNo have actual caffeine, never, never, never), Freddie cranks the car and says, "Want to go to Burke's?"

"We can't." I lean back as Freddie touches up her usually perfect hairdo. "He's grounded for coming in late and calling his sister a witch. Didn't he tell you?"

Freddie's hands freeze on her hair. She takes a few sharp breaths, then turns the Toyota right back off again. She swivels all the way around in her seat, until we're eye to eye. Her expression gives me a total chill.

"Is that what he told you about why he couldn't do stuff this week—that he's grounded?" She turns back around and bangs her hand on the steering wheel. "That coward-ass piece of shit, I swear to God I'll kill him."

My mouth falls open, and that chill turns into an uncomfortable numbness. It starts in my feet and spreads up my back and neck, all the way out to my hands and fingers.

I don't need to be a Sherlock to realize Burke has lied to me big-time. I can read it in every line on Freddie's smooth olive face. I can hear it in the frantic way NoNo's sucking on her frappuccino.

They know something I don't. Something major, and maybe something bad. It happens sometimes, the three original Musketeers sticking together and leaving out the fourth. Me. Only it hasn't happened since Burke and I got serious.

Burke *hasn't* lied to me since we got serious. Not that I know of.

Is he in trouble for something else? Going on some secret trip?

Is there another girl? God knows he takes enough shit from his sisters over seeing a white girl, even if that white girl is me and they used to like me. They just don't like me dating Burke.

"He's...not grounded?" I ask, feeling thick-tongued and a little unreal.

The world separates itself from me as I have a moment of sensing life-without-Burke. Which would be nothing. No life at all. No dances, no dates, no kisses, no hugs.

That can't be. It can't be that kind of lie.

Right?

The Wire

REGULAR FEATURE
for publication Friday, August 17

Fat Girl Fuming, Part I
The Hotchix Revelations

JAMIE D. CARCATERRA

Check out these pics. [insert image of saleswomen here; make Blowfish prominent]

These women did not want to sell me a shirt.

Why?

Because I'm fat.

And Hotchix clearly doesn't want fat people wearing their clothes. [insert image of me in the dressing room]

In fact, they didn't want to wait on me at all. And they had plenty to say, trust me, as if Fat Girl doesn't have ears and can't get her feelings hurt just like the next girl. [insert image of snottiest expressions]

Ask any Fat Girl you know, or any large guy for that matter. They'll tell you what it feels like to walk into a store like this and be glared at like you're nasty rotten gum on the bottom of somebody's pointy-toed witchy-poo shoe.

But before you go picketing outside Hotchix, know two very important things. First, Freddie Acosta already told those women off, and once you've been told off by Freddie, trust me, there's not much left to say.

Second, Hotchix is nothing special, nothing new, and definitely not alone. A few years back, a big clothing designer—who used to be fat himself, by the way—actually had a little snit when some of his creations were manufactured in "larger sizes." (Uh, like size 14? That's sooo large.) "What I created was fashion for slim, slender people," he said.

Seriously.

If you don't believe me, look it up.

So, many—maybe most—of the major designers don't offer "large sizes" (large being defined seemingly at random). If they do, it's only online, not in the brick-and-mortar stores. So, my friends and I, who are all different sizes, can't go clothes shopping together, even for the Senior Shoot.

Never mind the fact that large sizes are lots more expensive, so for those of us not rolling in dough, it's Diana's and the West

End or nothing. And I'm sorry. I'm too cool for Diana's and the West End. Besides, the air just doesn't smell good in there.

I need more options. I need real clothes I can actually wear and afford. I need a blue shirt with a wonderful pattern to match my skirt.

Is that impossible?

According to Hotchix and some clothing designers, I guess it is.

CHAPTER
THREE

"Nothing's bothering me," I snarl into my cell as I fold my column and tuck it into my skirt pocket. "I just got Fat Girl done. This one's gonna kick some ass."

Heath Montel stays quiet on the other end for a few seconds. I can hear him breathing. Imagine him sitting at the big brown desk in the journalism suite, talking on that ancient black phone with the handset and cord, and running his hand through the blond hair that hangs in his eyes. "You sure you're . . . okay after all that?"

No, I'm not okay. Everything sucks right now because my boyfriend's a rotten liar whose probably cheating on me, and Freddie and NoNo are freaked, and I'll never wear that pretty shirt, and now you called in the middle of everything.

Out loud, managing to keep my tone even and calm, I say, "I'm fine."

"Okay, good." Heath lets out a breath. "I was worried about you. That the whole Hotchix scene might have been—I don't know—traumatic, or something."

"It was for NoNo." I give her a glance to be sure she's

breathing normally. She is. Big relief. "She got way upset by animal skin. I owe her the best vegetarian meal ever, at some green restaurant that recycles everything."

Freddie nods.

NoNo sighs and fiddles with her recycled straw.

My grip on the cell eases, and I realize my hand's sweating. "Freddie came through okay, too, except the store clerks pissed her off."

Another nod from Freddie. A snicker from NoNo. Heath, too.

"I'm sure she'll handle them on her cable show. *That* I'm looking forward to." Another pause. Like Heath really doesn't want to hang up, but knows he should. "Will I see you tonight, Jamie? For layout, I mean."

Quick glance at the watch. My heartbeat picks up when I see I've only got about forty minutes to get back to the school. "*Wiz* practice is seven to eight thirty. I'll be there as soon as it's over."

"Okay, good. That's good."

Weird.

But then, Heath's weird all over, so that's no real surprise. I don't have time to figure him out right now. We're almost to Burke's, so I tell Heath good-bye, punch the phone off, and slide it into my pocket.

Freddie parks her car.

We get out and march up the sidewalk like a stiff, angry army.

The minute Burke opens the big double doors of his fine, fine house on the hill, he knows he's toast.

What with the three of us standing there, me with

arms folded, Freddie with hands on hips, and NoNo half-choking on her chewed-to-death recycled frappuccino straw, he can hardly miss that fact.

He doesn't even try to talk. He just lets us in and says, "Can we keep the screaming down? My mom's asleep."

His mom supervises the night shift at Garwood Hospital, and we all love her, so we nod. Then we stalk inside and make a quick visual check for Burke's sisters.

They're both in college, but they live close by—and visit a lot. They're a little hard to deal with, especially where baby-boy Burke is concerned. I'm glad neither of them is hanging around, claws extended, fangs at the ready. If I'm going to kill Burke for lying, I don't need any witnesses who won't help me hide the body.

He ushers us through their big living room and takes us into the fancy, stainless-steel kitchen, where he's chowing on a major plate of nachos and a two-liter bottle of Coke.

Guys.

I swear.

Haven't any of them heard of glasses? Or silverware?

We sit at his family's big round table, Burke between Freddie and me and NoNo on the far side, where NoNo just seems to belong. She plants her hands on the smooth maple and her expression says she'd rather die than keep sitting there, but she keeps sitting. Maybe the cheese on the nachos is bothering her, or the sour cream, or the upcoming conflict. With NoNo, it's hard to tell which phobia or fanatic belief has taken center stage.

As for me, the rich, spicy smell of the nachos bumps

against the tight knots of anger and dread in my belly, and I feel a little sick. For a few seconds, I look at the ceiling, at the cabinets, at the nachos, out the window—anywhere but directly at Burke, the boy who is supposed to be the love of my life.

It's dusk now, and the lights of Garwood, spread out below Burke's house, start to flicker and twinkle. The lamp over the table gives off a soft yellow glow, and his kitchen widescreen is set on the NFL Network. Of course. He taps a button on his remote and mutes the sound as Freddie gestures toward the nachos.

"Last meal?" she asks, sounding way harsh, even for her.

The little knots of anger bouncing in my belly turn colder and start to quiver.

I stare at Burke's handsome face, at his sad eyes and big frown.

Is something wrong with him?

NoNo says, "Fred, you're being mean." Then, "We shouldn't even be here. This is between Jamie and Burke."

Freddie cuts NoNo an evil glance. "It's all of us, okay? *All* of us. Nobody gets out of this in one piece, I'm betting."

"Freddie," Burke starts, but I stop him by putting my hand on his and looking him straight in the face. When he starts to hang his head, I pinch his fingers tight in mine.

"What's going on?" I ask, intending to sound forceful, but my words come out like a mouse-whisper.

Burke fidgets, but doesn't take his hand out of mine.

41

"I've been wanting to tell you, honest. I just couldn't figure out . . . didn't know . . . I can't—"

He hangs his head again, and I give him another pinch to bring him back to me.

This time, when he meets my gaze, he seems so sad I want to kiss him. But behind the sad, there's this weird sort of excitement, kind of like a fever.

I'm not sure I've ever been so scared in my whole life. And I don't like scared. I hate scared.

"I don't know how to tell you, Jamie," he murmurs.

"Oh, for shit's sake, Burke," Freddie snaps, "try words. Words usually work."

"Stop," NoNo instructs Freddie, a little louder this time, and, surprisingly, Freddie does stop. She fiddles with her dress and her falling-down updo, flops back in her chair, and spends her energy glaring at NoNo instead of hollering at Burke.

So I'm waiting now, to hear the worst.

He's cheated on me.

He's in love with some other girl.

He got some girl pregnant.

He has some disease.

Oh, God. He gave *me* some disease?

With each passing second, I want to kiss him more, or kill him faster. I can't decide.

He closes his eyes. Opens them. Opens his mouth, and says, "I've decided to have the surgery. I've been doing the counseling part, and I went in this afternoon for the start of the pre-op workup. Surgery date's in about a month."

For a while, probably a long time, I don't move or say anything at all, because I can't.

Of all the things shooting through my head, this so wasn't on the list.

Inside my stomach and brain, something like a riot breaks out. I feel like I can hear my own heart beating, screaming, shouting, and his and Freddie's and NoNo's and somewhere upstairs Burke's mother's heart, too.

Thumping.

Just blood in my ears, thumping away. My throat's so dry I want to drink a lake, or maybe a river, or even a beer, except I hate beer.

"You..." I finally manage as my hand slides away from his. "You can't."

Burke hangs his head one more time, and I let him.

"Oh he can, too," Freddie says. "And his parents and skinny-ass sisters are all behind it. He won't listen to me or NoNo or anybody."

The surgery, my brain echoes.

I know what he means.

And I just can't believe it.

Burke's about to have weight-loss surgery. He's going to get banded or stapled or tied or ballooned or whatever it is. He's going to let doctors cut him open and risk his life and give away his senior year of football to...to what?

Shop at the male version of Hotchix?

"I'm academically out of football," he says to the tops of his knees, as if hearing part of my thoughts. "Besides, this is more important."

43

When he does look up, that fever has taken over his features, making him almost unrecognizable to me. "Jamie, I don't want to be fat anymore. When I graduate, I don't want to be a big black elephant just lumbering across the stage. I want—I want to look buff. I want to look *good.*"

"You're a god now," I say, trying to figure out who I'm talking to, who this alien being is, that's taken over Burke's body, my boyfriend's body, and plans to change it in ways I can't even begin to imagine or understand.

"I'm a god to you. But not to myself."

"To me—isn't that enough?" I turn my chair to face him straight on. "Burke, does my opinion count for anything?"

"Okay, yeah, we shouldn't be here," Freddie says to NoNo as they both stand up. "We'll, um, be in the car, Jamie. As long as it takes."

I barely notice them leaving, except for NoNo dropping her chomped frappuccino straw on the tile floor of Burke's kitchen. The slobbery piece of red recycled plastic seems to bounce in slow motion, and I wonder if I lost my sanity five minutes ago, and how I'll ever get it back.

Burke's talking before the front doors even close, but I'm not hearing all of it. Just pieces.

"...nothing to do with you, with us, I swear, I just didn't know how to tell you. How to convince you it's what's best for me." He cups my cheek, then runs his fingers from my cheek to my chin while I can't move and wish I could cry and tell him to stop or slap him or something. Anything.

"You'll be my goddess, no matter what, Jamie. You

know that, right?" He leans forward and kisses me, but my lips don't move.

This backs him off.

He shakes his head and sighs. "I knew you'd be like this. All mad."

"Mad?" My own voice sounds like it's coming from Mars. "That's what you think I'm feeling?"

A breath. Two breaths. He doesn't interrupt me. Smart boy.

"I'm mad you lied." Still on Mars, but getting closer. "I'm mad you decided all this without talking to me. Yeah, I'm mad. But Burke, I'm—I'm scared. That's what I really am."

"No fear, baby. I'm Burke Westin." He opens his arms. "Nothing's going to happen to me."

"You're black," I say.

He lowers his arms, surprised. Then he glances down at himself and back up at me. "You just noticing that, Jamie? Because—"

I finally do smack him, hard, right on his muscled shoulder. The *pop* jars me back to earth, and the pain in my fingers gives my voice new power.

"Black people die from this surgery, Burke."

"White people die from it, too." He rubs his arm where I hit him, but smiles at me in that way that always melts me.

Not tonight. I'm melting in a different way already. I'm dissolving.

"I know white people die from it!" I pop his arm again. "One in two hundred, and that's only counting patients who die on the table or right after they get the surgery.

You *know* those surgery centers manipulate statistics. Lots more people die in the first year after bariatric surgery. One in twenty. Maybe more!"

Burke starts to say something, but I cut him off.

"And you're black, so you're *three times* more likely to die from it—and the doctors don't even know why." This time I don't hit him. I grab his arm and squeeze, then just hold tight, feeling the warmth of his skin against my cold, shaking fingers. "Don't do this. Don't."

Burke peels my fingers off his arm, then holds both of my hands in his. His big, strong hands that cover mine so completely. "I've thought about all that, I swear. And read about it."

"You? Read something other than *Sports Illustrated* and *ESPN Magazine*? Be real." I laugh, but only because I'm fighting so hard not to cry.

"Hey, my American lit grade is aced." He fakes being wounded by my words. "I'm young. I'm obese and borderline diabetic, but otherwise, I'm pretty strong and healthy. I don't smoke. I know how to exercise. My mom's a nurse. My dad's CEO of a self–help company— and my sisters are friggin' drill sergeants in training. Hell, you'll be a drill sergeant. I've got a lot going for me, Jamie. A lot that says I won't die." He grins. "Black or not."

He leans forward, and we go belly to belly, chest to chest, with only the chair arms between us as we kiss.

Slow. Not deep. Just soft. I love his lips.

I love the feel of him against me. His size. His strength. The way he makes me feel little and dainty and protected, yet still big and powerful, all at the same time.

Damn him.

Does he think kissing me will shut me up?

When he pulls back, his dark, dark eyes are misty and wide as he gazes into mine. "I'm gonna need you, Jamie. Say you'll be there. Say you'll still love me even though I'm doing this."

Damn *him.*

"I hate you," I say out loud, then take it back, and finally do cry, and he scoots forward in his chair to hold me.

He lets me get snot all over his shoulder, and tears, then lets me curse him a few times before I promise I'll still love him even if he does this stupid, stupid thing. I promise I'll be there, too, provided his sisters don't rake out my eyes or put some sort of unbreakable sister–curse on me.

Then Burke says, "I know you're gonna write about this in Fat Girl. I want you to. It might help people, maybe even help you get that scholarship. You deserve it."

A little more snot. A few more tears.

"Promise you won't run out on me, Jamie." Burke's voice drops low, thick with need and hope and fear and that weird, scary fever.

I really wish his nachos would fall into a hole and die before they make me vomit.

"I won't run out on you," I whisper. "I promise."

REGULAR FEATURE
for publication Friday, August 24

Fat Girl Fuming, Part II
The Hotchix Revelations

JAMIE D. CARCATERRA

I've got lots of reasons to fume. If I listed them, you might fume, too, or freak out. But first, I need to congratulate Freddie for her school cable-news piece on Hotchix. Another congrats to NoNo Nostenfast, for surviving contact with animal flesh and doubling the circulation of *Green Revolution* with her outraged account of the life-shattering experience.

Hotchix, well, their corporate offices have yet to respond. *Big* surprise.

Which brings me to the psycho clothing industry in general.

Hey, fashion freaks! Answer me one question. What the hell size am I? Go ahead. Measure me. Enlighten me.

Can't do it, can you? Because there are no standard clothing sizes in this country. Even NoNo the stick-bug wears a 2 in some clothes, a 4 in others, and still larger yet, a 6 in some brands (provided they have no animal parts or child labor involved). Part of this is just normal variation in styles and fabrics. But part of it is much more sinister. A plot. Seriously.

A nationwide marketing plot called "vanity sizing."

Even though most everyone in the United States is getting bigger, sizes are getting smaller. Cheesy retailers figured out that when women feel good about themselves, they buy more. So, the simple solution is to inch down the size on the label, even though the garment really isn't any smaller, and voilà. Women feel better about themselves even though their bodies haven't changed at all, and they buy more clothes.

Some retailers are even coming out with "double zero" and "subzero" sizes. How can somebody be a minus size, for God's sake? Are we that desperate to believe we're thin? Thanks to this kind of crap, I have no idea what size I really am, except that for sure I can't wedge my curves into *anything* at Hotchix—even though I'm a hot chick.

Here's what I do know:

- Most grown women in the United States, and most older teenage girls, wear size 12 or larger, however you want to measure it.

- The standards for what little standard-size clothing there is for women in this country were developed in the 1940s. Yeah. Over sixty years ago.
- Designers stopped using standard sizes because we so pathetically need to feel thinner. Clothes come in straight sizes, extended straight sizes, plus sizes, and now superplus. Never mind the whole women's, misses, junior, etc., categories. The difference? Who knows? Fat Girl doesn't. Most skinny girls don't know either.
- It goes something like this. "Straight sizes" (not a comment on sexual orientation) are designed using models supposedly "normal" in weight and height, but the industry had to stop calling them normal when they realized over 40 percent of women in this country wore sizes larger than those.
- Plus sizes tend to be less form fitting, especially up top and in the hips.

Now, we could argue for years over where "plus" begins. According to those my-clothes-are-for-skinny-people designers, probably anything over size 6. According to many other designers, it's size 12. According to most sane humans, it's 16 to 18 and above.

All of this adds up to some very important truths.

Guys, give it up. You can't buy clothes for your girlfriends. Sizes won't help you, and you'll invariably buy the wrong thing and piss her off. Sound familiar?

Girls, get real. Do you really know what size you wear? Even more important, do you really know why it matters *so much* that somebody would create subzero sizes?

Fashion industry people, stop the insanity.

United States of America, wake up!

And Fat Girl . . .

Well, Fat Girl, in all her fatness, may have fewer body-image issues than people who wear "normal" sizes.

CHAPTER
FOUR

In the windowless brown cinderblock cave that is our domain, Heath Montel leans over the drafting table next to me and doesn't say a word as I snip and arrange my post–Hotchix Fat Girl feature into its assigned spot. We've got three desk lamps blazing over the layout, but half the ancient fluorescent bulbs in the high ceiling fixtures above us are burned out. Useless. And we can't get maintenance to change them, and we don't have a ladder high enough to do it ourselves. It's hot, too. Hot enough that some of the old articles taped to the walls are peeling off or sagging.

When I glance at Heath, his blue eyes seem sharp, awake, and focused as he edges in sports headlines and a breaking piece about a health department investigation of an *E. coli* outbreak traced back to spinach our cafeteria actually served. I squint to see if the spinach was cooked or raw, not that it really matters, but my brain's been sticking on stupid things since I found out about Burke's surgery.

I feel weird.

I don't feel like me.

I don't feel like Fat Girl, either.

I'm not sure what—or who—I feel like, and I don't want to figure it out. It just makes me mad. Everything's making me mad. Even the music Heath's playing makes me want to scream. Retro rock. Usually my favorite. To-night it sounds like *clatter* and *bang* and makes my hurt-ing head hurt worse. I'd turn it off, but I'd screw up Heath's rhythm and mind-set, and we're too close to deadline for that. If we don't get the rag finished and driven down to the printers by tomorrow morning, it won't come out on Friday.

Ms. Dax would just love that. About one less letter grade's worth, I'd bet.

"Screw her," I mutter.

Heath doesn't so much as twitch when I talk to myself. His blond hair hangs forward over his forehead, and his tan seems smooth in the harsh desk lights. He's not on a Garwood team like Burke, but he looks like he's into sports. Maybe he plays something outside of school.

I've never asked.

God, I'm such a bitch.

When Heath and I talk, it's always newspaper, news-paper, newspaper. But damn it, he seems so . . . so . . . calm. Even when we're down to deadline. I hate him for being calm. I hate him for being tan. I hate everything. Except maybe Burke and NoNo and Freddie. And sometimes my family.

"We should get a grant like drama did for the cable

retro radio. The radio with the busted antenna. It's probably forty years old, that radio. Heath won't replace it, either.

Why? It works.

Idiot.

At least I have a cell phone, when I'm not grounded
from it. Heath doesn't even have that. He says it's because
he doesn't want to be that connected. Maybe it's a money
thing, even though his family is supposed to be rich. That
I could really understand, given the way my family struggles with the budget. My mom calls it being "overextended." I've heard people say that about the Montels,
too. That they're overextended.

I guess being rich—or looking rich—isn't so easy.

I wipe my forehead. It's hot, and I'm still tired from
play practice.

Do I stink?

God, don't go there.

I've been thinking about stinking lots more since the
whole Hotchix dressing-room nightmare, and I really
don't want to stink up the room and gag out Heath. Not
that he smells like roses himself. If he lifts his arm again, I
might have to faint on general principle. Except Fat Girls
never faint. Fainting is for delicate skinny girls.

Am I feeling delicate?

No. More like exhausted. I don't think I've had a good
night's sleep in the two weeks since Burke's big announce-
ment about his surgery. I could so easily go face first on
the layout table and start snoring. The smell of glue and
developer makes my eyes—which still have glitter stuck all
around the edges from the makeup chick practicing on me

about Burke, and thinking about Burke makes me want to cry. And I'm not friggin' crying, especially with friggin' green glitter still stuck to my Evillene eyes. Instead, I sing along to the retro. Three Dog Night, I think.

Heath sings, "The window. The window. Throw her out the window." Then he starts another nursery rhyme, and it always ends with throwing whatever's in the rhyme out the window. Mary and her little lamb, Humpty Dumpty, Georgie Porgie—doesn't matter. They all go out the window. He told me once about the group who did the song. Trout Fishing in America. Only Heath would know a group named Trout Fishing in America.

A few minutes later, I realize something's wrong and tear my attention from the drafting table, even though Heath's layout looks good.

The problem is, he's stopped singing, and so have I. There's only the radio, playing some old Meat Loaf song now.

I turn my head to find Heath looking at me. His hand's resting on the Fat Girl feature, and he's just looking at me.

"What?" I open my palm and almost drop my X-Acto.

He glances down at the piece, then back to me. "This is really good stuff, Jamie. You know that, right?"

I clench the X-Acto in my fist like I'm planning to stab something or, worse yet, somebody. "Uh, thanks. Your spinach–diarrhea piece is a work of art, too."

Heath frowns, and when Heath frowns, his whole face gets into the act. "I'm being serious. You've got real guts, putting this stuff out there. Putting *yourself* out there for people to take their shots."

57

"I've gotta have that scholarship." I manage to lower the X–Acto, but my hand's shaking.

Heath gives me a half–angry look, like that wasn't his point, but then his face relaxes and he nods. He goes back to looking at my part of the layout.

I go back to proofing his section, but I can't concentrate. The radio's pissing me off so badly I want to hurl it against the concrete block wall. Stupid thing probably wouldn't break.

"So he's really gonna do it?" Heath's voice flows underneath a Beatles song. "Burke, I mean. A couple of weeks ago when we talked on the phone, you were really upset, and then I heard he's not playing football. And there's this rumor—he might be having bariatric surgery?"

"Yeah." I squeeze my eyes shut, then make myself open them. I wish the radio would die. I wish I had never heard the word *bariatric*. I wish Heath would shut up.

"I feel like I should say something," he says, ruining all my wishes at once.

My teeth don't come apart when I growl, "Like what?"

Heath smacks his X–Acto and highlighter down on the drafting table. He braces himself with both arms and looks straight ahead, away from me. "You don't have to be such a bitch all the time, Jamie. I'm trying to be nice."

"All right, all right." I make a point of putting *my* X–Acto down gently. "This is me not being a bitch. What do you think you should say about Burke's surgery?"

Seconds pass.

They feel like long, miserable days, but I'm not being a bitch, so I keep my mouth shut.

"I don't know." Heath turns toward me a little. "I mean, I guess—I'm sorry. I know you've got to be worried about him. Like you need all that angst and freaking out on top of everything else we've got going this semester."

My bottom lip trembles.

I really hate Heath now, because he just said more than Freddie (*I don't want to talk about it but you need to*), NoNo (*It's his decision*), and my family (*That's the stupidest thing I've ever heard*) all put together.

Heath made the tears come.

All of a sudden I'm blubbering like when I was a freshman and got stung on the nose by a bee, and I really do want to faint or fall down or just...quit. Completely quit.

Instead, I sit down on the linoleum tile floor and lean against the wall, with the drafting tables and the newspaper layout above my head like a big, woody, gluey print umbrella.

Heath sits under the tables beside me, so close his leg touches mine. A few seconds later, he actually offers me a handkerchief. A real one. White. The damned thing's monogrammed with a curly *HM* in the corner.

This makes me stop crying and roll my eyes.

"It's my dad's," Heath says. Then he laughs. "It looks stupid, but it holds the snot. That's what matters, right?"

"Are you really rich?" I blurt.

Heath leans back and rests his head against the concrete block wall. His shoulder presses against mine as I actually use his stupid monogrammed hanky to wipe my eyes and nose.

"No," he says. "Not anymore. But my parents haven't ac-cepted that yet. My dad's company is downsizing and he's losing his job. Mom's gone through her trust fund. Our house is up for sale, but they're trying to keep it quiet."

Oh great. And here I was, trying not to be a bitch. "I'm sorry."

"I'm not." Heath launches into an explanation about dwelling size and SUVs and wasting energy that reminds me so much of NoNo I actually wonder if I should get the two of them better acquainted.

Before I can even wrap my brain around that little plan, he asks, "Will you deal with the whole Burke's-bariatric-surgery thing in Fat Girl before some asshole writes in and asks about it?"

Good point.

Very good point.

I use the hanky again. "Probably. Yeah. Definitely. I should."

"You are so getting that scholarship, Jamie. I know it. I feel it."

"Thanks."

"You should have been editor-in-chief this year, just so you know." Heath's tone is matter-of-fact and relieved, like he's been waiting weeks to say this.

"Yeah, well, that was never going to happen."

"Dax didn't do it because you're fat or anything. She just likes guys better."

"Duh."

He laughs.

And that makes me laugh again. Then cry a little more.
I've definitely entered an alternate universe.

We keep talking about college at first, then scholar–
ships and the clock ticking down on the National Feature
Award.

Then we're chatting about other stuff.

He plays soccer in a city league.

I've never touched a soccer ball, but I've always
wanted to.

He thinks I sing better than the chick playing Dorothy
in *The Wiz*. She played the lead in last spring's *My Fair Lady*
and he didn't like her then, either.

I tell him how I wanted that role but couldn't have it
because, of course, Dorothy isn't a Fat Girl. Fat Girls are
always villains in plays. At least every play I've been in.
Villains or mothers or grandmothers. Once I got to play
Mother Nature, though. At least that costume was way
past great.

"Maybe I'll write a play for you," Heath says. "You can
be Dorothy and do all the damned singing. How would
that be?"

I turn my head toward him a little and find myself
looking into his blue eyes and tanned face, and a quirky
smile I'm not sure I've ever seen before.

It's nice.

And I'm still in that alternate universe, but sliding
slowly, slowly out of it.

"If you write it, I'll sing it," I say, intending to sound
loud and goofy, but my words come out quiet. "Swear."

He keeps me pinned with those blue eyes. "Okay. One day, like twenty years from now when I finally have time to get it done, you're so gonna regret saying that."

On the radio David Bowie sings, "Ground control to Major Tom."

Heath reenters the atmosphere before I do. "Listen," he says in a more normal Heath voice, kind of flat and distant and who-cares. "I'll take the paper to the printer, okay? You get some sleep."

"Are you serious?"

"Yes." He holds out his hand for his hanky.

I ball it up in my fist. "Uh, I'll wash it first, okay?"

That quirky smile sneaks back for a second. "Fine. Good idea."

He edges out from under the table and stands, and I follow him. My legs feel shaky, but they hold me up.

I'm at the door of the cave, with Heath's monogrammed hanky still balled in my fist and my hand on the door frame when I ask—without even turning around—"Heath, do I stink?"

What the hell did you just do?

Are you nuts?

Of course you're nuts. Friggin' delirious.

Now he'll have a ton of questions.

But he doesn't.

He just says, "Nope. Most of the time you smell like vanilla."

And that's that.

And I leave, before I can make an even bigger idiot out of myself.

REGULAR FEATURE

for publication Friday, August 31

Fat Girl Answering, Part I

JAMIE D. CARCATERRA

Dear Fat Girl:

I don't understand why you're doing this column. Do you just want to embarrass yourself?

I'm doing this feature because of people like you, for people like you, and because I want to bleed enough on paper to win the National Feature Award. It *all* goes in my final portfolio. And of course I don't want to embarrass myself. I'm *not* embarrassed. Better look in the mirror on that one.

Dear Fat Girl:

Do you glory in being fat?

Would you? Duh. No. I don't glory in being fat. I just am. Am fat. It's a fact of my life, and before all the "obesity epidemic" hoo-ha in the news, it was a fact I didn't have to think about every minute of every day.

Dear Fat Girl:
Is being fat an eating disorder?
It can be, but compulsive overeating is not officially recognized in any diagnostic manual or by any insurance plan I know of. God forbid. If it got recognized by anybody other than people like Fat Girl, somebody might have to design and pay for treatments that really work.

Dear Fat Girl:
Do you think fat people get discriminated against?
Absolutely. But I don't know where I stand on whether or not we should be discriminated against in some situations. We take up more space and cost more money. It's just a fact of life.

Dear Fat Girl:
Have you tried any of those diet plans I've seen on television?
Probably all of them, if they didn't cost money. I don't have the bucks for glitzy systems. And people who need to lose five pounds—die, die, die. My left boob weighs more than you.

Dear Fat Girl:

What do you think about gastric bypass surgery?

I'm so not going there right now. Lots of people die. Dying is *not* on Fat Girl's consideration list, for me or anyone else. Just shut up about gastric bypass surgery until I say otherwise.

Dear Fat Girl:

Obesity is a serious health problem for our whole nation. Are you trying to deny that?

Obesity can be a serious health problem. However, there are a lot of conspiracy theories about the current news frenzy being driven by the diet industry. This would be the same diet industry that makes billions for doing nothing to help and usually making things worse. Apparently, the diet industry funded some, maybe a lot, of the studies "raising the alarm."

Then there are the conspiracy theorists who say all the obesity-isn't-so-bad articles are funded by the billion-dollar food industry.

Probably a little truth to both.

Read the bloggers. Read the scientific articles. Make up your own mind.

CHAPTER
FIVE

"Again!" barks Mr. Dunstein, our director, starting every-body over on Act I. Everybody calls him dog names behind his back, because he looks so much like a nervous little lapdog, with his comb–over brown hair and giant eyes, and the way he twitches and hops around the auditorium, yapping at everyone.

I'm sitting just offstage in a wobbly folding chair while the freshman idiot doing makeup practices on my eyes *again*. She's stuck them together twice already. I don't know how she's ever going to get her act together before opening night, but I swear she'd better not glitter–glue my lids shut that night.

When I've had all I can take, I push the makeup girl aside and pull on Evillene's big hoopskirt. Dunstein wants me to wear it every rehearsal so I get used to the width and movement, and look natural and comfortably evil on opening night.

Then I go sit on my throne, which is for now behind the last curtain, facing downstage.

I so like sitting on my throne. Especially when it's not my turn to make an entrance. I listen to the action, and figure I've got ten minutes before anyone yanks on my chair, so I slip out my cell and dial Freddie to check on her. Another girl dumped her three days back, and she's been down.

Freddie answers with, "Fashionista Services. If you can't spell muslin, you're so last year."

"M–u–s–l–i–n." I shake my head. "I can spell crinoline, too. I'm on my throne. In my hoops."

Freddie's snort makes me hold the cell away from my ear but I hear her say, "Get 'em, Evillene."

Keeping my voice low so Dunstein won't catch me talking during practice, I murmur, "You feeling better today?"

"Shit, yeah." I imagine Freddie waving her hand back and forth, all attitude. "I've had ice cream. I've run three miles to get rid of the ice cream. I even got NoNo to stand in Mickey D's while I fortified with a milkshake." She lets out a breath. "Now I need to run again, don't I? Damn."

The lightness in her voice makes me suspicious. My stomach tightens. "You've already got another date, don't you?"

Pause.

Laugh.

"Well, *yeah*. Nobody keeps me down for long, Jamie."

I roll my eyes and wonder how much glitter that underclass fool stuck to my lids and cheeks. "Just promise me this one doesn't already have a girlfriend. Or a record."

"She's clean, I swear. And she's only twenty. I met her at the bar last weekend. Thought she might be interested . . ."

And Freddie's off, telling me all about this girl. Who sounds a lot like the last girl, but that's okay, because Freddie's happy again, and that's what counts. As for NoNo, if Freddie made her go to a fast-food joint, she's probably home showering, to wash off all the negative energy. My stomach loosens. All's right with the world again. At least for my friends.

"Cue the witch!" Dunstein hollers, and I tell Freddie bye in a hurry.

My throne lurches as I cram my phone back in the pocket of the skirt I've got on under the hoop costume. It lurches again, moves a few inches, and I arrange myself.

Hey, sitting in a hoopskirt is not easy.

By the time the chair jerks again as the prop guys drag me toward center stage, I've got my witch-smirk firmly in place, my left hand held up beside my face, my whip raised in my right hand, and the hoops around my legs instead of over my head. Small triumphs.

"Three, four, five," the prop guys are counting, pulling on six to keep everything smooth.

Think evil. Think evil. Think evil.

Breathe. Two, three. Breathe. Two, three.

Keeping it even. Keeping it calm.

The throne glides.

Well, it rolls on wheels, but to the audience, it'll look like it's gliding.

My music's starting, soft and low in the background.

No Bad News. Think evil.

I breathe more, deeper, getting ready to sing.

The prop guys swing the throne around to face the audience.

Only it doesn't stop where it's supposed to.

The auditorium chairs spin by in a blur.

My brain whirls with the throne.

I drop the whip. Swear *really* loud, and fall against the flimsy wooden throne back. Something cracks. Hoops fly up and smack me in the nose. Fabric sticks in the glitter paint left by the underclass fool.

"I swear I'm killing her," I shout over lots of other shouts as my throne creaks and groans, bashes one prop guy sideways, and almost flattens Dunstein before two more prop guys and half the cast get it under control.

"No Bad News" blares from the orchestra pit—recorded, not live, like it'll be on opening night. We don't start rehearsing with the orchestra section of the band until next week.

"Where's my whip?" I fight down the skirt and hoops and find myself face-to-face with Dunstein.

He's purple. His jaw's working hard.

"Whip?" I ask again, not worrying about Dunstein. He always looks like this a month before we open, when stuff goes wrong.

And it *always* goes way wrong, until about a week before the curtain goes up.

Somebody pops the whip handle into my outstretched hand.

"Again!" Dunstein bellows.

I tuck the whip between my knees and hold tight as

the prop guys yank my wobbly throne backstage for another go.

. . .

Freddie picks me up from play practice around 8:00 PM, and it takes me most of the drive home to scrub glitter off my eyes. Thank God for cleansing cream and Freddie's stash of junk cloths (kept mostly for me), or every bit of that itchy makeup would have been wiped on my expensive Diana's blue two-piece dress.

NoNo's belted in the front seat holding some *Ecology Justice Democracy Nonviolence* fliers. "I'm hand coloring the Green Party logo," she explains as we pull into my driveway. She taps the upper left-hand corner of the stack of papers. "Printers wash out all the vividness."

"What-ev-er," snipes Freddie. She parks behind our car—we only have one, a Ford even older than the antique Freddie inherited from her sister—and shuts off the engine with a slam-and-jerk. A buzzer beeps, so she slams off the headlights and we get out of the car.

Lights from my house spill across our tiny front yard, and I smell fresh cornbread and something rich and buttery and meaty. Brunswick stew. My stomach rumbles. I could eat my weight in cornbread and stew, and I will eat in front of Freddie and NoNo at my own house—just not very much, even though they're my best friends. I'll have a bowl, maybe. No seconds. Even though I worked my ass off at practice.

"I'm for dinner." Freddie sniffs the fragrant air. "Apps can wait long enough for us to grab chow, right?"

"Your mother is such a good cook." NoNo clutches her flyers against her dye-free T-shirt and hemp jeans as I unlock the front door. "Do you have any lettuce?"

"Yeah." I knew she wouldn't touch the stew (meat) or the cornbread (buttermilk, eggs, grease on the skillet). "And three cans of vegetarian beans, just for you."

We let ourselves in and weave through the stacks of junk my mom keeps in the front room, "just in case we need something." She never throws anything away, which comes in handy sometimes, but mostly gets on my nerves. Freddie and NoNo never mention the mess in my house.

I'm not sure if that's good or bad.

At least my room's fairly clean, and we make Mom keep her stacks out of the hallway.

Mom greets us in the kitchen with a big hello and hugs.

"Dinner's on the stove." She's wearing her gray hair pulled back in a bun, and when she gives me a squeeze, she smells like fresh soap and powder. As she lets me go, she glances at NoNo. "I'm so sorry I made something with meat. We'll get your beans from the cabinet. I—um. Yes. Sorry, sorry. We do have some lettuce, and there might be some raisins in the fridge."

NoNo grins at Mom. For some reason, NoNo always smiles at my mother even though she rarely smiles at anyone else. The two of them head to the far cabinet, with Mom babysitting the fliers while NoNo gets her food.

"Your mom's a saint," Freddie whispers when only I can hear her. I roll my eyes and stop looking at Mom, because she has on blue sweats like my dad, with lots of stains and holes. *Home clothes.* No way would I put mine on until my company leaves, even though my bra and underwear dig trenches in my shoulders and legs.

I wish my parents wouldn't wear their old sweats in front of my friends, but that's a lost cause. I know I'm as big as they are, but I do my best to look clean and put to-gether. It's sort of a fat person imperative—or maybe just a Fat Girl imperative. Never look sloppy because every-body expects fat people to be slobs. I completely refuse to be a stereotype.

But my parents...

It's our house, Jamie, they've told me when I've asked. *We're going to be comfortable in our own home.*

Mom's a secretary at a car plant where they have to wear uniforms that barely come in her size. Dad works for a freight company delivering packages, but at least his uniform fits. They're tired and sore when they get home, and I know what they think about home clothes at home, so I don't bother saying anything.

Mom's stacks of junk terminate on either side of the kitchen table, and Freddie and I steer around them to get to the bowls and the stew. A small television flickers on one cabinet. Dad stays glued to some game show, but he nods and waves. Dad's eating out of a mixing bowl, and he has three pieces of cornbread stacked on a plate beside it. Mom doesn't have a bowl. She never serves herself un-til everyone else is finished.

Freddie and I dip stew out of one of the two pots bub-bling on the stove and snag the last pieces of cornbread dumped from Mom's cast-iron skillet. Another skillet finishes and the timer goes off before we get spoons and napkins. Mom slips past us to rescue the cornbread. NoNo's beans *ding* in the microwave, and she's found enough lettuce for a small salad with raisins and no dressing.

"Yuck." Freddie's voice cuts beneath the game show hollering, echoing my exact thoughts. "Who eats plain lettuce with raisins?"

Behind us, the television volume goes up, and Dad says, "Yes!"

"Has anybody ever told you plants have feelings, too?" Freddie asks as we cart our spoils out of the kitchen, down the hall to my room, and close the door behind us—which still doesn't totally tamp out the game show. "They react with all kinds of plant endorphin stuff when you slice them or tear them or whatever."

"That isn't a scientific fact." NoNo balances her bowl of beans and plate of lettuce *and* her spoon without dropping her stack of fliers as she plops her bony butt on my ugly brown carpet. "It's still being studied."

From the kitchen, the game show *bing-bing-bings*.

Freddie settles on the floor across from NoNo and puts her bowl on the old squished shag carpet, too. Her cornbread's mashed up in the liquid, the way she always wants it. "Well, if they ever prove plants feel pain, are you going to starve yourself to death?"

"Of course not. I'll consume nuts and fruits collected after they fall from trees." NoNo looks at Freddie like she's stupid, which compared to NoNo, she is. So am I. Everyone is.

"Oh, God." Freddie gestures for me to help, but I ignore her eyeball crossing and think about going back to the kitchen and smashing the loud television.

Instead, we listen to background noise from an appliance commercial.

I hand Freddie the half-finished application packets for Vanderbilt and the University of Ohio that I've been keeping on my desk so she wouldn't lose them. "Do you think that would make a good essay topic? Plant-pain research starving vegans to death?"

Freddie and NoNo blink at me without speaking. NoNo crunches on her lettuce and raisins. Freddie gulps a mouthful of stew.

I eat my cornbread in a hurry, grab a few sheets of paper and a pen and settle myself on the floor where I can prop my tired back against the desk. "Seriously. I keep coming up empty on my Northwestern essay ideas."

"Aren't you going to do something from Fat Girl?" Freddie shrugs. "What about that column on pornography? It's great."

After a bite of warm, rich stew, I say, "That's going in my portfolio. All of Fat Girl is. I've got to write something fresh, something new."

The stew swirls inside my mouth, all the way down to my belly. So good. I eat it in quick spoonfuls, loving the meaty taste, wondering how NoNo survives without animal products or by-products. Outside my door, the game show revs to life again with clapping and yelling and bells ringing, and lots of bouncy music.

NoNo gobbles another leaf of lettuce, then fishes her crayons out of a box she keeps under my bed. She'll use crayons because all art supplies for children have had to be toxin free since 1990, so long as they aren't imported from China, which doesn't have those safety regulations. "But you could still do a Fat Girl piece, just one you aren't using in the paper."

"I don't know. It doesn't show much range." I suck in more stew.

NoNo gives me a stern look, if that's possible with crew-cut red hair and a mouthful of beans, raisins, and dry lettuce. She swallows hard. "It shows dedication to a cause. That's important, you know."

She has a point. And she has a 33 on her ACT and straight As, and she'll probably have acceptances to every college she's considering. Why would I argue with her?

My stew's gone in a minute or two, but so is Freddie's. NoNo will be eating her dinner all night. She takes a while with food.

Screaming from the game show, a moment of silence, then a loud, bellowing used-car ad. I know it's probably killing Dad's hearing. He'll be deaf by the time he's sixty.

"I think you should write something about Burke and his gastric bypass." Freddie doesn't look up, and I see her muscles get tense in case I start yelling like those used-car sales guys. I sort of have every time she's brought up the subject.

I've talked to Burke about his surgery, but that's a little like talking to a zealot about religion. It bothers me, that wild sparkle in his eyes, when he talks about being "normal" soon, but what can I say to him? It would be nice to magically be normal. I can't deny that.

"The stuff with Burke, it's private," I grumble, trying not to think about Heath and his warning that I need to put my feelings about Burke's surgery in *The Wire* before people start writing in to ask about it.

"Nothing's gonna be private for long," Freddie shoots back. Her olive cheeks tinge red, and for once, her black hair isn't hanging frizz free around her face. It looks a little messy, like she's picked at it. "He'll be out for weeks, and when he comes back, he'll be shrinking like crazy."

My jaw clenches, and I have to force myself to stop gritting my teeth. Whenever the subject comes up, I just want to cry. "It's private for now, okay?"

Freddie gets a stern expression that's much worse than NoNo's. "He goes under the knife in a little over two weeks, Jamie. You can't pretend it's not happening."

"I can until they roll him away. He could always change his mind."

We all go quiet.

The television in the kitchen doesn't. Somebody won big money.

Freddie, NoNo, and I all have the same look on our faces about Burke changing his mind on the gastric bypass.

The look says, *Yeah, like* that's *going to happen.*

No matter what we want, no matter how we feel, short of divine intervention, Burke is having that surgery. I glance down at my belly-spread and the way my thighs look bigger than NoNo's whole body, at the awful brown "landlord carpet," and finally at the blank essay paper. All proof that God has never been too fond of answering *my* prayers.

Freddie shifts tactics faster than I can work up a good feeling–sorry–for–myself attitude. "Are you going to the hospital even though Anastasia and Drizella will be there?"

"Damn straight." I can't help grinning at Freddie's Cinderella's wicked stepsisters' nicknames for Burke's older siblings. Their names are really Mona (oldest) and Marlene (meanest—as in, she really could drink blood and take over the vampire world with no guilt at all), M & M for short.

"Good." Freddie scratches something on her Vanderbilt application. "We'll be there too. Early."

Which draws a horrified look from NoNo, who views hospitals as vile pestilence–spreading ecohazards—but she knows better than to argue with Freddie and me about something this important.

After a few seconds of trembling disgust, NoNo closes her eyes, opens them, and looks at me. "When's opening night for *The Wiz*?"

"October sixth," I say, then fish around for something witty and Evilleneish to keep it light. Find zero. Nothing. My brain is flashing *almost three weeks after Burke*, but I shake it off. Burke isn't going to die on September 18. He'll come out of the operating room just fine, except his stomach will be stapled into two parts, with the food–getting part about the size of my thumb.

He'll feel full after two tablespoons of food, especially at first.

I've done my reading.

The thought of a thumb-sized stomach, *two tablespoons*, completely freaks me out. I like to eat. Especially if something tastes good. I like to eat until I can't eat anymore, if something's perfect, like Mom's stew.

My hand goes to my belly, until I realize Freddie and NoNo are both staring at me. I jerk my hand off my stomach and stuff my fist into the brown carpet. "I don't want to talk about Burke's surgery." All of a sudden, my stew isn't sitting well inside. My arms and legs and chest tighten, and it gets hard to breathe. "Tonight, I just want to finish these damned applications, okay?"

Freddie gives me another shrug and scrubs her palms against her jeans before going back to her Vanderbilt application. NoNo lowers her head and colors Green Party logos on her fliers.

Through the end of one game show and the start of another, I stare at my blank paper and reswallow the stew that's burning up my throat. My chest pulls and squeezes whenever I try to breathe.

The only thing I can think about is Burke and Burke dying and Burke not being in the world anymore. Even if he survives, our world will change so much. Our world together, I mean. We won't be going out for pizza anymore after he has that surgery, or sharing a milkshake and fries, or anything much to do with food at all. He probably won't even eat popcorn at the movies, and he definitely won't be scarfing down his absolute favorite: four plain chocolate bars, snapped in half, two bites per half. That box of chocolate bars I keep in my closet just to take candy to him—it'll have to go.

Two tablespoons.

Tighter chest. Blank paper. What am I going to put on the blank paper? I have to put something there.

We can always go to movies with no popcorn, or find other stuff to do. Get a grip. He said you were his goddess. He asked you not to leave him.

But I'm scared.

Burke's scared, too, at least somewhere in those glittery–zealot eyes, or he wouldn't have been worried I'd leave him.

Me leave him?

Stop it. Not thinking about it. Applications only, at least for to-night.

On my blank pages, I write *TWO TABLESPOONS.*

Then *THUMB.*

And glance at my thumb. And at my big fat belly.

Thumb.

The sounds of a weight–loss commercial drifts down the hallway. One of those advertising the newest fabu-lous miraculous, lose–fifty–pounds–in–one–week pill. The kind with the writing at the bottom in two–point mi-crotype that flashes by so fast you'll blink and miss it. If you freeze–frame and whip out a magnifying glass, it'll say something like:

These claims have not been evaluated by the United States Food and Drug Ad-ministration. Do you think they would touch us with a ten-foot research beaker? This product does not treat, cure, or prevent any diseases or medical conditions. Taking this pill does not guarantee you'll lose weight, but we know you'll spend the bucks anyway because you're desperate. Individual weight loss will vary with how much you diet and exercise, because any fool knows pills don't make you lose weight. Our spokespeople are probably paid actors but we call them compensated voluntary endorsers to confuse the hell out of you. Testimonials are total bullshit and for informational purposes only and we don't even endorse, research, or verify them (Bob's uncle wrote them all anyway). If anybody does manage to get results from this bit of pressed sugar and herbs—other than indigestion and high blood glucose—they aren't typical. Don't crush or snort this product. Don't stick this product in your ear. Don't heat this product and spill it on any part of your body. If you do, you're a dillweed and we're not liable. The guys in white coats talking to you are not medical doctors. Duh. We can't believe how many stupid asshats will actually buy this RIDICULOUS trash.

I laugh and look up.

Freddie and NoNo are gazing at me, seeming relieved.

Freddie nods to the notes I'm making on the paper that used to be blank. Fast notes. A satirical diet ad, only the sad part is, the real commercials are so much worse if you really read and listen.

I whip a clean page over my notes, write the title in big letters, and hold it up for their review.

I LOST 500 POUNDS OVERNIGHT WITH HOODWINKIA!

Freddie's grin gets huge. "Go, Fat Girl."

And I take my pen, and I go.

The Wire

REGULAR FEATURE
for publication Friday, September 7

Fat Girl Freaking
Fat Boy Chronicles I
JAMIE D. CARCATERRA

My freak-out cauldron is approaching rapid boil.

I've been gigantic since I was born, and the biggest health crisis I've ever had was the first day of my freshman year, when I got stung in the nose by a bee. Nothing like a Fat Girl with a big red swollen nose, wailing and blubbering all over study hall. Took me a while to live that one down—but I did, because I'm not just any fat girl. I'm *the* Fat Girl. Remember?

My boyfriend Burke, who has given me permission to dub him Fat Boy, must feel like he has a lot to live down. He's tired of assumptions, stereotypes, snarky comments, and attitude thrown in his general direction. He's tired of the things people say.

Mostly, he's tired of being Fat Boy.

Yeah, that's right. Fat Boy has had

enough. He's so sick of it that he's going to risk his life to change his outsides.

What do you think of that?

Fat Boy's giving up football.

Fat Boy's giving up a chunk of his senior year, and some of his counts-for-college grades.

Fat Boy's going under the knife, and all Fat Girl can do is watch and pray and make sure all of you, every one of you in this whole school, get this one crucial point: Obesity surgery is *not* an easy way out of being fat.

Don't even think it. Don't even imagine it.

You have no idea what Fat Boy is about to go through to look more "normal," to feel more "normal." Never fear. I'm going to tell you. I'm going to report as Fat Boy works harder than most Marine recruits, hurts worse than most people in horrible car wrecks, and risks so, so much.

By this time next year, because he's choosing surgery, Fat Boy has a one in twenty shot of being Dead Boy.

Dead and buried from surgical complications.

But he's had enough, and he'd rather be dead than fat.

So, here's the thing. I have to support him, because he's mine, and he needs me to be there.

If he makes it through this and comes to graduation all buff and healthy, every damned one of you better stand up and cheer like crazy monkeys, because Fat Girl can find out where every last one of you lives. If you don't cheer, I'll know, and I'll find you.

For now, instead of looking up your addresses (yet), Fat Girl will just freak out about Fat Boy and worry. I want you to worry with me, and think good thoughts.

Don't make me hunt you down.

CHAPTER
SIX

Two teacher–chaperones, about a dozen junior class "hosts," and the entire senior class minus a few cowards who didn't show up, stumble onto the football bleachers at daylight.

Senior Shoot. Woohoo.

Burke, Freddie, NoNo, and I rub sleep–grunge out of our eyes and squint at the finished versions of seven different "fantasies" the guys from set design constructed for the event. Then we stare down at the selection form and try to focus. We can choose who we take fantasy shots with, and three of the fantasy sets. I check off "Sultan and Sultana," the set with the big tent and red velvet cushions, my first choice out of the whole bunch. Second, I mark Burke's pick, "Rah-Rah" (the football-player-and-cheerleader set, of course). Third, I scratch the little eraserless pencil lead on Freddie and NoNo's choice, "Wild West Shootout." We'll leave "Dungeons, Dragons, and Wizards" and "Otherworldly" to the fantasy/sci-fi nerds, "Wall Street" to the math geeks, and "Victorian Afternoon" to anyone stupid enough to try to lace up a corset so early in the morning.

Besides, thanks to my years in the drama department, I have decent costumes for the three we agreed to choose. Always an important point, where my luscious, curvy body is concerned. The costumes are in my garment bag, which Burke carries for me, along with his own, Freddie's, and NoNo's, too. We girls have our makeup kits to worry about.

The four of us will dress up, pose together, and hope we make weird enough shots to get picked for the yearbook spread. But even if we don't, we'll have copies for our own memories. Then come senior class photos in various states of insanity and goofball posing and, finally, the serious class shot. Last of all, we do group shots, which for me will be drama and newspaper, and individual portraits, which will get sorted for use if we win some honor or other.

One long friggin' day ahead, but hey, at least we don't have classes. Not a bad deal for a Wednesday, if you think about it.

It takes the junior class hosts about an hour to collect the forms, put the groups in order, and hand out donuts and orange juice, the traditional ceremonial breakfast for Senior Shoot. Burke and I lean against each other until the food shows up, while on the metal bleacher step below us, NoNo whips out some kind of vegan bar with soy nuts to eat instead. She gives her sugar-coated donut to Freddie, who breaks it in half, pops a piece in her mouth, and hands the other piece to me. Because of the absurd hour, and how nobody's really that close around us, I do eat it. In fact, I kill Freddie's offering before my donut and juice even make it down the row, hoping the sugar will prop my eyes open another centimeter and make me feel like putting on a harem costume.

Burke takes our food off the tray when it arrives, then passes the tray to me, and I stand up and walk it on down the row. The guy who takes it from me, one of the math geeks, stares at me for a few seconds, then smiles and says, "Thanks, Fat Girl."

People have started that since the newspaper articles.

Some kids seem to mean it in a nice way, like Math Geek, so I don't knock him backward off the bleachers. I just give him a blazing Fat Girl glare, which makes him smile bigger.

When I get back to Burke, he holds on to his donut, napkin, and juice cup as I sit and eat. When I'm finished, he offers me all of his stuff.

"You aren't eating?" My eyelids finally do move a fraction higher. I collect his food and juice, but nothing's computing.

He reaches into his pack on the bleacher step behind us and pulls out a bottle of water. "I have to get ready," he says. "You know, start eating better, so this whole surgery thing doesn't shock my system."

My eyes open all the way. The first bite of Burke's donut turns heavy in my mouth, and I don't think I can swallow it without choking. For some reason, my eyes dart from his dreads and smooth forehead down across his cheeks, to his broad shoulders, belly, and finally come to rest on his powerful legs. I wonder how long he's been "eating better." Is he already smaller? Has he already started to change before he even has that god-awful stomach-stapling thumb-sized-two-tablespoons night-mare?

Christ, Jamie. Does that even matter when he might die in six days?

Smile at him, damn it.

So I smile, and force down the bite of donut, take a swig of juice, and wish I had some idea what to say, because Burke obviously wants me to say something.

"Good for you." NoNo breaks the silence, and I could kiss her, but I'm too busy letting the rest of Burke's donut slip out of my fingers and fall to the grass and mud un-derneath the bleachers. The ants can have a feast. I don't want anything else.

NoNo finishes her whatever-it-is bar and stretches. Her T-shirt is totally colorless today, with a consistency that reminds me of burlap. Her jeans, though—still bright blue hemp, high waist, and totally dork. "It's important to prepare for body trauma," she continues.

Freddie's face puckers. "Body trauma. God that sounds gross. Don't make me hurl my sugar and animal fat into your lap, 'kay?" She wipes donut crumbs off her chin as NoNo gags. To Burke Freddie says, "I'm glad you're doing that. I wondered when you'd start—well, worried that you wouldn't, really."

"I don't want to be one of those people who gains twenty pounds before they go in." Burke shakes his head, and his dreads brush the shoulders I love to squeeze and poke and rest my head on when I'm tired or sad, or even really happy. "That would make my risk of complications higher."

Everybody looks at me.

My turn to talk.

Only my words fell through the bleachers with Burke's donut.

Guess he doesn't want the four chocolate bars I automatically packed in my makeup kit for him. He probably doesn't want them anymore ever, does he?

I could eat the ones I have left, or give them to Dad. My stomach lurches, and I taste orange juice when I swallow a burp. Nothing sounds good right now, even chocolate. *It'll be nice to save that fifteen bucks a box every week, right?* Because that's pretty much where I spend the lunch money my parents give me, on Burke's candy, since I don't eat at school.

After a few awkward seconds, I manage to squeak, "I want you to take care of yourself." Then, after a slow breath, "Can I do anything to help?"

Please say no.

As if reading my mind, Burke shakes his head. "I have to do this part on my own." He takes my hand and gives it a squeeze, his eyes already far away again, studying the crowd.

Fifteen or so minutes later, Freddie gives me hell as we dress in the back corner of the visitor field house. It smells a little like gym socks, boy-sweat, and heinous foo-foo perfume from all of us, which does nothing to help Freddie's mood.

"You need to be more supportive, Jamie, I swear." She glares at me over the jeweled veil of her purple belly-dancer costume.

She and NoNo automatically stand in front of me, to give me a little privacy as I struggle into last year's *Aladdin and the Wonderful Lamp* costume. I played Fatima, a healer chick who gets killed, then is impersonated by a genie's wicked brother. *Fat*-ima. Of course. I'm sure the whole school thought that was a kick, but at least I got a neat custom-sewn blue jumpsuit, jeweled belt, and silky blue face-turban thingee out of the deal.

"I offered to help him." I wrap the turban thingee around my cheeks and chin, realize I'm sweating, and hope I don't stink. "And I tossed the chocolate bars I brought him in the trash. What do you want from me?"

"Oh, I don't know." Freddie folds her purple-draped arms and taps her flip-flops on the field house's stone floor. "How about a hug? Some warmth? Some looo-oove?"

NoNo, who is dressed in a green costume that reminds me of that old *I Dream of Jeannie* television show, only faded-looking green like all her stuff, nods. The tassel on her blah green hat flips forward. "You need to tell Burke what you feel, everything you feel, so you don't have any regrets if something bad happens."

Freddie and I stop glowering at each other and laser-eye NoNo instead. "Don't talk like he's going to die," I say, but Freddie's louder with, "Shut *up*, you morbid bitch!"

NoNo reacts with a twitch in her right eye. "Prepare for the worst, and be grateful when it doesn't happen."

Freddie's next comment isn't even printable.

Both of NoNo's eyes twitch. "Is what she said even possible?" she asks in a mousy voice.

Every conceivable social group has stopped chattering and dressing, and all the senior girls in the field house now stare at us.

I push my way between Freddie and NoNo and strike a pose. "If you want a picture, assholes, that'll be twenty dollars for a package of two eight-by-tens."

Four hands shove me forward before I get any louder, just in case one of the teacher-chaperones happens to be within earshot. Geeks, brains, jocks, freaks, and everybody else scatters before the might of Fat Girl and her entourage.

· · ·

All the way through the "Sultan and Sultana" and "Rah-Rah" shoots, I try to figure out how to be huggy, warm, loving, tell Burke all my feelings, prepare for the worst, and hope the worst doesn't happen.

The whole thing makes me want to spit orange-juice-donut burps all over the football field.

Right about the time Burke plants an illegal kiss on me even though I'm wearing his last-year's football uniform and hitting him with his own football helmet (you didn't seriously think I'd dress like a cheerleader, did you?), I decide being normal is probably the best bet. Normal, with a healthy dose of it's not happening, it's *not* happening thrown in. As long as I don't let Burke or Freddie or NoNo hear me, I can say *it's not happening* as many times as I want, damn it, and hope God decides it's a prayer and that, for once, my prayers might be worth answering.

During the "Wild West Shootout" photos, a couple of news vans pull into the drive that leads to the football field. Two of the three local stations usually run our Se-nior Shoot as a humor/human-interest sort of piece. Nothing new or unusual, except there are more cameras than I remember from last year, when we had to play hosts to the seniors. Looks like at least one of the big-wig reporters has come, too, instead of the pathetic newbies that usually show up for something like this.

During the serious class photos, a van from the third news station pulls into the drive.

"Man, we're popular," Freddie mutters just before we split up for group and individual photos. The teacher-chaperones float around the edges of the field sucking on tea and lemonade, and still eating leftover donuts off and on. They don't seem concerned about the news vans.

It's getting hot, but the breeze smells like fall and cold air and brown leaves coming soon. I try to keep my focus there instead of on Burke or the hovering news crews, which, oddly, are not approaching any of the kids already done with group and individual shots. Drama photos go fast, since we're all natural hams who so know how to pose.

Journalism, however, isn't so smooth. Heath and I are the only seniors, and he's about as camera-comfy as a plastic doll with a stick up its butt.

"Loosen up, Roboto," I whisper as the poor yearbook guy tries again to get a decent shot of us standing next to each other, holding a copy of *The Wire*—at least one with Heath's eyes open. Other seniors collect around us in small groups, talking and laughing. Some of them look at me. I distinctly hear the words *Fat Girl*.

What, they never noticed I was fat before my column? I don't get it.

When I glance at Heath, he's blushing. "I arrange photos. I never said I look good *in* photos."

With a loud sigh, I slip my arm around his shoulders and goose him hard in one armpit. He jumps, throws the newspaper straight up in the air, wheels on me, sticks his finger in my face and yells, "Damn it, Jamie, don't *do* shit like that!"

Click, click, click goes the digital camera.

"Print one of those," I instruct the shocked photographer, who has pulled the camera from his eye. "They're more true to life anyway."

But Heath snatches hold of the photographer and makes him delete the last three pictures.

One of the news crews filters through the whispering groups of seniors already finished with their photos. Channel 3, from the big sign on the front camera. The rail-thin reporter has thick black hair cropped just above her shoulders and a red big-shoulder dress that makes her look way too much like Lois Lane. Only Lois doesn't try to interview anybody. She just stands there, gazing at Heath and me.

Heath and I look at each other.

What the hell?

Five slow, hellish minutes pass before we finally get a

shot of Heath without an I–have–menstrual–cramps expression. The yearbook guy finally waves us on toward the
individual portrait setups, but Lois Lane waves at me and
jogs in my direction, dragging her camera crew behind her.

"See?" Heath mutters from behind me. "They saw what
you did to me, and now you'll pay. There is justice in the
universe."

"Can it," I snarl just as Lois reaches me. Behind her, the
clumps of finished seniors gawk, along with the yearbook
guy, who is now ignoring the waiting Beta Club.

"Excuse me, are you Jamie Carcaterra?" Lois sounds
out of breath. "Are you Fat Girl?"

My mouth runs before my brain works. "Well, I'm sure
as hell not Skinny Girl, am I?"

She pauses, huge television smile frozen on her
sculpted face. Those poofy, puckery lips so can't be real.

"She definitely has ass fat pumped into that mouth,"
I tell Heath in low, private tones. "Seriously. That's how
they do it."

He bursts out laughing, but covers it by coughing. I
get another *don't–do–shit–like–that* look.

My eyes flick around the gathering crowd, hunting for
Burke. Or Freddie. Maybe NoNo would be better. She
loves to have platforms for her Green Party educational
talks. What better venue than Channel 3, complete with
Lois Lane? Television interviews aren't really my shtick.
I'm print–media all the way. Unless it would help me get
that scholarship...

Sweat coats my face and neck, and I think about how
I'll shine and look pale next to pancake–Lois, but oh well.

Lois thrusts the microphone forward. "Can you repeat what you just said?"

I clear my throat. "Yes," I enunciate in my stage voice, "I'm Jamie Carcaterra, aka Fat Girl."

"Fat Girl, can you tell me the real motivations behind the provocative column you're writing for Garwood's school newspaper, *The Wire?*" Lois beams after her question. It's enough to blind a person, the way the sun blazes off her whitened teeth.

Her question and the mouth-glare catch me off guard, so much so that I don't know what to say. "Uh..." comes out clearly, as well as "I—well..."

Heath steps up beside me in a hurry. "I'm Heath Montel, editor-in-chief. Jamie's writing Fat Girl so people know what it's really like being overweight in today's society."

Lois gives him a look that says, *Okay, thanks. Now move.* I recognize it, because I've used that look many times myself.

Ever polite, Heath fades back without being asked out loud.

"Ms. Carcaterra, by medical definitions, would you consider yourself overweight or obese?" Lois asks without skipping a beat. "Morbidly obese?"

"I... don't really like clinical terms and distinctions. I'll just stick with fat, thanks." I work up a first-class stage smile, one I hope looks decent on camera.

God, I wish Burke and Freddie and NoNo would show up.

Lois moves in a little closer. "Are you affiliated with

the National Association to Advance Fat Acceptance that you mentioned in your first column?"

Quick search of the growing crowd. Still no Freddie or NoNo in sight. "No, but they have a lot of great articles and resources on their Web site."

"Why did you choose a column name and a term that most children use to poke fun at overweight females?" Lois's tone gets more strident. "Was that a political statement?"

"No," I say honestly. Then, "Yes. The fat part, but not the girl part, or the whole fat-girl name. It's just what I am. I'm a Fat Girl. I wanted to put the words into print."

Lois blinks like she's not following me.

Freddie so needs to steal this bitch's job.

Whip-fast, Lois's voice switches from confrontational to sweetly sympathetic. "You must have suffered terribly from teasing and bullying due to your size. Is that why you're so angry?"

I'm angry? The sun seems hotter across my cheeks, and I fidget in my Diana's skirt and blouse, one of my best, a silky brown with tribal prints woven across the belly, arms, and waist. *I'm angry right now? Am I?*

I shrug. "If I'm mad right this second, it's because you're asking questions that don't make sense. And actually, no, I haven't been teased or bullied much at school. I have good friends. People seem to like me. I'm usually the one doing all the teasing—and the bullying, too."

"You admit you're the bully. I see." Back to confrontational now. "Are you biased against thinness and thin people? Did that bias motivate your sneak attack on the Hotchix clothing chain, because they serve primarily *normal*-sized teens?"

"Sneak attack?" Who *is* this chick? Has she been bribed by the fashion industry or something?

Beside me, Heath steps forward again. I glance at his way-red face as he pushes his hair out of his eyes and says, "Hey, lady, you know what you can do with your attitude and your—"

I take hold of his arm to cut him off. After letting him go, taking a second to calm myself, spending another second wondering how red my own face has turned and estimating how brightly my sweat is glowing on camera, I respond with, "Can you define normal for me? Because—"

"I read your column on vanity sizing, Fat Girl," the reporter interrupts. Her voice gets louder, even more forceful, and a little sarcastic. "Tell the truth now. Isn't that just another cop-out to avoid limiting your diet and increasing your exercise?"

My smile goes cold. I feel it, and I don't care. Fine. She wants Fat Girl, then it's Fat Girl she'll get. "That's a first-class boundary violation. You have as much right to ask about my diet and exercise as I have to ask why you got ass fat injected into your lips. Care to share?"

Lois looks flapped. Before she can open her enhanced mouth again, I add, "Did you see Freddie's cable piece on Garwood's channel? I'd say I was the one who was attacked at Hotchix. How fair is it that larger teens have to buy clothes from expensive specialty stores—stores that target older women who enjoy looking like fruit?"

This time the poofy lips say, "Is it true your boyfriend Burke Westin, one of our local football stars, is about to have gastric bypass surgery?" Lois-Lane-from-hell looks directly at the camera. "A very controversial procedure for teens."

That question yanks my words away again, and I suddenly hate the reporter even more than I was already hating her. Tears pop into my eyes. A hundred responses fly through my mind, each nastier than the last, but my chest gets so tight I can barely say, "Yes."

Eyes glittering with triumph, she moves in for the kill. "What are your feelings about Burke's potentially tragic choice?"

When I don't answer, when my hands start shaking, Heath's hand clamps on my shoulder. "Read her column and find out like everybody else," he says, loud enough to get the attention of one of the teacher-chaperones as she drifts close enough to hear. "Come on, Jamie."

Commotion.

People talk louder and louder, but I'm not processing as Heath forcefully moves me away from the reporter.

The chaperone takes over behind us, insisting that Lois and her crew back off.

I hear the principal's name, and something about harassing students, and police.

We get a few yards away, then a few more, toward the visitor field house the senior girls have been using to change clothes. Tears spill down my cheeks. Near the goal post, I pull back from Heath's firm grip and double over, trying not to puke many-times-reprocessed juice. He drops to one knee beside me and keeps one hand on my back.

I hear giggling from the field house.

The hand moves. Then it comes back.

"You okay?" he asks quietly. "Want to go hide out in the journalism room?"

I shake my head.

Freddie's voice rises over the low rumble of chatter and more giggling from the field house. "What the hell happened, Jamie? Hey, Jamie!"

By the time I stand up, Heath has faded into the crowd before I can even thank him. I squint, trying to pick out his blond head, but no luck. Then Freddie and NoNo surround me, Burke grabs me and holds me tight.

For a few seconds I float away and breathe in that scent I love, and enjoy how strong and powerful he is.

At least for now.

Soon I won't fit in his arms. He'll get small, and I'll be so big I won't fit right here against him, where I belong.

Both of my hands slide up to his chest, and I push back from him before I break out sobbing like a complete idiot.

He looks so handsome in his three-piece suit and tie, required for his football picture. I'm glad the coach let him take a medical out instead of academically disqualifying him, so he could still be in the picture and do stuff with the team.

"Want me to bust somebody up, baby?" he asks, totally serious. "Because I will. You just point the way."

He flexes his fingers and makes fists, probably without even realizing what he's doing. And once more, I'm aware that seemingly the whole senior class has gathered around us to stare.

Okay, I might have been a ghost once upon a time. Maybe they didn't really notice me past my bylines or my stage roles. Maybe they didn't pay that much attention to me or my friends or my size, or whatever.

But they're damn sure noticing Fat Girl now.

I'm not liking it much. Not this way.

It takes Freddie a few minutes to insult them all enough that they go away. NoNo chats with the teacher–chaperone, giving quick–witted reassurances and urging the teacher to "man the perimeter" to make sure the re-porters don't come back.

Guess she's been to enough protests to know the strategies.

Sometimes NoNo really surprises me.

I wait for everybody to gather close again. Then, clutching Burke's hand for support, I tell my friends what happened.

Without crying. Getting madder as I talk.

NoNo mentions the word *lawsuit* once, but Freddie mentions it twice, along with volunteering to help Burke bust somebody up.

When I get to the part about Burke's surgery, though, he grimaces.

My heart bumps against my ribs as I study his pained expression. "What?"

"Nothing, really." He lets go of my hand. "I guess it

doesn't matter if all of Garwood knows I'm having the surgery. With *The Wire*, it's not like it was some big secret. It's just . . . television feels different."

Hot waves of shame wash through me. I reach for his hand and snatch it back to me. "I didn't even think about your privacy. I'm so sorry!"

"Don't be." He squeezes my fingers. "If I can't hold my head up in public about it, I shouldn't do it, right?"

"Can you hold your head up in public about it?" Freddie's tone is hopeful, but she can't see that fanatic gleam inching back into Burke's eyes.

"Not a problem." This time, he kisses my hand.

Freddie blows out a loud breath. Her face shifts from hopeful to resigned to best–friends–till–the–end. "Okay, then. I guess that's settled."

NoNo nods, her eyes roving around us as if she's expecting an army of Lois Lanes and cameras.

That's settled.

Yeah, right.

It's anything but settled for me, but what am I supposed to say?

A hug, some warmth, some looo-oove. What I feel, everything I feel, so I don't have any regrets.

God I hate this!

But Burke . . .

I scoot closer to him, lean my head against his shoulder, where, for now, I still fit.

"I love you," I whisper.

He says he loves me too, but when I close my eyes, all I see is that gleam in his eyes.

REGULAR FEATURE
for publication Friday, September 14

Fat Girl Dishing
Fat Boy Chronicles II
JAMIE D. CARCATERRA

I have a few things to say to the investigative reporter from one of Garwood's news channels who ran that insulting piece on me two days ago. First, please feel free to eat my pink, size 5X, cheeky, stretchy, lacy undershorts. Second, you edited that piece to make me look like a thin-hating axe murderer. Third, you're an unethical sensationalist wench, and one day Frederica Acosta will take your job.

Now forget you.

The purpose of this piece is to tell all of you what Fat Boy is about to go through, so you'll get those positive thoughts flowing.

Some of the stuff is standard hospital crap. No food or drink after midnight, arrive at the hospital at an ungodly early hour so you can sit around and wait, put on an embarrassing ass-flashing cloth gown with broken snaps and two laces that aren't long enough to tie, and wait for the anesthesiologist to knock you into next week with a shot and some very stiff gas.

Once they get Fat Boy into the operating room, they'll slice his abdomen in several places, stick in some tubes, and pump him full of gas. That's so the surgeon can see what he's doing.

After turning Fat Boy into Fat Gas Boy, the surgeon pokes a teeny lighted camera and little surgical tools through those slice holes, and watches what he's doing on a computer monitor.

Are you sicked out yet?

Keep reading.

The surgeon will then proceed to staple Fat Boy's gut together to make a pouch at the top, which at first will hold about two tablespoons of food or liquid. Eventually, it'll stretch out to hold about one cup. Think about that tonight while you're ramming down the typical four to six cups of chow.

After that gross-iosity, the surgeon will snip open a piece of Fat Boy's small intestine and hook it up to his newly stapled stomach pouch. Everything will now bypass the bottom of the stomach and the top of the small intestine—that's where *bypass* surgery gets its name. Yum.

Fat Boy, assuming he's still alive and having no other major problems that require bigger cutting, will get stitched or stapled. Then he'll get shoved out to the recovery room and shot full of pain medication, which will make him Legally Stoned Boy. Perhaps the only redeeming moment of this whole nightmarish experience. At least until they yank him out of bed and make him march around to prevent nastiness like blood clots in the legs.

For one to two days, no matter how much he marches or begs, he'll get no food or liquids.

Then he'll get liquids. Milk, broth, maybe juice, and maybe if he's very, very lucky, cooked cereal. This lasts two to three days.

He'll graduate to gelatin, then pureed food—*for a month*. Delish, yes? And so it goes. He'll have no idea what he can tolerate, or how much. He'll have no idea what he still likes or doesn't like. He won't ever eat an entire pizza again. No megasized milkshakes or large fries with that, or vats of chili on homecoming night. He'll even be giving up his very favorite meal: the Bag'o'burgers from Hotstop Grill.

All of these delights, Fat Boy surrenders—
not just now, but forever.

So, like I told you, send positive thoughts
to Fat Boy, and do it now.

CHAPTER
SEVEN

My eyes rocket open, and I sit up in bed.

Did I oversleep?

Christ, did I miss Burke's surgery?

But the glowing green clock display says 2:00 AM. I've only been asleep for a few hours. My breathing slows down, and I rub my tight chest. It's still two hours before I need to shower, but I figure what the hell and get up. No sense trying to sleep. I'm wired and fired like I could run ten miles, if my boobs wouldn't give me black eyes the second I tried.

After my shower, I put on one of my dad's old robes and sit in the kitchen, as far from Mom's piles of junk as I can get, and work my way through a whole pot of instant coffee by myself. With each hot, bitter sip, I think about Burke. I wonder if he's sleeping. If he's scared.

Maybe he needs me. Maybe I should call?

But if M & M stayed over...

They probably did.

So if I call Burke and they hear his cell ring they'll throw a giant bitch-fit about how he needs his rest before surgery, and make his morning miserable.

I go back to my coffee and make some bacon and biscuits, and finally a couple of boiled eggs. By the time Mom staggers in for her morning snack, I'm dressed, the second pot of coffee's already brewed, and I'm polishing off some half-stale donut holes Dad's probably counting on for his breakfast.

Mom mumbles something that sounds like, "Up early."

When I nod, she grunts, sucks down the touch of coffee she likes with her cream, and stumbles back out to get dressed. She wanted to drive me to the hospital this morning instead of Freddie, but I don't know why. I hope she doesn't surprise me with *I took the day off to support you*, or something equally sweet but crazy-making.

The whole time she's digging for her keys, I go back and forth between worrying about Burke and sweating Mom's motives. Then I start glancing at my watch, because it's closer and closer to the time, and I do *not* want to be late.

She finally locates the damned keys under a pile of magazines beside her kitchen chair. "Knew they were around here somewhere."

Yeah, like five hundred other things we've lost in stack-hell. But I smile and wish I'd thought to buy snacks to take along with my notebook, pens, pencils, phone, and the book of Yeats poetry I need to finish for English. At least I did stuff a few diet soft drinks in my pack, in case the hospital machines run out.

106

Mom gets the car started in record time, and we leave our driveway in the weird, gray light before sunrise. If Burke has to be at the hospital at 5:00 AM, so do I—M & M or no. Mona and Marlene will just have to get a grip. They aren't scaring me away from my guy when he most needs my support, even if I'd rather die than watch him get rolled away on a surgical gurney, bound for a gut stapling.

It's his decision.

That's my latest phrase.

It's not for me to judge, or rant or flip out or beg. It's his body. *It's his decision.*

Mom's asking me if I've got money for meals, and I'm nodding, barely listening.

It's his decision.

That's a hard argument, though. I mean, if you're a couple, if you've been together and you're tight, shouldn't one half of the couple have a say in what happens to the other half? Do people have to be married for that rule to kick in? Would I feel this way if I was the one having the surgery?

It's his decision.

"... angry with us?" The tail-end of Mom's question drifts through the car like the ever-present smell of rust and old fabric. She turns onto the road heading for the hospital. Rain starts to spatter against the streaked windshield, turning oncoming headlights into kaleido-scopes.

"What?" I ask, trying my best to remember what she might have said before the angry part. "Why would I be mad at you?"

107

Mom sighs. "You're a million miles away. I'm sorry this is so stressful."

All I can do is blink at her.

"I asked if you're angry because Dad and I haven't ever considered this surgery for us, or for you." Mom guides the car into the hospital parking lot and up to the front entrance, which will be unlocked, per Burke's paperwork, right at 5:00 AM, the hour he's due to arrive. A small crowd mills in front of the door, probably today's surgery patients, and pathetic people like me, scared to death they'll lose everything that matters.

I squint, but I don't see Burke or his family.

"Never figured weight-loss surgery was an option for any of us," I mutter to Mom, scanning the crowd for Burke, his parents, and his evil older sisters.

The *we can't afford bariatric procedures* part of that thought goes unsaid.

Mom's fingers tap against the steering wheel. "Dad's asked for a copy of the policy his company bought, just to be sure, but he doesn't think it's covered by the benefits."

My head swivels toward Mom like I have no control of my own neck.

She's gazing straight out the rain-streaked windshield, tapping her fingers. Her gray hair falls against her broad shoulders. I think she's wearing Dad's home clothes, because her black sweats look a few sizes too big for her.

What she said, about the policy...my mind combs over the words, trying to make sense of them. Something inside me shifts left, then right, and my head throbs like

my brain's expanding. "So . . . you're saying bariatric surgery *might* be covered by Dad's insurance?"

Mom swallows hard. Her face looks pinched in the
rainy gray dawn and parking lot lamps. "Maybe. Eighty
percent of it, anyway. The other twenty percent, we'd
have to pay ourselves."

"Oh." *Pop* goes the expanding brain.

"Jamie, if you want to do this, we'll find a way." Mom
finally looks at me. Her expression tightens, turns desperate as she lets go of the wheel and clenches her hands. "I
don't want you to go through life unhappy with yourself
like I have, and Dad. We didn't even realize kids could
have this operation. If we had—"

"Mom!" I raise both my hands and almost choke to
death on the sudden lump in my throat. "I don't know if
I'd do it, even if the insurance *will* pay, okay?"

In my mind, Fat Girl snaps, *Who says I'm unhappy with
myself?*

Am I?

Brain expanding . . .

Head throbbing . . .

I mean, yes, I've admitted I'd love to be magically thin,
but this way? From a surgery that could kill me, that no
one even knows the long-term consequences of?

Dad's insurance might pay. If I want to try this, maybe I can.

Mom's nodding. She gives me a lame, trembling smile,
then a kiss on the cheek. "I wanted you to know we're
checking things out. We'll do whatever we can."

When I get out of the car, my legs shake. My head

feels too big and heavy for my neck, but I shoulder my pack, stuff my hands into my skirt pockets, and try to breathe as I walk toward the hospital's front entrance.

Today's for Burke. I need to remember that and support him, and take good notes for Fat Girl.

But if I want this surgery for myself, maybe I can have it.

The front doors open, and the crowd surges inside, leaving me behind.

I think I see Burke and his family now, so I walk faster.

By the time I get inside, people have scattered, following colored lines on the floor to different areas. Remembering Burke's instructions, I follow orange, for surgery. Rainy, wet smells give way to cool, canned air and that antiseptic, alcohol scent. There's a touch of pine, too, probably from floor wax, since every white tile shines like glass.

Two gleaming hallways later, I enter the auditorium-sized surgical admissions area, and find Burke standing by the long wooden front desk with his family. He's wearing jeans and his football jersey, and he's got his arms folded across his chest like he does when he's nervous. The sight of him makes my stomach clench. Somehow, in this huge room Burke seems smaller than he should be, like a little boy instead of big man. I want to hug him. I want to grab him and shake him and talk him out of this. But his mom and dad are signing things, and M & M hover like bees around everyone else, buzzing at each other.

They see me, and the buzzing gets louder and more ominous.

When Burke spots me, he breaks into a big grin, un-folds his arms, then holds them out to hug me.

Seconds later, my face presses into his shoulder and I take a deep breath, savoring his sandalwood–leather guy smell. His strong arms tighten around me, and I hug him back hard, hard, harder, trying not to think *what if this is the last time?* But I think it over and over and hold my breath to keep from crying. I'm still shaking from what Mom said and seeing Burke look so tiny in the big room, and because I'm half–scared of M & M no matter how I act to everyone else.

"Everything's gonna be fine," Burke whispers in my ear, and his low, sexy voice gives me shivers. He kisses the top of my head and pulls back until he can see me. "You know that, right?"

"Sure," I lie, and somehow keep the tears back. My heart's pounding, thumping, hurting. I so don't want any of this to happen. But what can I do? Everything I think of is so selfish and stupid.

It's his decision. It really is his decision.

"By noon this'll all be over, and I'll be stoned out in re-covery." Burke leans down and brushes his lips against mine. His big hands grip my arms gently, and I love how they feel. "Then I'll be in my room, and you'll be there with me, okay?"

All I can do is nod, which Burke takes to mean I be-lieve him, because he's Burke, and a guy, and guys can be so totally stupid sometimes. Especially about important things. He lets me go after another quick kiss.

M & M mutter louder and head toward us, matching

frowns decorating their perfect, thin faces. They both have on suits. Mona, brown, and Marlene, forest green. Compared to my family, they look streamlined and modern. Twice as mean, too.

I go stiff and plan my verbal defense, as much as I can with these two.

"*Hey*," Freddie's voice rises from behind me and fills the space around us. M & M pull up short and actually smile toward the door, where I assume Freddie and NoNo have entered. So not fair. M & M *like* Freddie and NoNo. I guess because they aren't dating Burke.

Freddie and NoNo look streamlined and modern today, too, with Freddie in a sharp lavender skirt and blouse and NoNo in khakis with a form-fitting T-shirt. Only I'm un-streamlined, un-modern, in my flouncy blue broom skirt and flowing white blouse, with my hair loose and messy like Mom's.

Burke's parents join us, and everyone's talking but me.

Why can't I talk?

Why can't I chatter and smile and act like this is just peachy? I *need* to. I really do.

But there's a nurse with a chart standing at the desk, and she's calling Burke's name, and taking him, leading him away. He's waving.

No.

The nurse directs us toward the surgical waiting room down the hall, and Freddie and NoNo tug at my arms, and I'm trying to smile at Burke and blow him kisses and say something, like *I love you*, or *be safe*, or *be well*, or *please*

GOD *don't do this*, but I can't, and all I really want to do is scream.

No. No!

I don't want to watch the doors close behind him. But I watch. Not listen to M & M talk about how wonderful this will be, or Burke's mom the nurse worrying that they won't have compression hose to fit Burke's legs so he might be at more risk for clots and all the other technical medical stuff she obsesses about. But I listen. And then I walk, numb and quiet, trying to hold Burke's big grinning image in my mind, ignoring the shiny hallway all the way to the waiting area.

The *family* waiting area, M & M point out, but Freddie and Burke's mom say something to them about promises they made to Burke, and they chill, at least a little bit.

The waiting room's almost as big as the surgery admissions room, only there's light brown carpet and light brown chairs, and tribal-looking prints on all the walls. A nurse sits at a desk reading, and beside her there's a phone for the doctors and surgical nurses to call with reports or to tell families about problems. My eyes steer away from the phone.

It won't ring for Burke-problems. It'll just ring around noon, to tell us he's through.

This room smells like antiseptic, too, only with an overlay of sweat and perfume and aftershave and the coppery, tense scent of raw nerves. The lamp lights are soft, and probably meant to be soothing, like the subdued colors and the scattered bunches of magazines on end tables.

I'm not soothed.

When I look at the clock, it's 6:00 AM. Two hours until the surgery begins.

I sit a few chairs away from everyone else, pop open a diet soda, and take my notebook out of my pack. The blank pages seem to stare at me, and no matter how much pen tapping I do, I don't have that flash of inspiration I need to start a column. My eyes drift to the clock. 6:15...6:20...6:31.

Freddie's talking to M & M about college choices, and I can't help listening. They're pushing her to go for law as a first major instead of mass communications.

"Once you get to law school, you could specialize in communications law or even intellectual properties." Marlene waves a hand like the matter's settled. "Law will pay the bills, honey. Everything else can be a hobby."

"I'm thinking about environmental law," NoNo says with her gaze on the ceiling, like she's counting the panels, or assessing whether or not they're energy efficient.

"So it's law now?" I ask, surprised. "I thought you were fixed on conservation and ecology."

NoNo nods. "That too. I want to keep my options open."

"Definitely career tracks for the future," Marlene agrees, even though Mona glares, because she's heading toward corporate law. Sort of the mother ship for NoNo's vast array of enemies, the way I see it.

M & M don't react when I scoot closer and join the conversation. Even they look nervous, in their narrowed eyes, and in the tight, stiff way they sit. Pressed and starched, like their brown and green suits. Burke's mom and dad stay quiet, and check the clock more often than I do.

7:00.

7:10.

7:30.

I try to chat, but I wonder what Burke's doing. If they found those bizarre tight hose he's supposed to wear in a size that will fit him. I wonder if they even have a gown Burke's size, or if he's mad because his butt's hanging out.

The conversation turns to whether or not college majors are really important, since grad school or professional school is what makes all the difference, career-wise. Noise doesn't travel much in this room, and the other clusters of family–friends–bystanders sound like they're whispering. They probably think we're whispering, too, except for Mona, who gets loud when she's passionate about something.

As much as I can't stand M & M sometimes, I can't help admiring their brains. Burke's whole family—college people. Professional people. Nobody works at the local Cost Cutters or grocery store or delivery service. They don't watch television when they have a family meal, and they probably don't eat beans and cornbread that often.

I want to go to college.

I *really* want to go to college, then on to whatever graduate school or professional school calls to me. I want to write for a living, about life and the weather and Burke and our children and academics and the state of the world. More than anything, I want to sound like these smart, educated people, look like them, be around them, *be* them.

Burke and I will have a family like this.

Finally it's 8:00, and we all go church-quiet as the clock hands tick into place. Burke's getting gassed and knocked out, and it'll be four hours before I know for sure that he'll wake up again.

"Intense," NoNo mumbles, and Freddie nods. Burke's mom holds his dad's hand, and M & M glance around the room at other clusters of people.

Freddie asks the question I don't dare put into words, and she directs it at M & M. "Are you sure this is okay?"

Silence expands around the group of us, our light brown chairs and our private patch of light brown carpet.

Nobody answers.

Marlene gazes at me like I put Freddie up to asking the question, but I meet her eyes with no guilt at all. My mind slides back and forth between her angry face and wondering what's going on with Burke.

8:05. Is he asleep yet? Has the doctor started cutting?

If I have this surgery, who will be out here in the waiting room for me?

Mom would probably insist on going in with me, but Burke threatened his folks about that. Maybe I would, too.

I'm so not having this done.

But maybe I could.

My stomach aches. I should have eaten more breakfast.

Mona finally starts answering Freddie's question, and

she uses the phrasing I've read on hundreds of Web sites when I researched Burke's surgery. "The risks of staying overweight far outweigh the risks of this surgery."

Marlene picks up the party line right away. "It's curative for diabetes, and it might keep him from getting hypertension—which you know kills black men more than anyone else. And it lowers cholesterol. Burke will feel better about himself. He'll live longer."

"If he comes through the procedure in good health," NoNo adds in the same thoughtful tone she used when discussing law school.

Everyone, me included, glares at her. "No bad energy," I remind her. "No hexing."

"There's no such thing as hexing," NoNo shoots back, but Marlene pats her hand.

"Just for today, honey, there is. Let's be positive."

"The studies only cover like sixteen to twenty-four months, by the way." I can't help myself. It's my nature. What can I say? "You can't make the leap to words like *cure* and *prevent*. Not yet."

When everybody takes a turn staring at me instead of NoNo, I explain. "The studies that talk about 'curing' all those problems and 'preventing' other stuff. They only cover a short span of time. A lot depends on long-term diet and exercise, which would be true with or without bariatric procedures. Now that weight-loss surgery is big business, it's almost impossible to get solid, unbiased information."

Marlene shakes her head. "I knew you'd be negative about this. I asked Burke not to let you come."

"Marlene," Burke's mother says in a warning tone.

"I'm not being negative." My face is getting hot. I can feel it. I'm probably red as an overripe apple, and Freddie's expression turns severe, warning me just as surely as Burke's mom warned Marlene. "I'm just stuck on the actual facts, not the hype, and it worries me. There is a downside to bariatric surgery, and that's why doctors argue over whether or not teens should have it."

"I think that's enough from everyone," Burke's father says in his deep, calm voice. "The boy did his research, and so did we, and so did his doctor. For Burke, this is the best choice."

"Teens do better with the procedure anyway." Mona locks eyes with me. "Because they're in better health to start with. Did you read that *fact* in all the hype you're talking about?"

"Yes." My fingers curl on my empty, wordless notebook, and my pen drops to the floor. "I'm not being negative, really. I'm hopeful. I'm—" I look away from her. Let her win the damned staring contest. I don't care. Maybe it'll make her feel better.

And what am I, anyway?

Mad?

Scared. Terrified. Half-sick inside. Wishing it would turn 12:00 in a hurry, and we'd hear how Burke was doing.

For some reason, Heath's voice pops into my head. *You don't have to be such a bitch all the time, Jamie. I'm trying to be nice . . .*

"I'm just worried," I finish, in as not–bitchy a voice as

118

I can muster, which loosens the tense you-promised-you'd-shut-up lines from Freddie's face and brings NoNo a few lightyears closer, back from Planet Nostenfast.

Burke's mom gives me a sympathetic look. "We're all worried, honey. It's okay. I know it means a lot to Burke that you came, that you're supporting him."

I'm sweating now, my face is hot, and my throat's tight from trying not to say anything else. Do I stink? I probably do.

8:31.

9:47.

10:02.

When noon comes, my nerves fizz like shaken soda. We're all clock watching now, all sweating.

The nurse informs us that Burke's been moved to recovery, and I slide down in my seat. Flat soda now. Drained. Listless. He lived. Thank God he made it through the procedure. Thank God.

But now more waiting, for him to get stable and wake up, so we can see him. His parents first, then his sisters. Then me. I can handle that. I can wait my turn, so long as he's alive and okay and Burke, and he doesn't die.

After fishing some change from my pack, I shove out of my seat, leave Burke's family and Freddie and NoNo, and go in search of a snack machine. A pack of peanut-butter crackers will kill a little time and take the edge off. But I end up wandering halfway around the hospital trying to find the snack room, which I never do, and then can't find my way back to the waiting room.

Damn it.

I'm following the orange line!

What if that phone's ringing and there's news about Burke, and I'm not there? Shit. Shit and a half.

I keep weaving down the hallway, following the or-ange line, until I'm finally back at surgical admitting. When I ask, the nurse points the way back to the family waiting area. Exactly two steps later, I nearly bang into a guy standing dead center on the orange line.

When I jerk my head up, shocked, I see Heath Montel.

He's so out of place with his floppy blond hair, relaxed-fit jeans, and monogrammed polo shirt, that for a long moment or two I don't recognize him.

When I finally regain my wits, I shake my head and ask, "What are you doing here? Aren't you supposed to be in school?"

He hesitates, and his grin seems as out of place as the rest of him. "School business. I got a pass to come see if you got this week's Fat Girl done yet."

Blank stare from me. I know I'm doing it, but I can't stop.

Way to go, Miss Superior-Intellect College Girl.

"Burke's still in recovery, Heath." My lips feel numb.

Heath gives me a nod. "Yeah. Well, that's okay. I mean, I didn't exactly expect you to have it done." Dashes of red slide across his cheeks. "What I really mean is, I came to see if you were okay. If you needed anything."

A Valium, no, ten Valiums, a pack of peanut-butter crackers, and some antistink body spray. Got any of that handy? "That's sweet." I do mean that as I say it, I just don't really know what to do with him. "I'm . . . you're . . . that's just sweet. Thanks."

"You've got my number, right? You can call if you need something later. And tell me how things went?"

"Sure." The word comes out too slowly. "I'll call."

"I can bring you guys dinner." Heath clenches his fists like he's mad at something, but I know it's not me. He looks generally freaked out and nervous, which is even sweeter.

"I'll tell Burke's parents. They'll appreciate it." I want Heath to move so I can get back to the waiting room. But at the same time, I want him to stay, to walk me back and sit with me. He's more comforting than the light brown color scheme and low lighting, though I can't really say why.

Before I see what's coming, Heath gives me a fast hug, then takes off down the green line, back toward the main entrance.

When I look up, Freddie's standing a yard or so away with her mouth open.

"Heath came to see if we were okay," I babble, not sure why I'm talking so fast.

"I'm sure he's worried about *us*, yeah." Freddie eyes me with one eyebrow cocked. How does she do that? I can't, even when I try.

Her face shifts from bothered to worried. "Come on back to the waiting room, Jamie." She beckons for me. "The surgeon called from recovery. There's a problem."

REGULAR FEATURE
for publication Friday, September 21

Fat Girl Screaming
Fat Boy Chronicles III

JAMIE D. CARCATERRA

Burke stopped breathing.

Not during surgery. During recovery.

He.

Stopped.

Breathing.

No air. No breath. No nothing.

The nurses said he lost his color, started gasping, and grabbed his chest. His heart rate shot up, his blood pressure tanked, and he passed out.

He's back on the operating table while I'm writing this. Live and raw. This is it, folks. This is the real deal.

A pulmonary embolism. Which, according to the surgeon, is "an occlusion of the pulmonary artery—in Burke's case, one of the short segments—by fat, air, or a blood clot."

Translation: Even though Burke wore those stupid old-people support hose during the surgery, something broke loose, got stuck, and BURKE CAN'T BREATHE.

Because it's big and bad and he's young and it's only in one of the short segments, and because Burke won't be able to take the anticlotting drugs to fix it, the surgeon has to CUT THE THING OUT.

"Don't worry," Mr. Surgeon said. "It's a common complication in our teen patients. We'll get in there, fix it, and he'll be good to go."

Hello?

Common complication?

Teenagers who have gastric bypass have trouble breathing after they get cut? Did I miss this somewhere in my reading?

It seems to me the ability to *breathe* would be essential to all these good outcomes I read about, all these wonderful cures for so many medical problems.

Let's take a poll, okay? To keep me sane for the next five minutes. Here it is.

  1. If I was fat, I'd rather be
     A) fat
     B) dead
     C) sent back in time to the Middle
        Ages where everybody wanted
        to be fat and happy.

2. Bariatric surgery is
   A) psychotic
   B) demented
   C) what, you expect me to give you
      another option?

3. Burke will
   A) live
   B) die
   C) it doesn't matter, Jamie should
      kill his family and his doctor
      anyway.

4. I would ____ this surgery.
   A) do
   B) never do
   C) OUTLAW

Are you praying for Fat Boy?
I am, and you'd better be.

CHAPTER
EIGHT

"He looks so...so...." Freddie can't finish. She's about to crack the fingers on my right hand, she's squeezing them so tight.

Helpless, my mind supplies. *Flat. Still. Burke's too still.*

I don't know what I expected, but not this. Not near this.

Burke looks dead.

Except for his chest, which jerks up, then down, up, then down, in time with the ventilator's pumping and clicking sounds.

I feel dead just looking at him. The universe drains down to empty, like somebody sucked out all the air and rightness.

Why did this have to happen?

Freddie's grip digs into my skin, but I don't care. The pain keeps me here, reminds me I'm not dead, he's not dead, but he looks it, oh my God, he looks lifeless and helpless and pitiful. Not Burke. Not my Burke.

Why did he have to do this endlessly *stupid* surgery—and why, why, why did it have to go wrong? My ribs ache from the force of holding in my screams.

I knew this was wrong. I knew it was bad.

All I can do is stare at Burke and his breathing machine through the door of his glass room in the Intensive Care Unit. He's hooked to intravenous drips on both sides, and the ventilator joins his throat at a little knot of bandages. The surgeon explained about the ventilator. Temporary, to help his lungs recover from surgical trauma.

The surgeon explained about respiratory complications for teens—totally normal.

The surgeon explained everything, yeah, and assured us Burke will be just peachy, but right now, he's sedated and breathing through a friggin' tube in his throat. Actually, the surgeon said "mechanically assisted respiration." He probably said other stuff, too, but I only caught bits and pieces after "mechanically assisted respiration."

He'll have a scar on his throat, small and round.

Assuming he wakes up with normal brain function and ever gets out of that bed, like he's supposed to.

God, I need to stop this.

Standing in the door of Burke's glass cubicle, I don't feel totally sane or even real. Freddie and I keep not moving, not talking.

Should we whisper to him so he knows we're here? Yell to wake him up? Are we supposed to be bouncy and magically cheerful so he doesn't think we're scared shitless he's about to die?

One-two, one-two, one-two, one-two. Up and down,

jerk, jerk, jerk goes Burke's chest and belly. It has to hurt to breathe that way, with a machine jamming oxygen into your lungs. It has to.

Is he in pain?

Please don't let him be in pain.

I wonder if he can still smell anything with that ventilator attached to his throat. I hope not, because the nurse's station behind us reeks of alcohol and fresh cotton—and even that doesn't mask the sweet-rotten stench of blood, infection, and other body stuff I'd rather not think about.

"Burke probably thinks he died and went to hell," I whisper to Freddie.

"He's fine," she shoots back. *"We're* in hell."

"Shhh," says a nurse from the nurse's station, and Freddie and I slip inside Burke's glass cubicle before we get shushed again. My breath jerks along with Burke's, like a machine's pumping stuff into my lungs, too.

Freddie says, "Oh, my God, I'm suffocating," and I want to hit her. Blood pounds in a vein standing out on her left temple.

My body seems to be following everybody else's lead, so my blood pounds in time with hers. My eyes study the windowless back wall, the two glass side walls, the square white ventilator with its blue tubes, the IVs, the hospital bed. No televisions in here. No chairs. Just the machines, and places for nurses to stand, and wires and tubes and monitors. I notice everything in glowing, etched detail, except Burke, because now that I'm closer, I can't look at him at all.

I don't want to look at him. But I don't want to leave either. I never want to leave him again, because what if I leave and he dies? Nobody should die alone.

He's not *going to die.* My eyes flick to flat, chest-jerking Burke. *He is* not *going to die.*

He's been out of his second surgery and recovery for about three hours. Only two people can visit at one time, and only once per hour, for fifteen minutes. His parents took the first slot, and M & M got the second.

"Do something, Jamie." Freddie interrupts my distracted thoughts as she gestures to Burke's hand. "Maybe he can hear us."

I know she's not expecting me to heal Burke or work any miracles, but it feels like a huge miracle that I can even stand to touch him. My eyes stay on his hand, which seems as still and flat as the rest of him, except it jerks, jerks, when the ventilator pushes air. Forcing the brightest smile I can force, I take his hot, dry fingers in mine. His hand twitches with each pump of the machine.

"Hey," I whisper to him in between ventilator clicks and *whooshes*. My gaze drifts from the blue baggie-thing pulled over his dreads to his smooth, perfect forehead, and lower to his nose and mouth and broad shoulders, covered by a white hospital gown. Louder, over the machine noise, I tell Burke, "You need to wake up, seriously. You're wearing something that looks like a towel. It's kind of cute. I know you hate being cute."

No movement but the jerks from the respirator.

I glance at Freddie, who gives me a *keep going* expression, all wide-eyed and fearful like I might ask her to say something.

"Freddie's here," I tell Burke. "She's a total chickenshit, but not as bad as NoNo. NoNo was worrying there was blood on everything she touched."

"Blood products," Freddie corrects.

"Whatever." I'm pretending Burke's eyes are open now, and he's looking at me, and he's smiling. Will I ever see that again? Will he ever be able to smile again? "That's why we had to send NoNo home. I know you understand."

Nothing.

But I imagine there was something. I want there to be something, so, so badly. A small move of his lips. A glimmer of awareness.

"I've got to get this week's Fat Girl turned in, but I wanted to have next week's ready, too, since we're moving to longer practices with *The Wiz*, and I'm afraid I'll run out of time." When I squeeze his fingers, I wait for him to squeeze mine back, but he doesn't. God, how can he already look smaller? "Wake up and talk to me, so I can give my next column a happy ending."

"He's not in a coma, Jamie." Freddie moves closer to the bed and puts both of her hands on Burke's leg. "He's sedated. He can't—"

"Just shut up, okay? I know that." But it still feels like a soap opera, where the hero's in Twilight Land, and the heroine wakes him with a passionate speech and gentle kiss. I wish I could wake Burke with a kiss. He's my prince, right? I should be a better princess, with a powerful, magical kiss.

129

Hoping past logical hope, I bend down and brush my lips against his soft cheek. So hot. So still and tight. I've kissed Burke that way a thousand times, but usually he makes a noise way down in his throat, like some big, happy tiger.

Now, there's nothing.

I can't wake him. I want to, but I have no power at all.

He twitches with the ventilator, but makes no sound, no indication he hears me or feels me, or knows I'm alive.

After he's skinny, it'll be like this, says the mean part of my brain. *He won't know you're alive.*

My breath jerks with Burke's.

But maybe I'll have the surgery, too, and get skinny with him. Maybe he'll have to stand beside *my* ICU bed after some nasty complication.

Jesus H. Christ and his brother Mervin, too. Have you lost your friggin' mind? Do you want to die?

I don't, I don't, and I don't want Burke to die, either. I want his surgeon to take him back to the operating room and undo this nightmare. Put him back like he was, walking and talking and on his feet, holding me, hugging me, smiling at me, and kissing me back.

"Are you hurting his hand?" Freddie tugs at my wrist. "Ease up, chica. You're cutting off blood flow."

"Come back to me," I whisper to Burke as I let him go. "Don't worry. You won't have to do this alone. I won't let you. I'll be right here."

Damn it. I wish I could be. Fifteen minutes at a time, I will be. Once an hour. I hate this!

Since we don't know what else to do, Freddie tells him

about her cable piece on teen bariatric surgery. She says she's doing it over, this time an exposé about the hidden risks. She orders him not to be her bariatric surgery horror story poster child.

One of the nurses pops his head into Burke's room. "Time's up, ladies."

The sound of the nurse's voice makes us both jump. It's like the guy took a hammer and shattered a perfect moment—if you don't count the Burke-breathing-through-a-tube thing.

Freddie glares at the nurse even worse than I do, but she steps out of the glass room after giving me a little push back toward the bed. "Take a second with Burke," she instructs before she walks to the nurse's station.

Okay, finally.

I open my mouth to start yelling, but my gut twists and my throat catches and tears jam into my eyes. Coughing, choking, I spin away before he can see me or hear me, but he has to hear the sobs. I can't stop them. I can't even breathe until I lean down, hang my head, and squeeze my eyes shut so tight I see stars.

With each deep, sucking breath, my sobs break off a little sooner. I'm dizzy. I want to puke, but I can't puke in an ICU. It might hurt Burke, or freak out his nurses, or make them say I can never come back to see him again, and then I *would* die.

Finally, finally, my words come back and I manage to turn around and tell Burke, "I hate that you're in this ICU. If you were in a regular room, I wouldn't have to leave you."

Burke doesn't move.

I take his hand and squeeze it and flop his arm, careful not to dislodge the IV stuff. "Please open your eyes. Please try to say something. I need to know you're in there. Please, Burke. *Please!*"

Burke still doesn't move.

I sob all over again like a giant moron and stroke his dreadlocks through the blue baggie-thing while I kiss his cheek over and over. At least it's warm. I don't know what I would do if his skin got cold. I'd probably lie down on his bed and freeze solid with him. I couldn't stand it.

Shivers hit me in fast rushes as I think about a quiet, colorless, soundless world with no Burke. He's a light for me, an oasis, a place to stay when all the other places close me out. I'd be homeless without him, in an inside-way. I'd be less than I am, in ways I can't even imagine.

"Don't get cold, baby." I'm probably cutting off the blood flow in his fingers again, but I don't care. I want to yank his hand until he notices me. Until he notices *something*.

"Wake up for me. Burke?"

Another nurse steps into the cubicle and clears her throat. She looks a lot more serious than the other nurse.

She tries to talk nice for a second or three, but Freddie's voice is louder when she says, "Hey, Fat Girl. Get your ass out here now. You want the vampire twins swooping down here to suck your blood?"

I'm not sure what freezes Nurse Serious and the first nurse in their tracks—the vampire blood-sucking part, or the Fat Girl part. They stand aside, kind of stupefied, as I give Burke's motionless hand one last kiss before placing it gently back at his side. I make sure his covers are pulled up and tucked under his arms, run my fingers across his forehead, and tell him I love him.

Then I hold up my head and start walking past the silent, staring nurses with as much dignity as I can muster.

Jamie can't leave Burke's room. No, not me, not the me who loves him so much I feel like I got my own gut stapled.

It takes Fat Girl to do something this brave and painful.

Feeling?
Something tells me
That it's more than I can deal with.

"Can I Go On?"
from *The Wiz*

FEATURE SPREAD
for publication Friday, September 21

Fat Girl Wondering
Fat Boy Chronicles III—Addendum
JAMIE D. CARCATERRA

(Update)

Fat Boy survived surgery number two, to remove the clot lodged in his lungs from surgery number one. To quote his surgeon, "He's currently requiring mechanically assisted ventilation."

Translation: Fat Boy's breathing because a machine pushes air through a tube crammed down his throat.

He's trapped in a smelly glass room with smelly glass nurses who wear rubber shoes and want everybody to have "patience." He has needles in both arms. He doesn't turn his head, open his eyes, or notice when somebody kisses him.

If Fat Boy feels anything, it's pain. If he smells anything, it's raunchy. If he sees anything, it's scary. If he hears anything, it's moaning. He can't taste anything, of course, because he's not eating anything.

He's out. Not awake. If the power went off, his lights would go out, too—literally.

This is what THIN is worth to Fat Boy. More than agony, more than breath, more than love, more than life. This is what THIN is worth to his doctors, his family, maybe even some of the people who call themselves his friends.

What is THIN worth to you?

And for God's sake, *why*?

CHAPTER
NINE

I can't stop crying. My eyes feel swollen, like I'm seeing through aching slits, but Fat Girl parts the seas of ICU nurses like Moses having a big, nasty fit. Maybe they're afraid to get too close to a blubbering fat girl.

Obsesophobia, my stressed brain suggests.

Well, that's fear of getting fat, not the blubbering girl part. What about *ephebiphobia*—fear of teenagers?

Freddie and I have almost reached the automatic ICU door when the bravest of nurses stops us. He looks sad and sympathetic when he says, "This will take time. You have to be patient, hope for the best."

"The best will happen," Freddie tells him, sounding pissed. "No hoping to it."

The nurse lets us go without saying anything else, which is good, because Freddie's wound up tight. My lame consciousness comes up with stupid words or just stops talking when I'm flipped out, but Freddie gets capable of premeditated first-degree verbal assault.

I'm still half-crying and churning out weird phobias

and she's still bitching about Nurse Patience–Man when we round the corner back to the waiting room.

And pull up short a few feet from the door.

Heath's at the hospital again, this time waiting with Burke's parents and sisters, sitting and chatting like he belongs here now, with our group.

Pieces of my brain crash together, trying to adjust to the sight of Heath and Burke's family hanging out together, and I can't grasp it.

I want to run back to Burke, where things are weird, but not this weird.

Yet I want to run to Heath, too, and beg him to sit under a drafting table with me and say funny things until my gut unstaples a few notches.

What is he doing here?

"What is Heath doing here?" Freddie echoes my thoughts out loud. "He should be—I don't know, at the paper or something, right?"

"He probably wants my Fat Girl feature," I mumble a few seconds later, after I find my voice. "I told him I'd have it later."

Heath still doesn't see us. He's lounging, all relaxed and not intimidated, right in front of M & M, and his blond hair hides the top of his eyes.

He's not here for the feature. I know that.

He's here because he's worried about me, and I think that's so sweet. So sweet I totally don't know what to do about it.

Freddie studies Heath like a professional reporter, like she's calculating weight and height and all potential juicy quotes. "You did Fat Girl for this week, didn't you? While Burke was in surgery the second time?"

"Yeah. It's in my bag." I take a step toward the waiting room door.

"Wait." Freddie grabs my arm. When I stop and turn around, her face looks tense and suspicious. "You were pale and shaking, and now you're all pink and *Heath's here* and *Fat Girl's in my bag.*" Her eyes narrow as she glances from Heath to me. "What's going on?"

"That's a dumb-ass question." I pull my arm away from her, breathing fast but as deep as I can, trying to chill, trying to get a grip. I didn't know I had been shaking, or that seeing Heath made me stop. "It's Burke. The way he looked. The way he was."

"You should still be upset," Freddie says, getting louder.

"I *am*." I turn my back to the waiting room door and stare her down. Fat Girl, all the way. "I don't know what the hell you're talking about. Right now I have to write a quick addition and turn in my feature. I don't have time to freak out all over the hospital hallway."

Freddie's eyes stay narrow, but she nods and gestures toward the waiting room.

When I turn back around, Burke's parents and sisters are staring at us. So is Heath.

He looks glad to see me.

I start shaking again, and this time, I know it.

.   .   .

"More scholarship assurance right here." About fifteen minutes after I sit down and start writing, Heath takes my

Fat Girl feature and the post–emergency surgery update, tucks it into the folder he brought, then slips the folder under his arm. "After Channel 3 News called to verify you were writing about a real boy having real bariatric surgery, I didn't want to run this week's *Wire* without Fat Girl. We might get some major coverage on this."

He smiles at me, and I can't help smiling back. I'm amazed, because Heath and I aren't under a drafting table, but he's still managed to get me distracted and make me feel a little better. We're sitting in the back of the surgical waiting area, near three small groups of people I don't know. A different nurse sits at the desk by the phone, writing, writing, writing on a clipboard. My stomach's hurting and growling, but I'm not really hungry, not with everything that's happened.

"I think I made an enemy out of that one reporter," I say as I lean back in my chair and stretch. "But I guess she's over it."

Heath gives me an old–guy mature look. "Those reporters probably have lots of enemies. Adult ones, who sue them and stuff. We're lightweights."

He turns red when he realizes the term he just used, but doesn't say anything to make it worse.

It's cute, how Heath acts when he makes a goofball comment. I wonder if *he* hates being cute, like Burke? Maybe it's an all–guys–feel–that–way thing. One day, I'll ask him. I seem to ask Heath a lot of things I'd never ask anybody else.

My stomach twists, and I look toward the waiting room door. Burke's parents have gone to see him for the fifteen minutes allowed this hour, and Freddie's chatting with M & M. All three of them give me looks now and then, and I hope they aren't talking about me.

Heath's eyes are so bright and so blue when I look at him again. He seems so alive and full of motion and breath and health, it's hard to talk to him, but nice, too. I don't have to worry about Heath.

I point to the folder. "Will you bring me a copy of the paper once it's set?"

"Yeah, sure, but..." Heath fidgets in his seat, and his smile slips away. "That'll be Wednesday or Thursday. You'll be back by then, right?"

I shift in my chair too, numb and tired of being still. "Depends on how Burke's doing. If he doesn't wake up, or things go wrong, I might still be here."

Heath's eyes get a fraction wider, and his mouth stays open three or four seconds before he says, "You can't just stay out of school, can you?"

"Yes, I can." I feel a Fat Girl rush of will and determination, and I know my tone sounded Evillene bitchy. All I need is green glitter eye shadow to complete the effect.

"Okay." Heath raises one hand and makes a peace sign. "It's just with class and the play and senior stuff and ACT studying, I didn't think—but I'm sure you know what you're doing."

Brain explosion. Brain explosion.

I shove both of my fists against my eyes and shake my head. "Jeez, don't remind me about all that stuff."

"Sorry. Bad idea. Cut the text. Change the font." Heath's embarrassed face swims before my eyes, covered in spots, when I move my fists. He's got that cute *oops* look again, and it almost makes me want to laugh.

"Well, I've got to go," Heath says. "Will you walk me out?"

The thought of getting out of the waiting room, walking with Heath, maybe getting fresh air and a snack sounds way past excellent, but I'm afraid Burke's parents will come back and I'll miss the update.

"I can't. Sorry." I gesture to Freddy and M & M. "I need to be here in case we get news."

Heath looks unhappy, but he shrugs, and after a few seconds, gives me a too-serious look. "You call if you need me. I'm keeping my phone next to my bed all night, just in case."

"That's completely beyond sweet. You're the best." I want to lean over and hug him, but that feels a little weird, so I don't. But I know I'm looking at him hard, maybe funny, maybe desperate. The wrong way. Enough that I notice Freddie and Burke's sisters staring.

Get a grip, get a grip, keep a grip, look away . . .

But I can't.

Instead, I stand when Heath does, and walk him to the door of the waiting room.

When I pass Freddie and M & M, one of them sniffs. Loud.

What the hell?

I had to get the article written. Deadlines wait for no man . . . or surgery. They're college women. They ought to know that by now.

At the waiting room door, Heath stands close to me for

142

a count of three, maybe four, looking at me. Before I can ask him to stop, he says, "I'm sorry about all you're going through—and call if you need to."

Then he makes a quiet exit, folder still tucked beneath his arm.

I watch him go and wish I could be as relaxed and calm as he always looks. Like the world is no big deal, like life is easy and fun and just one big endless movie.

It must be amazing to be Heath. Or at least he's good at giving that impression.

Somebody grabs my elbow, and it's Freddie. She pushes me forward a step, out of the waiting room, into the hallway. "We need to talk, Jamie."

"No way." I hold my ground. "Burke's folks will be back any second. Whatever it is can wait that long."

"Now," Freddie says through her teeth.

"No!" I use the elbow she's holding to nudge her backward.

Red streaks form on both of Freddie's olive cheeks. "Fine. We'll stay *here* and you'll tell me what's happening between you and Heath, right here, right now."

"Wha—?" Like a guppy, I work my lips but don't do anything besides blow air bubbles. My face feels so hot it might as well be on fire.

Freddie's unguppy lips pull tight, and she almost growls out, "You heard me."

Now it's me walking away from the waiting room door, dragging Freddie with me by *her* elbow. When I finally stop, almost at the end of the hall back toward the ICU, I wheel on her. "What do you mean, what's happening between me and Heath? I told you, he wanted the piece, that's all."

Freddie twists out of my grip and rubs her elbow. "Piece of what?"

"For God's sake, Freddie!" Heat blasts across my face. "I've been waiting at this hospital all day for Burke, and he might be dying, and you're freaked out about *Heath*?"

Freddie stares at me, evil-eyes me, and scowls. "Wrong answer."

"What the hell do you want to hear?" I wish I had something to throw, since throwing Freddie's not an option. "What's the right answer?"

"Don't be stupid, Freddie, of course I'm not hot for Heath." Freddie props her hands on her hips. "Or how about, *Are you nuts, Freddie? I'm totally in love with Burke.* You should have seen yourself, Jamie, the way you looked at him—the way he looked at you. Something's up. Admit it."

I'm feeling like I could turn green and spew in a heartbeat. "You know me," I tell her, hearing the death-frost in my own voice. "You know exactly how I feel. Besides, do you honestly think Heath Montel would be interested in me?"

At this, Freddie gapes for a second, then pops back with, "Not everybody's stuck on the fat thing like you are."

Okay, now throwing Freddie does seem like an option. "What's that supposed to mean?"

"Nothing." Freddie backs down a little, lets her arms fall, and shakes her head. "Everything, Jamie. And the question isn't whether or not Heath could be drooling over you, because he is. Are *you* drooling over *him*?"

"You *are* nuts," When I glance back toward the ICU, a huge knot ties itself in my belly, just thinking about what's happening to Burke. "Of course Heath's not drooling over me."

As I turn back, she just stares.

I think seriously about finding out if I can turn her into a fastball.

"You don't even hear yourself, do you?" Freddie keeps staring. "Heath can't be attracted to you. Heath's not drooling over you. Fine! Who cares what Heath does? What about *you*, damn it?"

"I'm in love with Burke." My glare ratchets up five levels, daring her to say anything back, to doubt me.

All the red drains out of Freddie's cheeks, and suddenly, she looks as tired as I feel, except she's still glowering. We eye duel for a few seconds, then turn away at the same time and start back toward the waiting room. Stiff-like, almost marching beside each other.

Freddie mutters, "You still didn't say outright that you aren't interested in Heath."

"For Christ's sake, I'm not interested in Heath," I dutifully say to Freddie, but the whole time I'm wondering what I do feel. And why. And my brain starts spewing idiotic crap again, like *philophobia*, fear of falling in love. Then, *metathesiophobia*, fear of change.

Heath's face dances in my consciousness—his blond hair and blue eyes, and that smile. Checking on me. Leaving his phone beside his bed all night, in case I need to call.

Oh, why don't we add one more freak-ass word, while we're at it?

What about stygiophobia, *the fear of going STRAIGHT TO HELL?*

"I'm absolutely not interested in Heath, Freddie. He's just a friend." I stop her at the waiting room door and whisper, "Good enough?"

"Yeah, I guess," she says with her words, but her expression says *doubt, doubt, doubt.*

When we get into the waiting room, I check with Burke's sisters to make sure Burke's parents didn't slip past us while I was gone. Then I sit down with Freddie and M & M and we talk about little stuff—school, and play practice, and the math and science parts of the ACT giving Freddie and me fits, and the whole time, I'm thinking about Fat Girl and Heath Montel.

My eyes keep flicking back to the chairs where we sat, where I wrote the update for him.

Thank God, thank God, Heath's gone, and I'm done with that for now. One thing off my plate. I'm relieved. I was relieved when I watched him wander away down the long hospital corridor.

Right?

Definitely.

I was relieved.

I've got to be more careful about impressions, though. If Freddie wondered about Heath and me, then M & M might, too. As much as they hate me dating Burke, if I act like I might ditch him for another guy, M & M definitely would grow fangs and suck my blood. I have no doubt.

Besides, I would hate myself for doing something like that. Not that leaving Burke for Heath is remotely an option. Heath is my friend, nothing less and sure as hell nothing more. He's weird and he can be a pain, and there is so totally no way he would ever be interested in me. Heath isn't a date–the–Fat–Girl type of guy. Not an option on his part, or on mine.

FEATURE SPREAD

for publication Friday, September 28

Fat Girl Frothing
Fat Boy Chronicles IV

JAMIE D. CARCATERRA

Fat Boy lives.

I hope you cheered. Don't forget I'm watching. Fat Girl has spies *everywhere*.

So, like I said, Fat Boy's breathing. Fat Boy sits up in bed. He can eat a handful of ice chips. He can drink a few sips of sugar-free noncarbonated beverages (find some of those other than water, I dare you). He can suck a few tablespoons of sugarless gelatin through a straw.

Yum.

He can stand, but a therapist has to help him walk. His wounds hurt, especially the second place the surgeon cut Fat Boy to help him breathe again. He has to blow air in and out of this little spirometer thing and move a little blue ball in a tube to be sure he doesn't get pneumonia.

And today, after three days in the ICU

and four days in a regular room on ice chips and gelatin, Fat Boy got to try pureed food. Not sure what it was. Some kind of pasty-pale goo.

Of course, nobody told me about the frothing. I'm not sure anybody told Fat Boy about it, and for damn sure nobody told NoNo, who fainted, and Freddie, who barfed. Fat Boy's sisters and parents turned kinda green, too, though his sisters always look a little—well, witchy.

Frothing works like this:

Normal stomachs make acid to help with digestion. Stapled guts fail to make enough acid, so the teeny pouch manufactures mucous to help digest food like pureed pale goo. Mucus builds up in the tube between the pouch and Fat Boy's mouth, called the esophagus. He sucks down goo, feels sick, and back the goo comes, mucus and all, bubbling up the esophagus and blowing out his mouth and nose. No, scratch that. Frothing. Like what cappuccino machines do to milk to make that foam on top.

Only out the mouth and nose.

I thought it would come out his eyes and ears before it was done. Fat Boy yelled and said he felt like somebody turned him into an exploding soda can.

Not fun. Not pretty.

Ruined my lunch and scarred NoNo for life. Freddie's talking about therapy.

Raise your hand if you think this surgery ought to come with a full-page, all-caps FROTH WARNING.

Well, that's unanimous.

Time Postsurgery: 10 Days
Pounds Lost: 16

CHAPTER
TEN

Burke studies me with his dark eyes, which seem wider and bigger as the days pass. He's propped on pillows in his hospital bed, and he has one arm draped across his belly to hold everything still. Every time I see him do that, I want to yell at him for choosing to have this procedure, but I don't because he's trying so, so hard to get better.

We're alone in his clean white hospital room with its clean white tile, because it's morning. I get before nine and after play practice, by agreement with M & M and Burke's parents, even on Saturdays and Sundays. Freddie and NoNo usually come with me at night, but in the morning, Burke's all mine.

"What time do you have to leave?" His voice sounds hoarse and weak, but at least he's been upright for my whole pre–ACT visit, and that breathing–tube hole in his throat is closing up.

I glance at my watch and taste a backwash of the coffee and pretzels I ate for breakfast. "Ten minutes. Mom's picking me up out front."

Burke coughs. The wet, rattling sound gives me cold chills.

"Is Freddie taking the test today, too?" He blinks those big eyes at me, chasing the chills away.

"Are you kidding?" I smile. "This is Freddie we're talking about. She's waiting until three Saturdays from now. The absolute last moment she can get a score turned in with her applications on time."

"Yeah, should have figured." He shifts his weight and winces. "You're ready. You're gonna kick major standardized-test ass."

Is his hair getting thinner? My smile fades to nothing even though I'm trying to keep it. I mean, I understand this whole losing-weight thing, how the pounds are falling off of him. He does have a stapled gut, and he's had complications, and he's been sick as a dog and frothing every other time he tries to eat. With all of that, nineteen pounds in eleven days isn't completely unreasonable.

But Burke won't lose his hair, right?

I didn't read anything about losing hair. Anorexics lose their hair and get all hypoglycemic and stuff—but I didn't think that was such an issue for bariatric patients.

I'd go check the top of his head and make sure his dreads are still firmly attached, but that might freak him out. After all the volcanic goo eruptions, I don't want to do anything to stress him. Stress makes mucous bubble like Evillene's cauldron.

After a few seconds, I realize we've stopped talking, and he's back to studying me. It's strange not to be eating breakfast with him. I must have had breakfast with Burke hundreds of times, but how can I eat real food in front of him?

We probably won't share meals hardly ever now. We'll have to find other stuff to do while we talk, so we don't just stare. Staring is weird.

"Can you tell I'm losing?" Burke asks for probably the twentieth time in the past three days.

I nod, like I always do. "More and more."

And I *can* tell.

His cheeks sink in and his neck's starting to sag, and under the sheets, his legs don't look so big. I'm not sure what I'm imagining and what's real, and what's because he's been so sick. If I lose thirty pounds, or even forty, people don't notice. I lost fifty once, and only Freddie and NoNo and Burke and my family had a clue.

Can I really see Burke's missing nineteen pounds?

Or am I seeing the future?

The thought makes *me* want to froth.

"Gotta go," I tell him. When I get up to give him a kiss, my hip bumps the chair and turns it over. I grab it before it clatters on the floor, because that happens a lot. My body doesn't work well with hospital furniture. My body doesn't work well with hospitals, period. Too big for the beds. Too big for the rooms. Definitely too big for stupid little wooden chairs.

Too big for Burke.

I set the chair upright and lean down to kiss Burke. His lips feel moist and soft again, like they're supposed to feel. I linger, tasting hints of cherry Jell-O. Burke always liked whipped cream with his desserts, but he can't have whipped cream now. Too much sugar. Not enough room for extras in a thumb-sized stomach.

"Mmm," Burke says as I pull away. His gorgeous eyes are still closed. "You'll ace this. Good luck, babe."

A nurse comes in carrying a tiny bowl of pureed goo. It's green.

I glance from the goo to Burke, imagining green froth even though I'm totally trying not to.

"Good luck to you, too."

. . .

When I climb into our old Ford, Mom smells like garlic and she's dressed in home clothes.

With a sigh, I push at the pile of mail on the seat between us.

"Checked it before I left," she says as I rifle through the letters, still thinking a little about the goo and wishing Mom would wear better clothes to places where she might run into my friends. Or at least take a bath.

An envelope from Dad's insurance company catches my eye. When I pick it up and ask Mom, she says I can open it. I hear the sudden strain in her voice and know we're both thinking the same thing—that this might be the letter about bariatric surgery and whether or not we have benefits that cover it.

My back and shoulders tingle as I hold the monogrammed parchment and blink at our address on the front. The letters blur even as I'm trying to focus.

I don't want bariatric surgery. There's no way I'd go through what Burke's going through.

154

But here's the letter telling me whether or not my family could afford it—for me, or for Mom or Dad.

Why does it matter? Why am I even looking? Would I let any more people I know get their gut stapled?

The envelope won't give.

Finally, I just rip off the end like Dad does, tearing half the letter in the process.

"What does it say?" Mom asks as she drives slowly through the Saturday morning traffic.

"I don't know yet." When I glance up, I calculate the distance to the testing center over at West Memorial Library. About ten minutes. We've got half an hour, but taking the ACT doesn't seem important all of a sudden.

The paper in my hand feels monumental.

I gaze at it, hold it carefully, treat it like it's fragile.

What if the procedure is covered?

Will Mom and Dad push me to get the surgery? Will they want it for themselves?

Do I want it?

My eyes drift from the folded paper downward, to my big belly, spread across my bigger knees.

For a split second, I can see myself without the fat roll. I can see my own thighs, trim and sleek and muscled, like those underwear models on television. I'd pump a lot of iron, walk miles, go up and down stairs as fast as Freddie—and I wouldn't even have to hold on to the railings. Maybe I'd never have chafe marks again, or a heat rash, or new stretch marks.

Maybe I'd quit worrying about whether or not I stink.

Maybe I'd shrink as fast as Burke. How small could

155

I get, with a thumb–sized pouch instead of a stomach?

Would I be like NoNo, all sticks and bones, or like Freddie—just right, with wide girl–hips?

If I got small, I'd go back to Hotchix and buy that shirt with the blue pattern, even if NoNo disowned me for supporting animal torturers.

Hell, I'd about have to disown myself, buying from Hotchix, but that shirt would be worth it.

Little by little, I unfold the paper.

My eyes blur at the words, hoping they won't say we can have the surgery, and at the same time, hoping that we do have the benefit. My brain yanks in two different directions, toward thin me and back toward fat me.

The first thing I read is a salutation addressed to Mom, with a note that Dad's the insured, and the name of his employer. Below that, in straight, clear type, the print reads:

Dear Mrs. Carcaterra:

Thank you for your recent inquiry about bariatric surgery. At this time, GetLifeRight does not cover weight-loss products, procedures, or programs. These items are not scheduled for review during this calendar year.

We wish you good fortune in your pursuit of health, and urge you to Get Life Right!

Sincerely,

Ann Smith

Enrollee Representative Class III
GetLifeRight Enrollee Services Department

Energy drains out of me until I feel like a puppet with broken joints.

I sag back against the tattered seat. My face turns hot and I sweat worse. Probably stink worse than Mom's garlic-basted home clothes.

I should ball up the letter and pitch it to the floor. Should have done that when I first saw the envelope.

How is it fair that some fat people can afford to get treatment and other fat people don't even have a chance to make that decision? The news keeps saying that being fat is just as bad as having cancer, that I'll die young from my fat and have all kinds of miserable health problems— but cancer kids always get treatment, don't they?

Now I do ball up the letter and pitch it on the Ford's dingy floorboard. Then I step on it for good measure.

Clearly, fat kids and fat people are worth exactly nothing to GetLifeRight and Ann Smith, Enrollee Representative Class III.

"Guess that's a no." Mom sighs.

"That's a no." My voice bounces through the car, sounding bright and light and without a care. "Not covered."

Sometimes I amaze myself. I'd rather scream and throw a fit, but what's the point? Would it change GetLife-Right's mind? What about Ann Smith? Would she give one flying damn?

Mom lets out another sigh, and this time the sound lasts until my teeth grind. "I'm sorry, Jamie. I really thought—well, I hoped—we could offer you this option. I know it was important."

"What? No way." I smash my foot against the crumpled

letter again. "I don't want any of us to go through what Burke's going through. Even if that letter had said yes, I wouldn't have done it."

Would I?

My hands come to rest against my belly, which I guess will be a part of me probably forever. Smartass cheer-leaders and people like Ann Smith will get to ask me if I'm pregnant and call me Blubber after that Judy Blume character, and the Blowfish saleswomen of the world get to keep right on ignoring me.

I see Ann Smith in my mind's eye, all stick–skinny, probably wearing a halter dress with bright pink spring flowers, and white peep–toe pumps. I'd break my thick Fat Girl neck even trying on a pair of pumps. Most fat girls don't wear heels. Add that to the list of girl–shit I'm shut out from, thanks to being big, and thanks to GetLife-Right declining the only treatment known to have a shred of success.

Ann Smith merges with Blowfish in my mind, and with all the women who look like them, act like them, live and breathe like them, worry over two pounds, and whine about a tiny pooch just below their belly-button.

BWNTE.

Bitches Who Need To Eat.

Screw them. And GetLifeRight with them.

"Jamie," Mom's saying softly, over and over.

When I finally look at her, I realize the Ford is parked at the curb outside West Memorial Library. Droves of

BWNTE stream past our car, loaded with presharpened number two pencils.

"Damn," I mutter, fighting an urge to yell about something, anything, just to yell my head off. "I forgot my pencils."

Mom brightens and rummages in the pocket of her dirty black sweats. She fishes out three pencils, two of which are slightly used and chewed (my dad the pencil eater)—but all sharpened.

"Thanks." I take the pencils from Mom's hand. "You're the best."

I hate myself for how sad and worried Mom looks. All because our insurance company won't pay to nearly murder me like Burke's has, and I decided to be a sniveling dork about it.

If Ann Smith had to live with Mom's expression, she'd find a way to get that damned benefit reviewed. Tomorrow.

Before I get out of the car, I squish myself across the front seat and give Mom a big, sloppy hug. "You really are the best. You and Dad both."

Mom sniffs in my embrace and presses her face against my neck. "I'm so sorry, honey. If we could do this for you, we would. You know that, right?"

When I let her go, I make sure I'm smiling. "I told you, I wouldn't have had the surgery even if we had the benefits."

"Okay." Mom brushes a lock of hair off my forehead, and her mouth trembles. "I just—it has to be so hard for you, knowing your boyfriend's going to be thin, and you still having to struggle. I wish I could take that away from you."

How many times have I wished I didn't have her genes, or Dad's, or any of my family's biology? But right now, I don't care. I don't even care about garlic home clothes or the fact that she's crying in front of people who might know me.

"You don't have to take anything away from me, Mom. I can handle myself just fine." I give her hand a squeeze and hope that's enough, because my pencils and I have to go.

Mom wishes me luck as I get out of the car, and I'm terrified to look back because I might see her crying all by herself and I'd lose my mind completely.

Why does the sky have to get so gray in the fall? A little light would be nice. A little sunshine. Anything to perk up my mood. As it is, I barely have the steam to get in the Memorial Library door, follow the signs to the small auditorium, and make my way inside.

The first thing I see is a room full of chairs with attached desks.

Oh, no friggin' way. Not today.

The nearest proctor looks at me expectantly. She's dressed in a yellow pencil skirt and flowery white shirt, and I can tell it will never in a million years occur to this BWNTE that I don't fit in desks like that. She can't just offer a solution. Oh, no. I'll have to *ask*.

Then she'll probably talk loud about the solution, and I'll probably stuff her into the nearest pencil sharpener and crank her head to a fine point.

I scan the room in complete frustration, and my eyes land on a blond-haired boy lounging in one of those desks. He's wearing Dockers and a white T-shirt, and I'd know him anywhere.

Heath.

My heart does a lame skip-and-bump, and my skin heats with embarrassment.

The desk thing is bad enough, but now, today, in front of *him*?

Why do I care? I don't care.

But I do.

Being humiliated in front of Heath feels a thousand times worse than being humiliated in front of a bunch of strangers.

Maybe he won't look up. Maybe he won't realize what's going on with me—but of course he does look up before I even finish the thought.

When he sees me, he smiles.

I wave.

Heath mouths *good luck*.

You too, I mouth back.

He keeps gazing at me and smiling.

I'm so stuck. It's time to sit down. The proctors say so, several times, but if I try to sit in one of those desks, it'll be a disaster. I won't fit. I'll probably break the damned thing.

Christ. In front of Heath.

Somebody boil me in hot water. It'd be lots less painful than this.

"Take your seats," a proctor demands, sounding law-enforcement firm. "Now, please. Yes, take your seats."

I'm wanting to cram my pencils in my eyeballs.

Oh, screw *it*.

I straighten as much as I can, make myself as wide as humanly possible, and bowl my way straight down front to the proctors' table. The plastic chair I pull out looks small, and sure enough, it sags beneath me when I sit down. But it holds. And I'm at the table, where I fit.

I don't even glance at Heath. I don't want to see the look on his face now. He'd never laugh at me, I don't think. But he might feel sorry for me, and I really would rather die than see pity in his handsome blue eyes.

As for the proctors, let them say something about my seating choice.

The chick in the pencil skirt looks like she might, but another proctor catches her eye and shakes his head. When he looks in my direction, he smiles at me like he understands.

Okay.

Whatever.

Maybe his mom's a Fat Girl, or his sister, or his best friend. Maybe he used to be fat and got his gut shrink-stapled. Or maybe he's had to take three dozen sensitivity classes and the ACT people consider being fat a bona fide disability.

Heath doesn't exist. I'm not looking at Heath. No way.

All I care about is keeping my seat without any drama or big production, acing this test, and putting the ACT part of senior year nightmare finally, finally behind me.

Only by the time the test comes around, I'm so sleepy I want to close my eyes. Or leave. Or slap one of the forty or so people staring in my direction because I'm sitting at the proctors' table.

Don't look at Heath.

Nothing like trying to pull open a sealed test booklet on cue in front of an audience. Or reading passages full of "underlined material" I'm supposed to correct for the English section. It seems so stupid, deciding between "they're" and "there" and "its" and "it's" when Burke's in the hospital and Mom's probably still out in the car crying.

My stomach hurts.

I know I'm sweating.

Don't look at Heath.

The passages don't want to make sense, and I can't remember the damned difference between *further* and *farther*, and even more, I totally don't care.

My first pencil breaks because I'm pushing down too hard.

This is a nightmare. It's worse than a nightmare.

I need these scores. I need the highest everything I can get for scholarships and special grants and admission to Northwestern.

That refrain's getting old. I'm tired of singing it to myself.

For a while, I sing *Wiz* songs in my mind, and squint at underlined material, and hack at where to position adverbs in sentences and which words should have an *–ly* ending.

Stupid, stupid, stupid.

The proctors calling time on the English section is just white noise.

I finally look at Heath.

He's got his head down, working away.

Nothing gets into my brain. Absolutely nothing. It's like my eyes can't even see the questions.

After a while, I give up, turn the test answer sheet over, dig through my memory to remember some of the recent letters Fat Girl received, and start writing on the blank back side. I can always tag the letters later, and clean up the wording once I'm back at school and see the actual text.

For now, I'll do my best and worry about the rest later.

Burke may have given me no choices in whether or not he had his surgery and started all his changes. GetLife-Right, the yellow–skirted BWNTE, Blowfish—all of them—can get stuffed.

I've got a choice now, and I'm choosing not to suffer through this damned test anymore.

FEATURE SPREAD
for publication Friday, October 5

Fat Girl Answering II

JAMIE D. CARCATERRA

Dear Fat Girl:
How is Fat Boy doing now?
Time postsurgery, seventeen days. Pounds lost, thirty-five. He's still in the hospital. He has an infection in his left big toe, if you can believe that. A tiny sore, but it's getting better. Oh, and he got a haircut.

Dear Fat Girl:
How did the ACT go?
Don't ask. I'm banned from taking it again because I refused to hand in my answer sheet, which had the rough draft of this column on the back of it. Guess my last scores will just have to do. Play practice is getting too intense anyway. The ACT and its desks and its yellow-skirted proctors can all get stuffed. Like I said, don't ask.

Dear Fat Girl:
Does Fat Boy really froth like a cappuccino maker when he eats too much?
SERIOUSLY, don't ask THIS question anymore. Yes, he froths. Yes, Freddie pukes every time somebody brings it up. Next person who asks this gets to catch NoNo when she faints. Knock it off. You're all totally gross.

Dear Fat Girl:
Do you think Fat Boy did the right thing, having this surgery?
It really doesn't matter what I think about his decision, does it? He had the surgery, and I'll be right beside him all the way. Fat Boy made a choice for himself. At least he had the choice to make. Not everyone does.

Dear Fat Girl:
Can you tell Fat Boy's losing weight?
Definitely. He's still a big guy, but he's changing every time I see him.

Dear Fat Girl:
Are you on a diet to keep up with Fat Boy?
No. You can get stuffed along with the ACT people.

Additional Note from Fat Girl:
Choice.

166

I mentioned choice in one of my responses. When was the last time you looked up that word? According to *Dictionary.com Unabridged (*version *1.1), choice* is "the right, power, or opportunity to choose; option." The right. The power. The opportunity. The option.

Have you ever thought about what it would be like not to have the right, power, opportunity, or option to choose what happens to your own body? I particularly like the *power* part. The bottom line is, choice means power.

Take away somebody's choice, and take away her power. That's wrong, isn't it? To rob somebody of power? Of rights? Of options?

If you agree, please leave a message for Ann Smith at GetLifeRight Enrollee Services.

CHAPTER
ELEVEN

It's no easy feat, finishing a scholarship application and a college entrance application exactly one hour before mailing deadlines, in the hall, dressed in red and white striped tights, a green hoopskirt, and glitter.

"Damn it, damn it, damn it." I dab Freddie's whiteout pen against the date while NoNo rolls her eyes. She disapproves of whiteout pens. Too many chemicals. NoNo's very presence is getting on my nerves today, even though I don't know why. Maybe it's the perpetual worried look on her face when I'm already nervous. Or maybe it's the whiteout thing. Or maybe it's just that NoNo would never have to play the fat part in any play.

My hands shake. All I can smell is sweat and ink and whiteout. If I don't get this stupid application done and get back to the auditorium in time for final run-through, Dunstein will go Evillene on *me*. We open in three hours.

My first opening night without Burke who's still in the hospital.

Heath said he would try to come if the typesetter co-operates.

"It doesn't matter what date you put on the application." Freddie leans against a row of lockers in the deserted hallway as I doctor the date yet again. "They won't know for sure when you signed it."

"It matters if I wrote down the wrong year." I keep my glower directed at Freddie. I'd rather pretend NoNo isn't standing in front of me in her bright blue jeans and drab brown T-shirt, chewing her fingernail because I'm polluting the environment. She's probably late for some Militant Green or Save the Chinchillas rally, or maybe an old-fashioned Down with Anything Sane and Normal protest march.

"Just give me the apps." Freddie sounds tense. "The main post office closes in half an hour, and I'm not driving all the way out to the airport for the overnight drop." She gestures to her sharp pin-striped pantsuit. "I do have a date, you know."

"She goes to college," NoNo whispers, like somebody might overhear, or like Freddie cares if anyone knows she's dating a college woman.

"I'm just glad it's not that scary tattoo-chick from the library," I mutter, drawing a snort from Freddie.

At least Freddie's current girlfriend seemed calm when I met her, and like she might not tap-dance on Freddie's feelings if things don't work out. I hate it when Freddie dates snobby women, with or without studded dog collars, and ends up bawling and eating donuts for days when they dump her.

I smudge the last pen mark. "Crap!"

"Just give them to me!" Freddie thrusts out her hand.

Swearing, I hand over the applications. Freddie grabs the papers and hands them to NoNo, who holds them like they're toxic.

My ears buzz, and a wave of heat crashes across my face and neck. "Oh, for God's sake, NoNo, just fold them and stick them in the envelopes!"

NoNo flinches like I slapped her, which makes Freddie puff up like Blowfish from Hotchix. "Take it easy," she says, her voice quiet.

"Seriously, Freddie, don't you ever get tired of it?" I'm getting louder instead of quieter, and I feel light and free and heavy and evil all at the same time. My voice booms in the empty hallway, louder, louder, like I'm projecting to an auditorium the size of Carnegie Hall. "It's Wite-Out. Wite-Out. Not rat poison! Does everything have to be a friggin' catastrophe with her?"

NoNo's head droops until her chin touches her chest. Her arms sag, too, and my application smacks against the legs of her too-blue jeans. She doesn't say anything, which, insanely, makes me madder.

"Well?" I ask, taking a step toward her. "Do you have to freak out about everything?"

"Back off." Freddie projects better than I do. Her snarl hits me like a push in the chest. My teeth clamp shut, and I back up a fraction. My face cools off a little, but not much.

No words.

If I say anything it'll be bad, and bad wrong.

NoNo's shaking from head to toe, and I worry she's about to fall over, or drop the applications, or both. Freddie takes the papers from her, tucks them into the envelopes, and seals the envelopes tight, all the while staring straight at me.

Somehow, I keep my mouth shut and my body still. I want to rant worse than Evillene ever dreamed of ranting. I want to call NoNo names and beat Freddie into the tile. But I don't. I really, really don't want to do that. I want to snatch the applications, tear them up, and just...run away. Go away. Get away. No paper, no Heath, no play without Burke in the audience. No fat part. No skinny part. No bariatric surgery. No environmentally friendly anything. There has to be some place in the world without any of these things, right?

When she finishes with my applications, Freddie says, "We're leaving now."

They both turn away from me, and Freddie leads NoNo straight down the hall and out of the building.

I stand there and stand there and stand there. It seems like forever, but I can still see Freddie and NoNo through the glass panes in the door, walking farther and farther away, across the parking lot.

The sun's going down.

And Burke's still in the hospital, and it's opening night, and I just sent my applications to Northwestern University with a crummy ACT score and my National Feature Award portfolio to the judges without a Fat Boy wrap-up—and pissed off my best friends who are mailing them, and the show must go on.

171

"Evillene!" Dunstein yells from behind me.

By the time I recover from my heart attack and turn around, he's already gone, back through the auditorium's swinging doors.

I hurry after him. When I push through the doors, I'm surprised to see several back rows already filled with people, and what looks like a news crew from Lois Lane's station setting up in the corner.

Well. Guess we're going big-time here at Garwood.

Flashbulbs spark as I sail down the aisle toward the stage. Yeah, boys and girls. Evillene's on the move.

As I pass the aisle seat three rows from the stage, where Burke usually sits, I turn my head.

If he weren't stapled and sick, he'd be here by now.

More flashbulbs blaze through my consciousness as I make my way onto the stage, then behind the curtain.

What the hell?

Dunstein's waiting for me, and he's smiling.

I stop in my tracks. Look down at my skirts to be sure I don't look like a freak. Dunstein never smiles on opening night. Bark, yap, screech, shiver like a psychotic Chihuahua, yes. Smile, no.

"Sold out," he says. If the little man had whiskers, they'd be twitching. He beckons me toward the makeup area for a quick touch-up and more powder. "And most of the season ticket holders actually showed up. You did great."

"Me?" Total confusion. "I didn't do anything. Thespian Club and Drama Boosters do tickets and promo. Are we really a sellout?"

"First time ever, and *you* did it. Your column." He shakes his finger in the air. "What's it called?"

"'Fat Girl Manifesto.'" My lips and cheeks suddenly feel numb.

He nods. "A newspaper, a national magazine, and a re-gional television affiliate. They've all come to see Fat Girl."

My words melt away like a wicked witch drenched by a bucket of water. It takes a lot of my energy just to nod.

Dunstein's babbling about how my columns on Burke are starting to attract national attention and provoke de-bate about adolescent bariatric surgery.

He cannot be serious.

Is that even possible, that anybody outside Garwood would bother with our dinky school newspaper?

We still use a typesetter, for God's sake, and the princi-pal's tried for years to "retire" us.

But Dunstein is serious, and he won't shut up, and I wish I had a bucket of water to melt him. Instead, I do a quick self-check. Fists, unclenched. Mouth, closed. Smile, fake but present. Then I rehearse the lines to my opening number in my head over and over, until Dunstein finally lets me pass.

As I'm walking toward costumes and makeup, my cell buzzes against my leg.

I yank it out of my pocket and see Burke's number on the display.

A smile tugs at my lips.

He's the only one who'd call me on opening night. He didn't forget after all, even though he's sick and still locked up in a hospital.

Warmth edges out some of my nervousness as I punch the green button and lift the phone to my ear.

"Hey, baby." I'm still smiling.

"Hey back." He sounds pumped. "Guess what?"

I'm waiting for *it's your opening night* or *break a leg* or *see, I'd never forget my favorite witch on a big night.*

What he says is, "I got weighed again—and I've lost thirty-eight pounds. *Thirty-eight* in eighteen days. Can you believe that? And that's weighing late in the day. I'll be down even more in the morning."

"I—uh. That's great." The phone shifts on my ear as I force myself to stand up straight when I'd rather just pitch the phone and sit down.

When I don't keep gushing, Burke says, "Sounds like you're standing in a well. With a crowd. Did you go out?"

The noise of the audience and the murmur from the cast and props guys get on my nerves. They sound like water, rushing and roaring, then dropping to a whisper and rising again. "It's the first weekend in October, Burke."

"The first—*oh.* Opening night!" A slapping sound comes over the phone, like Burke popped himself on the forehead. "Well, I know you'll do great. Break a leg, baby. Give 'em hell, okay?"

My chest feels tight. "Okay."

Burke says he loves me, and I say I love him and hang up the phone.

Still want to throw it, but too many people crowd around me. It's time to move. Gotta go.

Give 'em hell. Yeah.

174

Maybe it would have been better if he hadn't called at all.

But that's stupid. I'm glad he called. And he did remember to wish me luck, stage style. That should count. He is in the hospital and everything.

Losing weight just by breathing.

I try to forget about that, about everything, as I force myself to the dressing area and pull on my costume.

Time zooms by as I get final wardrobe touch-up, makeup, hair, and green glitter nails poking out of red and white striped gloves. Then it's time for boots and whip, and I'm ready. I'm not Jamie or even Fat Girl. I'm the queen of mean, the master of monkeybats. I'm the Wicked Witch of the West, modern style.

I'm Evillene.

And I don't make my first appearance until the second act.

Fat girls, even wicked witches, rarely have meaty parts.

Tonight, though, I'm not sorry.

Every time I glimpse the audience, I can't help noticing the reporters in the back rows and Burke's empty season-ticket seat. The whole thing gives me a hollow ache way down inside, like the universe has flipped on its side and won't roll back over.

Lights blaze. Guys moving props swear under their breath. It's getting hot as hell like it always does, and I mentally dare my makeup to run. Music swells and falls, swells and falls, and the first act ends and it's my turn now.

I settle myself in my painted wooden throne, still out of sight.

It's barely big enough, but lots better than ACT chairs.

The Winkie chant begins.

Winkies (monkeybats) walk across the stage tugging ropes.

My throne starts to roll across the floor, just like it's supposed to.

The Lord High Underling whips the Winkies and yells at them to pull harder and finally bellows, "Make way! Make way! The Wicked Witch of the West. Make way for Evillene!"

Groaning and crying from the Winkies. Another big tug, and my giant-ass throne rolls into view and stops, center stage.

I give the world my best glare, squinch my face, shove myself to my feet and yell my first line without even having to work up the emotion.

"Shut up!" I sweep my pointing finger across all the Winkies. "Because I'm evil with *ev-ry-body* today!"

The music for "No Bad News" kicks up high and fast, I turn square with the audience to start the song—and Burke's reserved chair isn't empty anymore.

Heath's sitting in it.

My chin drops a fraction.

He's dressed in jeans and a blue polo, his blond hair hangs in his eyes, and I think he has glue all over his hands, but he's here. To see me be Evillene. And he's sitting in Burke's seat.

The music gets loud, pauses, and starts back. Winkies stare at me.

Shit. I missed my cue.

With a fast nod, I rearrange my face into hate, doom, and disaster, start my walk, and belt my lines as I pop my whip over everybody's head again and again. Lots of wide hip action. Lots of shoulder.

I so hope my boobs don't fall out of this green corset top.

Glitter rains as I *pop, pop, pop* that whip and sing, and Winkies scatter and duck.

I'm Evil.

I'm Evillene.

Take that, Heath and Burke and Freddie and NoNo. *Pop!* Take that, reporters and Dunstein. *Pop!* Anne Smith. ACT. *POP!*

"Don't nobody bring me, don't nobody bring me, no bad news!" I do a big whirl and sweep with the whip.

Heath probably thinks this is a total gas.

And *what* are those reporters writing?

Fat Girl: Feature Columnist or Whip Freak?

I free-fall through the rest of my lines, Evillene-ing on instinct. We're to Scene III and Heath's still here, and he's smiling whenever I peek at him through the tiny gap between wall and curtain.

I let loose a major offstage Evillene cackle, then barrel out to make my last grand entrance.

As I project my lines, demanding Dorothy's slippers, Heath's still smiling.

I can't see the reporters because of the angles of the lights.

My fight with the Cowardly Lion begins. He calls me crazy.

177

"Is that an insult?" I screech at the lion, loving the opportunity to yell without pissing anybody off.

"No, Your Fatness," Lion stammers. "It's just—"

"Your Fatness?" I bellow with real gusto. "Your Fatness?"

Man, did I ever put my soul into *that* line. I step on the carefully taped X like I'm supposed to, grab Lion's arm, and put him in a hammer lock. "I'll cut you up, kitty-man. I'll have your hide!"

Seconds later, I'm melting, melting, and disappearing. And the music and burning sound effects get deafening. The guys under the stage pop the platform cover back in place, and I'm in the dark, and I'm done. I'm finished.

Fat Girl has left the stage.

I pick my way around ropes and pulleys and props and stage guys whispering *good job*, make it back to the backstage steps, and head for the dressing area. It'll take about a year for the play to finish and for us to bow. It'll take another year for me to get this corset top unlaced and scrub all this glitter off my face. And another year on top of that to be willing to walk out from behind the curtain, head into the auditorium, face Heath, and fool with reporters.

Breathing hard. Definitely sweating. Definitely stinking. I brush past a stack of wood offstage, turn a corner into the hallway to the dressing area, and nearly plow full-Evillene-force into Heath.

He's just standing there with his hands in his jeans pockets, grinning like an idiot. His eyes drift from my wig to my glitter makeup, then down to my cleavage and back up again.

Males.

All males.

Boobs turn them into idiots.

"You were outstanding," he says quietly.

"Thanks. I can't believe you took the time to show up for this." I notice he smells good tonight, like aftershave. Like maybe his jeans and blue polo are Heath's current version of a nice outfit, and he actually dressed up to come to see me in *The Wiz*. Except for the dried glue stuck up to his elbows and all over the left knee of his jeans, he does look good.

Great, in fact.

Heath manages to keep his eyes where they're supposed to be. "Wouldn't have missed it. You were born for that part. You know that, right?"

"Wicked Witch of the West. My fondest dream."

"It's got so much flair and drama. Best part in the whole play." He slides a hand out of his pocket and jerks a thumb back toward the stage. "That's why I didn't stick around. Once you melt, it gets pretty lame."

My cheeks warm up under all the green glitter. "That's sweet."

He gets a nervous look, then asks, "You want to grab something to eat, or do you have to stick around?"

"I'd really like that, but I can't leave until everything's over." My frown is genuine. The first expression all night that feels like mine, my own, and not Fat Girl's or Evillene's.

179

"Curtain calls, and after–play meeting since it's opening night—and I'll have to get out of costume."

And write Fat Girl for early layout before you get stressed out and kill me.

He looks disappointed, but I can tell he understands. "Okay, well, if you've got any energy left, I'll be over in the cave. And I'll bring you back some chow just in case."

I shouldn't go.

But I know I will, even though I'm tired and wrecked and probably the last place in the world I should be is in the cave with Heath Montel.

"Thanks," I say quietly, like NoNo telling some big se–cret. "I'll probably be there, if I can dodge the reporters."

Heath's smile makes me feel like anything but Evil–lene.

As he walks away, he waves over his shoulder. Even though he can't see me, I wave back.

Why does it have to be so long to curtain call?

FEATURE SPREAD
for publication Friday, October 12

Fat Girl Leading

JAMIE D. CARCATERRA

Why can't a Fat Girl play the lead?

I mean, seriously, would it hurt your eyes for a large woman to be onstage for hours—other than in an opera or a play about being fat?

Why can't Dorothy from Kansas have love handles? Why can't Christine from *Phantom of the Opera* take up a larger section of the stage? Would she sing less beautifully because she's fat? Would the Phantom and the hero love her less?

Ah. See, that's probably the rub.

Nobody wants the Fat Girl. Or more to the point, nobody *should* want the Fat Girl.

Isn't that a rule?

Like the Fat Girl must be thin or well on her way to weight loss by the end of any book, play, or movie.

And yet, articles abound on why Fat

Girls feel bad about themselves, have a higher risk of suicide, and literally kill themselves to be thin.

Hello?

Want to stem this tide?

Next time you morph a famous book into a movie or a play, hire a Fat Girl to play the best role. Let Juliet wear a size 3X. Let Ophelia have a few curves.

Come on. Be brave. Break the mold.

Let a Fat Girl play the lead.

CHAPTER
TWELVE

Dunstein dismisses the play meeting after only thirty-two minutes of ranting, set changes, scene changes, and new instructions. This has to be a record. He was particularly pleased with Evillene's dramatic melt, which I translate to mean he was ecstatic over the sellout and press attention.

I fold up the column I wrote while he ran his mouth, but when I try to get out the door, he grabs my arm and whispers, "Be positive when they interview you. Be up-beat."

When I stare down at Dunstein, he lets me go and his brown eyes widen pitifully like a lapdog about to be spanked. "They're interviewing me?" I glance behind him at the empty room. "Just me? Not the whole cast?"

Dunstein gestures toward the stage door and does his nervous-dog tremble. "Just don't be an ass. For the sake of *The Wiz*."

Okay.

I thought those reporters came to see the show and write their own pieces and opinions. If my brain hadn't been total confetti, I would have realized they'd want to talk to me, and probably alone.

My legs and arms feel heavy, and my brain feels like a balloon losing air.

Visions of Lois Lane's nasty investigative report dance in my head.

My personality tears down the center. The left half of my essence wants to boil onto the stage in my Evillene glitter and hoopskirt and hold court, run my mouth, really have my say. Do something to get national attention for Fat Girl, and for Fat Girls. Give important, meaty quotes, and shine, shine, shine for the scholarship observation period.

This could be it. I could do it—make a difference and wow the scholarship judges, too.

But the right half of my essence wants to slide out a side door and call Burke. Or forget that and go directly to Heath to show him my column and get his opinion. The thought of seeing Heath, of finally getting to relax and talk awhile, even listen to stupid music, seems like rapture. At least Heath and *The Wire* and my column are still right. Maybe after a little chill-out time, I could face another call from or visit with Burke, or think of the right words to apologize to Freddie and NoNo for being a psychotic bitch in the hall before the performance. Maybe I could even go get Mom some flowers, or something to cheer her up, since she's still all flat and sad over not being able to afford a life-threatening surgery to make me skinny.

Dunstein's dog-eyes and my need for that scholarship finally win out.

After a few minutes of makeup repair (no sweaty streaks), a teeth check (no half-chewed glitter), and a pits check (no skanky fog), I head backstage, through the set and stacked props, to the curtain. When I peek out, the auditorium is mostly empty. There's only one news crew left, with a reporter and a camera man and another guy who probably works for a newspaper, since he doesn't have a camera crew handy. Nobody looks like Lois Lane.

Deep breath.

I push my way through the divide in the curtain and step onto the stage.

Both reporters in the far right corner of the auditorium perk up, but I raise one hand in a stop gesture. "Let me tell you the rules."

The television woman, who looks a lot like Barbara Walters, nods and lowers her microphone. Newspaper guy, a redhead with a mustache, raises his eyebrows, shrugs one shoulder, and waits.

When I take another deep breath, it smells like sawdust and makeup. "First, no quoting me without my permission, including these rules." I fold my arms and survey them like Evillene getting ready to go ballistic on some Winkies.

Nobody objects to the first rule, so I push ahead. "Second, no snark-ass nasty questions. Third, my *name* is Jamie Carcaterra. My *column* is 'Fat Girl.' Please don't get that confused."

This gets me a look of sympathy from Barbara. Newspaper guy writes it down.

"Fourth, you both have five minutes, because I have to go turn in my column."

185

Newspaper guy immediately says he's Todd Sanders from the *Huntville Harper*, which surprises me. Huntville is "big city" compared to Garwood.

Barbara gestures to both of us like, *go ahead, you start, I'll wait*, and she sits down beside her camera guy.

He scratches the edges of his red crew cut and asks, "Have you been overweight your whole life, Miss Carcaterra?"

Okay, that's easy. I ease to the center spot on the stage, a few yards away from him. "Yes, I have."

Newspaper Guy Todd writes that down, too, and moves on with, "Have you considered having bariatric surgery like your boyfriend, Burke Westin?"

I hesitate, but not long. "Yes, I have."

When Newspaper Guy Todd gazes at me like *give me a teeny break, please*, I remember Dunstein's *be positive, be upbeat* mandate. So I smile and add, "It's not an option financially, and after watching what Burke's gone through, I don't know if I could stand the pain."

It takes Newspaper Guy Todd a second or two to write all that down. He looks triumphant when he finishes, like maybe he's proud of the idea for his next question.

"Do you think children ought to be allowed to have bariatric surgery?"

Behind Newspaper Guy Todd in the corner, Barbara shakes her head as if to say, *I would so never make* that *mistake.*

Be positive, be upbeat. Be positive, be upbeat.

"We aren't children," I say without yelling as loud as I'd like to. My voice carries off the stage, through the empty auditorium like I used a megaphone. "We're a few months from adulthood, and our bodies are *our* bodies. I don't know if *anyone* should have bariatric surgery, but if it's legal, teens should be able to make their own choices about it."

This time, while Newspaper Guy Todd writes down my answer, Barbara walks forward, microphone up, cameraman gliding behind her, and takes over. The light over the camera blazes, and I feel the heat from the bulb even though they're several rows away from the stage.

When Barbara speaks, her voice sounds warm and flowing, almost comforting, and something about her reminds me of my mother.

"Miss Carcaterra, I'm Barbara Gwennet from CSC affiliate WKPX—Channel 3 News. I find your column brave and refreshing. Congratulations on such a bold step."

"Thank you." *God, her name really is Barbara. How funny is that?* I find myself relaxing despite the Lois Lane trauma.

Barbara brushes a wisp of ash blond hair out of her eyes, then asks her question as she looks directly into my eyes. "Where do you get your inspiration for 'Fat Girl'?"

"My life. Every hour, every day." Another easy question. Thank God. "When you're as large as I am, you have two choices. You can be a supersized, invisible mouse, or you can be Fat Girl. I think it's time for the Fat Girls to speak—and never shut up again."

Newspaper Guy Todd sits down so he can write faster.

Barbara nods, seeming more like Mom than ever, if you don't count the black silk suit. Freddie would kill for that suit. "Do you feel like the positive female empowerment messages in your column outweigh the negative health messages?"

"I don't think I'm giving any negative health messages. If you read all of the literature, and take out the research funded by pharmaceutical companies or the diet industry, the health risks of obesity, even the definition of obesity, are not that clear-cut." My legs start to ache, and I think about sitting down on the edge of the stage. No way to pull that off in a hoopskirt, though. "There are risks, yes. But how those risks tie directly into fatness just isn't clear. Besides, 'Fat Girl' isn't a health beat or a weight-loss column. It's more about mind and thought and attitude."

I glance at the clock at the back of the auditorium. "Two more questions and I have to go."

Again, a gentle smile from Barbara before she asks, "How is Burke Westin *really* doing? In your opinion."

The words sock me in the gut like an elbow-punch. My face gets hot in a heartbeat, and more heat rushes across my skin. A hollow pit opens down inside me, like when I saw Burke's empty seat in the audience. "He's— he's changing."

My throat starts to close. I'm blinking too fast because I know I need to say something else. Barbara doesn't interrupt me or try to stop me, but I'm trying like hell to stop myself before the camera gets pictures of me standing all alone on the stage, blubbering and stuttering. I should have made a rule about hard questions. No make-Jamie-cry questions, but I don't even know which questions will hit me like that anymore.

I manage to talk about Burke's complications and his pain, about how calm he is, how focused and determined, and how much I admire him.

"He's already smaller," I whisper to the reporters, rubbing my throat as I talk. "It's like he's a different guy."

Barbara gears up to ask me something else, but the kind look in her eyes makes me want to scream or call my mother, probably both, and not in that order.

While my attention's focused completely on her, Newspaper Guy Todd slams me right in the face with, "Miss Carcaterra, are you worried more about Burke Westin's health or about him becoming thin and no longer wanting to be with you?"

In real life, if my throat wasn't too tight to swallow and my arms didn't feel completely weak, I would have slapped somebody for asking me that.

But I don't have the punch.

I don't even have words to punch.

Instead, I back away from Newspaper Guy Todd, and Barbara Gwennet, and the cameraman, too.

Before they can react, I shove through the curtains, bumble across the dark backstage, grab the column I wrote off the top of a speaker, and get my big, wide ass down the hall and out of that building.

I need to get to Heath and the cave and the paper and the stupid music he plays. I'll feel better when I hear the music, or when he says something inane and totally Heath. My heart will stop hammering, and I'll breathe and I won't sweat or stink.

Half-walking, half-running, I cling to the column and

head across sidewalks and around corners. It's dark, dark outside, no moon, clouds blotting out the stars. The fall air's cold enough to make my eyes water. My teeth chatter as I imagine telling Heath about the Fat Girl interview. He'll be flat-out freaked that we're getting television coverage. He'll be stoked.

I hope he hugs me.

What would that be like, Heath's arms around me? My face against his shoulder. I'd find out what he smells like up close. Really close. I'd find out how strong and solid he feels. What his voice sounds like in my ear. Chills course up and down my back, spreading out to my shoulders and arms. Total head rush.

I'm in the right building now, in the hall, heading toward the closed journalism suite door. Light spills from underneath it, into the dark hallway like a candle in some mysterious, faraway window, drawing me home.

"Oh my God." I stop walking so fast I almost trip myself. My fingers tighten on the folded pages of my column, and the paper crinkles.

"Oh . . . my God."

What the hell am I doing?

What the hell am I thinking?

I've gone bat-shit crazy. Worse. Ape-shit crazy.

I press my fingers against my fat, glitter-crusted cheeks and run them down my thick neck, to my big chest, and farther, to the mammoth belly holding up Evillene's hoopskirts. I'm Jamie. I'm still me. Still the biggest girl in school. I'm one hundred percent Fat Girl.

And I'm thinking Heath wants to see me? Wants to *touch* me? To hug me and gaze longingly into my eyes?

This is no movie. This is life as a Fat Girl, and in real life, guys like Heath don't fall in love with Fat Girls like me. I get to play the fat part, which is best friend, confidante, sidekick, whatever you want to call it. I can be "the lesbian" like Freddie, or the "activist freak" like NoNo. I can be the wicked witch, the wicked stepsister, the fortune teller, the crone, or even the whorehouse madam—but I can never be the beautiful princess, the delicate flower, *that* girl, the girl everyone wants.

In this drama, Jamie Carcaterra never gets to play the lead.

Except with Burke. I'm in love with Burke.

So why was I just thinking about sniffing Heath's neck?

Ape-shit crazy.

I rub my eyes and try to see Burke but instead I see stars and colors and I can't make anything coalesce into Burke's face. I catch the image for a second, but his cheeks sink in farther and farther, and I can't imagine what he looks like right this second. He really is different. He really is changing.

He really is leaving me.

And Freddie and NoNo will probably leave with him because I'm such a bitch, and then there's Heath.

My . . . what?

Friend?

Editor?

Bud?

Crush...

I'd slap myself if I thought it would do any good.

The door opens, and there's Heath in his dress-up jeans and blue polo. He's got his hair pushed back. I can't see his eyes in the shadows, but his grin is obvious.

My heartbeat speeds up, and I'm breathing too fast.

Is he glad to see me?

Friend. Sidekick. That's what you are. Get a total grip, and fast.

From the angle of Heath's head, I think his gaze is pinned on my cleavage again. He gestures to my corset top and hoopskirt. "You'll never fit in the cave wearing that skirt."

No words. I'm speechless. I'm an idiot.

"I'll, uh, change," I say, sounding breathless and completely asinine. "My clothes are back in the dressing area, but I wanted to give you this first." I hold out the crumpled column.

Heath takes it from me as I blurt, "Channel 3 and a guy from the *Huntville Harper* just interviewed me about Fat Girl."

"No way!" Heath's closer now, and his blue eyes bore straight into my brain. "That's amazing."

His grin just keeps coming. I grin back like I'm apeshit crazy, because I am.

Heath takes two more steps forward, puts his arms around me, and hugs me tight.

Oh, God.

The hoopskirt shoves backward and tips into the air.

Heath's taller than I am, and my face really does press against his shoulder.

More muscular than I thought, in a firm, lean way. Hard. Tough. His arms feel light, but strong and comforting. He smells spicy and clean up close, even though he's been working all day and night on the paper.

The tang of glue and the eye-watering punch of processor fluid hangs in the air around us, but doesn't seem to touch Heath. I feel like I've stepped into a bubble of perfect smells and sensations.

And he doesn't let me go.

I raise my arms, which feel like they weigh a half-ton each, and hug him back, and he still doesn't let me go.

Heath shifts a little.

His lips press against the top of my head, soft and warm and firm. I shiver. Can't help it. A good shiver. A shocked shiver.

What's happening?

Who is this insane boy?

Who am *I*?

This can't be happening, but it's happening, and I'm frozen like my feet got glued to the hallway tiles.

When Heath pulls back from our embrace, he leaves his hands on my shoulders. I blink at the green glitter and makeup I left on his polo shirt.

This time when he looks at my cleavage, he's not discreet, and I don't care. I feel that stare like a touch.

Would I stop him if he tried to put his hands where his eyes are wandering?

"You look great in that costume," he murmurs, his voice low and quiet.

The sound of it wrecks me completely.

I don't speak at all. Can't even imagine trying to talk. I need to go. Change clothes. Get to work. I need Heath to kiss me. I need him to look at me this way forever and ever. I need a damned clue, and a brain transplant on top of that. And a fan while I'm at it, because it's sweatshop hot in the hallway.

"Should I walk you back to the theater?" he asks, giving me more shivers with that rumbly voice.

"I'm, uh—walk—what?"

"To change." He brushes my hair behind my ear. "So you can come back and work on the paper."

Forget speaking again.

Heath pulls me closer to him. My whole body tingles everywhere he's touching me. He gazes into my eyes so sweet and soft, like he might be thinking about kissing me.

Please kiss me.

Please.

But he doesn't.

My mouth throbs from wanting it so badly.

"You're coming back, right, Jamie?"

"Yes," I say automatically, talking like a movie-woman in a dream, all whispers and sighs. If I lean forward, we'll be kissing. I'll be kissing Heath, and tasting him, and I'll know for sure I'm not imagining this.

Freddie's voice chooses that moment to yell inside my head.

Who cares what Heath does? What about you, *damn it?*

She asked me about this in the hospital, and I lied to her. I didn't know I was lying, but I did. To my best friend. I told her I was in love with Burke.

B . . . u . . . r . . . k . . . e . . .

All the chills and whispers and sighs flow out of me, and I go stiff in Heath's grip.

Images of Burke pound on my awareness. Him holding me. Gazing at me just before he kisses me. The way he looks all dopey and perfect and happy when we're cuddled up together.

Burke's smile.

Burke's eyes.

He needs me now more than ever, and I will not let him down. I'm his. He's mine. That's the way it is, the way it's supposed to be, the way it has to be.

Right?

"I'll walk you," Heath says, turning me loose.

"No, that's okay," I shake my head. "I'll be fine."

Heath's grin fades to a frown. He shrugs. "Guess I'll be here waiting for you, then."

I can tell he knows I won't be coming back.

We need to talk.

We need to kiss. Jeez. Stop it.

Heath and I need to talk but obviously not now. I'm shaking again, this time from wanting to run to the theater, get into my real clothes, and run straight back to Heath. But I can't. I just cannot do something that wrong, even when I want to *so* much.

Heath doesn't wait for me to leave. He heads back into the cave and closes the door behind him.

My heart's still beating, beating, beating. My skin feels hot where his hands were pressed against my arms. I'm something past crazy now. Worse. Lots worse.

When I finally get myself out of that building, I feel like I'm shredding something inside me.

Is this how it feels to do the right thing?

Because it sucks.

Night air hits me in the face, cold and mean.

I don't have any answers. I'm not even sure what the right questions are, or what I'm supposed to do now.

Maybe playing the lead isn't such a great thing after all.

You can't win,
You can't break even,
And you can't get out of the game.

"You Can't Win"
from *The Wiz*

The Wire

FEATURE SPREAD
for publication Friday, October 19

Fat Girl Dancing

JAMIE D. CARCATERRA

Fat Girl has lots of reasons to dance, other than our annual Halloween bash—and I'm not telling you all of them!

First and best, Fat Boy arrived home at 3:22 PM yesterday, a few weeks later than scheduled, but he's home, home, home! That doesn't let you off the hook, though. You still have to send positive thoughts, and cheer and pray for Fat Boy. Get busy. More chronicles coming soon, with photos! Days postsurgery: thirty-one. Weight loss: forty-five pounds.

Second, *The Wiz* is a hit. Sellouts last weekend and this weekend, too.

Third, I never have to take the ACT again. (Yeah, okay, I'm banned, but I'm DONE.)

Fourth, my college applications and scholarship portfolios are in, with special thanks to Freddie, who mailed the first ones even though I was a PB from H.

Fifth, The *Huntville Harper* ran a spread on Fat Girl early this week, and Newspaper Guy Todd got all my quotes right. Print media. Yeah!

Sixth and second-best, the taped Fat Girl interview is scheduled to run on CSC affiliate stations during their Body Image Awareness campaign.

Now, consider this. What if Fat Girl decides to dance in front of you, without Fat Boy to pound you into the dirt if you get too close?

Would you laugh?

Apparently, laughing at fat people dancing is becoming an international sport. If you go online and look up "fat people dancing," you get over 150,000 sites with video clips and brilliant remarks such as, "Reminds me of watching a lava lamp."

And it doesn't stop there. We've found sites featuring fat people kissing, fat people with piercings, fat people with tattoos, fat people doing other stuff I can't mention— it's endless. As are the comments, with words like *disgusting*, *pig*, *gross*, *revolting*, and *ridiculous*.

Remember my piece on pornography? Yeah. File these Web sites under that heading, with a cross-reference to *idiots with too much time on their hands*.

Anything goes since fat is now the national health crisis of the new millennium. Eighty percent or more of people under the age of twenty-one believe obesity is the result of laziness, and all fat people have to do to get skinny is choose to live better.

Tell you a little secret.

I'm dancing anyway.

CHAPTER
THIRTEEN

The minute we get back on the road after dropping NoNo at her protest rally, Freddie taps the steering wheel of her old Toyota.

"What's wrong with you, Jamie?"

"Nothing." I stare out the passenger window and try to look carefree or bored or anything other than freaked out. The note from Heath that I'm holding gets crumpled and uncrumpled, crumpled and uncrumpled. I've already read it five or six times, but I'm not finished with it yet.

Freddie lets out a sigh that says *bullshit*.

I still don't look at her with her perfect hair and makeup. She's dressed like a runway model, blue silk dress and matching shoes, even though the people at HeartBeat have drapes for us to wear over our clothes for our formal senior portraits. All us girls will look like we're wearing gorgeous evening gowns, and all the guys have to tolerate a tux jacket and tie. As for me, I've got on my usual, a flowing skirt and shirt, but I did at least pick something blue to get close to Garwood colors. I don't think anything shows under the drape, but better safe than sorry.

Another sigh from Freddie digs at my guilt.

Okay, okay, I know I'm lying or not telling or violating two thousand friend-rules, but what am I supposed to say?

I know you're still half-mad at me for biting off NoNo's head but I almost kissed Heath the Hunk two weeks ago, I've been dodging him like a dog since that moment, I'm exhausted from *The Wiz* performances, I'm blowing my math grade all to hell because I'm too busy daydreaming to do my homework, and oh yeah, I keep having to spend hours hanging out with the incredible shrinking boyfriend who can't talk about anything but losing weight. How's *your* day, chica?

Not.

So I crumple and uncrumple the note, look out the window, and listen to her sigh more intensely *all* the way to HeartBeat Photos. As she's parking, her phone buzzes. She glances at it, frowns, then hands it to me.

"Hey," I say to Burke.

We have to use Freddie's phone, since I'm out of minutes again. She has an unlimited plan, so it's all good. Wish I could afford that. Life would be lots easier with endless minutes ... or endless money.

"Where are you guys?" Burke asks, sounding deep and strong and enough like his old self to make butterflies bounce in my belly. When I close my eyes, I see Burke, my Burke, big and beefy and grinning, ready to wrap me in a bear hug. On the phone at least, the truth can be what I want it to be.

"NoNo's at a dye-banning rally, and Freddie and I just rolled up outside HeartBeat Photos for our senior portraits."

I keep my voice light even though I'm wearing out that note from Heath. He left it in my box in the journalism suite after I dodged him all week, worked on the paper when he wasn't around, and dropped Fat Girl in *his* mailbox.

The note says, "This feature is weak. Get back to the hard stuff ASAP if you want the scholarship."

Beneath that in clear, bold printing, he added, "We need to talk. Soon."

He signed it "H."

Typical Heath. He's been "H" since the first note he ever sent me.

"Jamie?" Burke's mellow voice floats through the ether, poking into my consciousness. "You there?"

"Yeah, sorry."

"I was asking if you'd come by after the portraits."

"Sure."

In a low whisper, he asks, "Will you bring me a couple of candy bars? Just two—nothing major. They've got me in food jail here."

"Are you out of your friggin' mind? Your sisters would slaughter me." I shift the phone to my other hand. "I've got no desire to have my heart torn out and my brains eaten for dinner."

He lets out a breath, and I imagine him stretched out on the overstuffed leather recliner in his bedroom at home, where we've cuddled hundreds of times. "Please, baby? Just a little taste. I'm ready for a more solid food."

"You want contraband, you hunt it down yourself." I make kissing sounds into the phone. "If you need sweet, you'll have to settle for me."

Burke laughs. *"Sweet.* Yeah. Just give me a taste of you when you get here."

I'm smiling when I hang up, but the note in my hand seems to get heavier and heavier, until I ball it up and toss it on Freddie's floorboard.

When I look at her, she seems to have chilled out a little, but not much. At least the bitch lines in her face have softened. "This whole Burke thing, it's hard, isn't it?"

"That's an understatement." I hope I don't have bitch lines in my face now.

We're parked in front of the portrait studio, sitting in the Toyota, letting the sun beat in on our faces and arms. I'd rather just sit in the sun and not talk, but Freddie likes to pry and poke.

"You hardly talk about Burke." Freddie pulls her keys out of the ignition and drops them into her bag. "You don't talk about the crap that really bothers you—like home and your parents, or worrying about college. Mostly, it's right–now things, like grades and the play. Did you know that?"

My hand's on the door handle, and I want to jump out and run, but I don't. "I guess, yeah. I'm not a whiner. Is that a bad thing?"

Freddie shrugs. "Don't know. Sometimes I think you keep so busy, you run so hard, so none of the other shit can catch up to you. That might be a bad thing, 'cause one day you'll get tired."

204

Damn her.

Not what I want to hear. Not what I need to hear.

No making Jamie turn red and blubber before senior portraits. I'm tired of wanting to stomp and sob all the time.

"I'm not just running to run." I know I sound irritable, but I can't help it. "Being a senior keeps me busy,"

"Yeah, but you do a lot extra, with drama and the paper and Heath and stuff." She leans toward me, like she's about to whisper a secret. "Um, how is it with you and Heath?"

I lean back and think about running again. "Like al-ways. We get the work done."

Freddie says nothing. She just stares at me, waiting, waiting, until I do open the door.

Before I get out, I say, "He's my friend, Freddie. Well, not my friend, really—that's you and NoNo. He's like a business partner or an associate or something."

"You look funny when you talk about him," she says quietly, holding one hand over mine so I don't get out. "Just so you know. I wouldn't bring him up around Burke."

"There's nothing to bring up." I slip my hand from un-der hers.

"If there was, you could tell me. I wouldn't go nuclear or spill or anything. I mean, Burke's my best bud from way back, but you and me, we're...we're the girls. It's different."

"Thanks." That's genuine, even though my gut clenches when I say it.

Do I believe her?

Do I believe anyone anywhere is really on my side?

We both get out of the Toyota.

Freddie closes her door and leans over the top for a second. "Just do two things for me."

My turn to shrug and wait. I face her, keeping my back to the studio, and try not to turn red and get majorly ugly before this stupid picture.

"Quit trashing NoNo when you're freaked." Freddie holds up one finger. "And take some time to apologize to her for the last time. You know how she is—but she's loyal, and she really cares about you, and she won't get over it unless you tell her you didn't mean it."

Now I'm red. Shit. Oh, well. But it's not mad red. It's head-hanging red. "Yeah, all right. I'll do that first chance, I promise."

Freddie looks pleased, then changes back to way-far serious. Up comes the second finger. "If you fall for Heath or anybody else, keep things clean with Burke. Do it right. Up front. Break up with him honorably and stuff. Okay?"

My head droops. I can't stop it. She actually made me hang my head.

What can I say?

Except, "Yes. Okay."

My head keeps drooping all the way inside, through all the paperwork and while portrait-lady escorts Freddie back toward the dressing room. Then portrait-lady pops back to the counter holding a body drape that will never in a million years fit around me.

Damn.

That's why I called ahead and verified that they had large body drapes so I could match everyone else in my class and not have to do the pictures in my street clothes. Only portrait-lady's definition of large and mine must be different. I should have said supersized, or megasized, or big enough to fit a damned mastodon.

She smiles and holds out the drape. "One size fits all."

This is so gonna be fun, I can tell.

Kind of like dental surgery. Without the gas.

.   .   .

By the time I meet up with Freddie outside the portrait studio, I'm tired like I've run a marathon. Not that I'd ever be able to run a marathon even with vampires chasing me—but my imagination supplies the details.

"Sometimes it gets old," I tell Freddie as we drive toward Burke's big house on the hill.

Freddie gives me a look like she's got stomach cramps, which is Freddie for, *I'm totally sorry it sucks so much*.

Yeah. Me too.

So much for talking more about what bothers me.

My life turns into a nontopic, except for Fat Girl. Once a week, I pour it all out and hope somebody gets a clue.

Does anyone get a clue?

Freddie and I don't talk much the rest of the way to Burke's. It's hard not to think about the portrait studio and how my picture will turn out. I hate seeing myself in pictures, kind of like I hate seeing myself in mirrors. I wish I could be all Fat Girl about it and love my big body, find it beautiful like Burke does ... or did.

And Heath.

You look great in that costume ...

God! I try to chase Heath's image and voice out of my mind. The way he looked at me, the way his voice sounded, it's hard not to replay the scene over and over again. I shouldn't, but I do.

How much was real?

What did I make up?

Heath probably hates me now for avoiding him like he's got some disease. I've pretty much stranded him with the paper, except for writing my column. His crumpled note rolls around on Freddie's floorboard as she parks the Toyota.

Decision time's coming up. We need to talk. Soon.

I can hear Heath's voice saying those words, see the serious look in his blue eyes.

Why can't I get him out of my head?

We're at Burke's front door now, heading inside, and I'm thinking about Heath.

M & M gather in the foyer, apparently on their way out. Thank God. They're both wearing sleek stylish blue dresses. They look like college women, graduates, on their way up the ladder and, of course, they are.

Me, I couldn't fit in a business suit with a crowbar and plunger to assist, and I'd probably break a ladder if I dared set my foot on a rung. Don't most ladders have weight restrictions? Hammocks do. Trust me. Burke and I found that out the hard way at the lake last year.

Freddie exchanges hellos with the vampire sisters as I ease past them and make my way to the kitchen. Sunlight streams through the big windows, making the mosaic design in the tiled floor sparkle. Everything's dusted and polished. Everything in Burke's world is always so clean and fresh.

Burke's dad is standing by the table gazing at a bunch of clothes laid out across its polished surface—three or four shirts, some shorts, some sweats, and a couple of pairs of jeans with the price tags still on them.

Burke's standing beside his dad, only at first my brain doesn't register Burke at all.

It's some other guy, thirty-five days after surgery, and almost fifty pounds lighter. A leaner, taller version of Burke in stylish, cut basketball shorts and a sleeveless T-shirt. More muscles, or more muscle definition. I get so cold my teeth try to chatter, but I clench my jaw and refuse to surrender.

It's Burke. Not Burke, but it is. It's him.

I'm still not used to seeing him standing up. I can so see the missing pounds when he's upright.

And he's shaved his head.

Like, bald.

This makes me blink. A gnawing ache chews at my stomach. He had to chop his dreads because his hair really did start falling out, *a perfectly normal situation* per his surgeon.

But . . . bald?

Not that he doesn't have a handsome head. It's adorable. It's just not my Burke.

He scoots his palm over his shiny black dome and gives me a wide, goofy grin. "I'm smooo–ooothe, baby."

"You're a god," I say, and try to mean it.

"Check these out." He tugs at his shirt and shorts.

"Double-X. I've dropped like three sizes already. And they're big on me."

Ice is forming on my skin.

Smile. Have to, because he's so thrilled. I have to be happy for him, but tears blur my vision.

Burke's wearing smaller clothes than I do.

I can't wear his shirts anymore. I can't fit into his sweats or his shorts and parade around to make him laugh.

No more hanging out in my guy's clothes.

That's lost, like his dreads, and the cute roundness in his cheeks, and all the things we used to talk about and do together. Everything's about weight loss now. I hate that phrase, "weight loss," like Burke misplaced half of himself somewhere.

It's falling off. He's melting, like Evillene.

My brain registers a coffee cup on the table beside him, with a spoon sticking out of it. I realize that was probably Burke's lunch, or maybe his dinner. His food fits in a coffee cup.

Burke's dad, who looks even leaner than Burke, slips past me with a pat on the shoulder and a "Glad to see you, Jamie." I watch as he settles into his armchair in the living room and picks up the television remote.

Back to Burke, since I can't focus on anything else.

"What do you think?" Burke, still standing in his new clothes that won't fit me, poses like a magazine muscle-hunk. "Can you tell I'm losing?"

"Absolutely." My answer's as automatic as his question. So is my smile.

210

Burke walks stiffly toward me—he's still sore, "working out the kinks" as his dad says—and hugs me.

"Don't worry," he says. "You'll lose, too, if you want to. Get small like me." He grins. "Bring those curves down to a manageable level, Jamie. It's *do*able."

My smile stays stuck on my face even though I feel flat and cold all over and almost sick.

Manageable level?

Burke never found my curves unmanageable before.

All of a sudden, I feel twice as huge. And out of place.

I'm hating it here right now, hating it really bad.

Manageable level?

Me losing weight was never part of this deal, was it? When did that happen? I missed that part of the contract completely.

But Burke's hugging me.

I hug him back gently, afraid I'll hurt his healing incisions, and God help me, I think about Heath and how he smells like spice, and the way he kissed the top of my head outside the journalism suite.

Guilt twists like snakes in my gut.

I let go of Burke too fast, and realize he's talking. Well, whispering.

"...in food jail." Burke shakes his head. "They don't understand. I know I'm ready."

More snakes, twisting, writhing, making me half-sick, but I'm supposed to keep smiling. I'm here for Burke, like I promised. Got to keep it together.

"My sisters," Burke says. "You know how they are."

I glance over my shoulder, through the living room

and back toward the foyer. "Yeah. They can be major pains in the ass."

"I keep telling them I just want a little bit." Burke makes an inch sign with his thumb and forefinger. "Chocolate. But they're blowing me off. You gotta hook me up with a Hershey bar."

"Food jail." I'm putting the pieces together now. "You're still wanting me to bring you candy. No way!"

Burke opens his arms, pleading. "Come on, baby. I'm counting on you."

I jerk a thumb toward the foyer. "They'll bite my neck and bleed me dry if I bring you contraband. Not happen–ing."

"Please?" He gives me the puppy eyes.

Damn him.

Those eyes are still way wide and big, and totally pa–thetic when he wants them to be. "I'll think about it," I say to shut him up and make him quit with the puppy gaze.

"Jamie," Mr. Westin calls from the living room. "I think you should come here."

The snakes in my belly multiply.

Shit. Did he hear that about the chocolate bars? I'm so dead.

Burke looks as startled as I feel.

Busted.

"Sorry," he whispers, but I hush him with a wave of my hand.

Together, we walk slowly into the living room to face our doom. I can tell Burke's expecting the worst. And it gets better, because here come Freddie and M & M, who obviously haven't left yet.

Greeeaaaaaaat.

"...big controversy brewing at tiny Garwood High," the television news blares, "where senior Jamie Carcaterra defends her right to superobesity in her tart, irreverent 'Fat Girl Manifesto.'"

"Whoa," Freddie says, sitting down on Burke's giant leather sofa. "Fat Girl goes big-time. This is national news, right?"

Mr. Westin nods. "It's a segment called *Food for Thought.* The network features local reporters from all over the country with interesting pieces."

Burke whistles and makes *whoop-whoop* sounds, then whacks me on the back.

M & M gape at the set, eyes wide.

Barbara Gwennet, the reporter who interviewed me after opening night, fills the screen—with a backdrop of big bellies and butts marching by.

For a few seconds, she looks sweet and sympathetic and earnest. Then her eyes narrow and she lifts a copy of *The Wire* and reads, "I'm not chubby. I'm not chunky. I'm not hormonally challenged or endocrine-disordered. I do not prefer platitudes like large or plus-sized or clinical words like obese...I'm fat...Get used to it. Get over it."

The bellies and butts keep passing by behind her. Sometimes the camera zooms in on the largest specimens.

Barbara pauses, gazes into the camera, eyebrows raised, and reads more. "Fat Girl, in all her fatness, may have fewer body-image issues than people who wear 'normal' sizes."

Another deep stare into the camera, then more out-of-context quotes from my manifesto. "... compulsive overeating is not officially recognized in any diagnostic manual ... the same diet industry that makes billions for doing nothing to help and usually making things worse ... funded some, maybe a lot, of the studies 'raising the alarm.'"

Oh, I can so see where this is going, and I hate it already. My hands clench. All the cold is gone, and I'm hot instead. Burning up.

Burke's still making celebration noises. Freddie and Mr. Westin sit, obviously stunned. M & M look like a strong breeze would blow them both to the floor.

"The voice of our youth." Barbara shakes her head as the belly-butt parade continues. "Free speech, or the malicious opinions of one misguided girl who chooses to disregard a serious national public health crisis?"

As I stare, dumbfounded like everybody else, Barbara snips quotes from Fat Girl and splices in brief out-of-order sound bites from my interview until I sound like a screaming, rampaging fat activist who despises medical science, skinny women, and bariatric surgery. According to her I "mercilessly dig" at my "young male friend" who made the "incredibly brave decision" to have a weight-loss procedure.

"You digging at me?" Burke cracks up. "She's smoking something. I'd like to know what it is. Can I have some?"

"Be quiet," M & M order at the same time.

"Mmmm," Freddie agrees, leaning forward.

Mr. Westin rubs his hand over his chin.

Barbara misrepresents a little more, stating I "closed down" the local Hotchix in a "brazen sneak attack" with a few of my "radical friends."

Freddie swears softly, then covers her mouth.

On the television, Barbara again lifts the copy of *The Wire*. "Competing opinions and health columns are conspicuously absent. Will thin, healthy students be forced to picket this 'fat rag' to be heard?"

Long, dramatic pause as the fat bellies and butts fade slowly to a black screen.

"This is Barbara Gwennet, and Garwood High's 'Fat Girl Manifesto' is truly food for thought. Until next week, good night."

Seconds pass. Maybe minutes. Nobody speaks. Commercials flare and flash by, but I'm not processing any of them.

The news show goes off. A crime show comes on.

My cell rings. I grab it, glance down at the number, and see that it's my house.

I answer, feeling numb, like I'm hearing sounds *ping* against my ears from far, far away.

"Jamie, people are calling," Mom says without even *hello* or *how are you*. "Neighbors, reporters, the principal, and your editor, Heath. I think you need to come home. Jamie? Jamie, are you there?"

No.

"Yes," I say, quiet, dull, freaked by the sound of my own voice, doing my best not to see anyone or anything in the room around me. "We're leaving now."

FEATURE SPREAD
for publication Friday, October 26

Fat Girl Aiming

JAMIE D. CARCATERRA

Point that gun.

Squeeze that trigger.

It's so easy to shoot the Fat Girl.

After all, we make the biggest targets.

And that's just what Barbara Gwennet, Channel 3 reporter, has seen fit to do. She twisted facts to make me look stupid and dangerous. She twisted my words to make me look as unhealthy as possible. She shot Fat Girl. Was it fun, Barbara? Did it warm your icy little heart?

Not that I should be surprised. It's open season on fat people, no limits, and no restrictions. Hold on to your supersized butts, Fat Girls, because we're the last acceptable targets for bashing, snarking, and discrimination. Maybe it's the giant boobs, or the bouncing-across-the-television-screen bellies Barbara used for a story backdrop.

Maybe it's the way we smile when people like Barbara tell us we have beautiful eyes or beautiful hair (like we don't know what that means about the rest of our body). Maybe it's how easy we are to dupe with a little kindness and understanding.

Fat Girls are so desperate for approval, success, and acceptance, we'll believe anything, at least for a minute. Even that a reporter like Barbara Gwennet understands our Fat Girl pain.

Is the "naïve Fat Girl" another myth I'm busting?

A year ago, I would have said *yes*. Maybe even a few months ago. But now Fat Girls are in the sights of local media, national media, newspapers, radios, blogs, video Web sites—everywhere, all the time, it's an *obesity crisis,* an *overweight attack,* an *OMG-we're-fatter-than-ever rampage* through worldwide pages, screens, and sound bites. We're the reason for rising health-care costs. We're the cause of riptides and global warming. We're ruining the airline industry and wasting fuel. And now, God forbid, we're even *talking about it.*

This is a personal message to Barbara Gwennet, some food for your thoughts—if indeed you have any thoughts:

1. Thin people get plenty of press. The public gets bombarded daily with pictures of concave thighs, countable vertebrae, hollow cheeks, skull-like smiles. According to some facts and figures printed in *USA Today*, the typical starlet or cover model is around 30 percent thinner than an average, healthy woman and is likely struggling with issues such as hypoglycemia, hair loss, and even risk of bone loss from lack of eating. Did you know a few decades back models and stars were only 7 to 8 percent thinner than "normal" people? Wonder how that relates to our national size obsession and "obesity epidemic"? Food for thought.

2. According to journals that study obesity, even fat people hate fat people. Everyone does. It's called "antifat bias"—what you demonstrated yourself so perfectly, when you gave your report about me. A study by the North American Association for the Study of Obesity found that people would rather give up a year of life than be fat. Half of thousands of people asked in a survey agreed they would rather live a shorter amount of time thin than

218

be fat. In fact, 15 percent said they'd give up ten years or more of life to avoid obesity. Fat is now so horrid, so unacceptable that people would consciously choose to die younger rather than contend with obesity. Hence the rise in and acceptance of dangerous obesity surgery for children. Hence the brave, scary choice of Fat Boy, and all he's gone through. Food for thought.

3. It doesn't end there, Barbara. Thanks to attitudes and hypemongering reports like yours, 33 percent of people would rather get divorced than be fat, 20 percent would rather be childless than fat, 15 percent would rather be depressed than fat, and 14 percent would even pick alcoholism over a big belly. Food for thought.

4. *Nooo,* it's still not over. In that same study of thousands, 10 percent of people polled would rather have an anorexic child than an obese child, 8 percent would choose a child with learning problems over an obese child, and 5 percent were even willing to sacrifice a limb or their vision rather than be fat. Thank God nobody asked them if they'd hack off their

kid's leg or arm, or put out their infant's eyes. I'd be afraid to see those answers.

What would you give up to avoid obesity, Barbara? The life of your firstborn? A toe? A leg? Come on. What's it really worth to you? Now *that* would be some food for thought. Spell it out and I'll print it in this "fat rag" for all the poor, downtrodden skinny kids to read. I'll make it entry one in our new competing health feature: "Ten Steps to Hypoglycemia and Hair Loss."

CHAPTER
FOURTEEN

"Hypoglycemia and hair loss?" Principal Edmonds winces as he drops last week's *The Wire* on his desk.

He leans back in his leather office chair and folds his hands over his paunch. "A little harsh, Jamie? I don't want your manifesto to degenerate into anorexia bashing, especially not with this ugly television news thing exploding all over the place. The eyes of the nation are on Garwood High and your column—literally."

I grind my teeth and try to keep my mouth shut.

Principal Edmonds has been cool about the column so far, but it's mostly because he could care less about the newspaper. He'd be just as happy if we shut down *The Wire* and let it die a quiet, anachronistic death.

But right now, *The Wire*'s making news, not just reporting it, so he's stuck.

His cinderblock office is standing room only, with him behind the desk, Ms. Dax beside the desk in her best white Sunday dress, Burke and me in chairs in front of the desk, our parents behind us, and to my left, on the small loveseat against the wall, underneath a shelf of football trophies, Heath and Heath's dad.

Aftershave competes with perfume and leather and cleanser smells, and I wish somebody would open a window.

It's hot.

"The latest Fat Girl feature crossed the line." Ms. Dax fiddles with her bleached-blond hair. "We're sorry, Mr. Edmonds."

Enough with the hair.

And we're not sorry. I'm not, at least.

But I know better than to say that out loud. I'm Fat Girl. I'm not Suicidal, Get-Suspended Girl.

And Dax—to hell with her. She's only here because she got summoned. Otherwise, she could give a damn what Heath and I do. All her time gets spent with the freshmen and sophomores over in the classroom section of the journalism suite, not in the cave where the work gets done. Heath and I are responsible for the actual paper, not Ms. Dax. She primps again and acts like her panties are in a total wad. Everyone's worried about appearances at Garwood since reporters and news vans keep swarming the campus, and even the PTA security patrol can't keep them all out.

Heath doesn't say anything, but he's looking at me. I can feel his eyes on my cheek, my face, my shoulder. My skin tingles. The harder I try not to notice Heath, the more I do notice him, and it's driving me over the edge. Having him in the same room with Burke makes me feel squeezed flat, like there's not enough air left in the universe.

I should have talked to Heath by now, told him . . . told him what?

God, I have no idea what I want to tell him.

Yes, you do. You just don't have the guts.

"You ordered me to get back to the hard stuff." I glare at Heath mostly to make him look away so I can breathe, but when he meets my gaze, I want to die twice, come back to life, and die one more time.

He slowly looks from me to Principal Edmonds. "I don't think 'Aiming' is more over the line than Jamie's other manifesto pieces," he says in that calm, rational-sounding voice that makes me want to scream when we're late on layout. "It's cutting edge. We want people to get mad, think, rant. To talk and communicate about the issues. That's the whole point of 'Fat Girl Manifesto.'"

"Yeah," Burke agrees. He's decked out in new school-colors basketball shorts and a jersey, and he looks smaller, impossibly smaller, than the last time I saw him. "People need to start a dialogue about all this. I think—"

His mother shushes him with a pinch to the shoulder.

"I don't like my son's medical issues being national news." Mr. Westin puts his hand on Burke's shoulder, too. "It was one thing when this was a local matter, just for our school and community. The involvement of the major networks and outlets changes everything. Fat acceptance activists are actually picketing my business."

"The school, too." Principal Edmonds gestures toward

223

the front drive, where I know a group of fat acceptance folks are waving GO FAT GIRL signs at an opposing group of Trim the Fat America nutcases carrying BREAK THE POISON PEN posters.

It's insane.

The only way I could turn out more protesters would be to have Freddie write a feature on gay marriage. Hmmm. Maybe I should. We'd have Fat and Antifat and Up with Dykes and Down with Fags screaming at each other all over the place.

We'd probably get out of class for weeks, and I could go homebound and quit worrying about my damned math grade.

Mom tweaks my neck as if to say, *Leave the daydream, honey. Reality calls.*

I sigh.

Mr. Edmonds doesn't seem too upset, but then I didn't think he would be. As for me, well, all publicity is good publicity, according to my parents. The National Feature Award people can't ignore this, even if my ACT composite sucks. They've been mentioned about two thousand times as the "driving motivation" behind Fat Girl's diatribes, and that'll happen again tonight when the story headlines on a CableNewsNow segment.

I can't believe Fat Girl's about to be featured on News-Now. Unreal.

"We want it over." Mrs. Westin's intense expression and sharply defined face remind me of M & M all rolled into one person and multiplied. "No more Fat Boy—and hopefully things will settle down." She pats Burke's shoulder.

"The surgery was good for him, and this column makes it sound like some disastrous nightmare."

"That's not true, Mrs. Westin." I lean toward her and hold out one hand, palm up, pleading. "I'm trying to show everyone how hard it is, how strong Burke has had to be to choose bariatric surgery. It's not an easy way out."

"Well, we have an easy way out of this media mess, at least." Mr. Westin doesn't sound mean, just final and determined. "There will be no more articles about my son."

"Dad, I don't mind. I like being a star." Burke grins at me as if to say *I like being your star.*

I know I'm supposed to smile back, so I do, but my lips might as well be made out of wood.

Heath doesn't miss Burke's look or my stupid smile. His expression remains exactly the same, but something dark and unhappy flashes through his blue eyes.

I so feel like a tennis spectator, bouncing back and forth between the two of them. I feel like a shit, too, even though I haven't done anything wrong.

Yet.

"Jamie needs to bring the story to some sort of reasonable resolution," Mom, who is for once not in her home clothes but work clothes instead, speaks up for the first time. "All the mail and phone calls—students want to know how Burke's doing. I can't imagine leaving it all unfinished. At least settle the series on a positive note."

Dad, in his delivery uniform, mutters his agreement, and Burke and Heath chime in that they agree. The office door rattles, and I imagine Freddie and NoNo, ears to the keyhole, about to spill inside and shout, "Yes, yes!" to make the whole debacle complete.

Principal Edmonds presses his index fingers into his lips for a moment, then turns his attention to the Westins. "I believe the students and the Carcaterras have a point, that it would be beneficial to have some closure. Will you agree to a wrap–up feature about Burke's progress, if you get right of approval?"

"I don't see the point," Mr. Westin says. "It will just be more fodder for these reporters and gossip rags."

"They haven't gotten to see the new me yet." Burke pulls away from his parents and stands. He gestures to his shrinking gut, his whole shrinking body. "I want my success to get some play. I'm coming back to school after Thanksgiving. Give Jamie one more article, so everybody knows I'm well and healthier now."

When his parents don't respond, Burke says, "She needs this. Her scholarship portfolio's mailed, but the judges will still be watching." He gives me a sweet look, then turns back to his parents all serious again, with, "I need it, too. The truth in print. Please?"

He's trying to be my hero. He's always been my hero. Against my will, my eyes move from Burke to Heath. Heath and his dad both seem so quiet and reserved, like they're a notch above everything happening in Principal Edmonds's office.

Snobs?

But Heath isn't a snob. Is he?

More like shy, in his own way.

The Westins agree to the final Fat Boy Chronicle with

226

lots of conditions—things I can and can't mention—and I've got to get it done pronto, like right after this meeting, for their approval. My parents agree, and Ms. Dax gives her consent, too.

Heath looks pleased. His dad looks blank and disinterested.

Maybe Heath Sr. *is* a snob.

Principal Edmonds dismisses everyone under the age of eighteen, keeping the parents to "iron out a few more details" of how Garwood will respond to my little storm of media attention. We've gotten calls from big news shows and at least two talk shows, but so far we're saying *no, no, no way.* I don't want to do any television interviews or talk shows or recorded anything.

I don't trust any reporters now, for any reason. If I talk to anybody, it'll be print media, and I'll have approval rights, just like the Westins.

Burke leads the way out of the office, and we nearly trample on Freddie and NoNo. They aren't listening at the door, but they probably were before Principal Edmonds told us to leave.

The two of them crowd against Burke, Heath, and me, demanding to know everything that happened.

We scoot them out of the main office foyer into the hallway, where at last, at last, I can breathe. The doors are propped open, and a cool breeze swirls down the hallway. Everyone else is in class, so for the moment at least the hall is our private domain.

Burke says, "Jamie gets to do a Fat Boy wrap-up."

Freddie's eager smile turns huge. "And after that?"

Heath shrugs. "After that, 'Fat Girl Manifesto' continues. Nobody said we had to stop."

"*Yesssss.*" NoNo raises one scrawny, dye-free arm like she does when she's leading protest chants. "Victory for the people."

Burke puts his arm around my shoulder and pulls me to him. "That's my girl. My movie-star babe."

I feel stiff touching him, even though I don't want to, and I keep looking at Heath, who keeps looking at me.

Heath's eyes blaze, but his voice is quiet when he asks, "You coming to the cave to work on next week's layout, Jamie?"

He's been doing it alone for, what, three weeks now? I'm letting him down. Okay, I'm totally chickening out, but I can't go. Can't be alone with him. For lots of reasons.

"Freddie and I promised to help NoNo with some protest rally fliers, and my parents have me on lockdown because of the television stuff." I omit that we're meeting at Burke's to do NoNo's fliers. Don't want to say it, to see that flicker of discomfort in Heath's eyes again.

"Okay." Heath stuffs his hands into his jeans pockets, lingers long enough to give me another brief once-over, nods at all of us, and drifts away, Heath style. He heads down the main hall, toward the exit that leads to the journalism suite. The way he moves, so quiet and fluid, like liquid flowing downhill, makes me wonder if I imagined he was just standing here with us.

I'm still staring in Heath's direction when Burke says, "Aw, man, I forgot all about that flier stuff. I've got a group meeting tonight."

Freddie, NoNo, and I give him a look.

"Group meeting?" Freddie says slowly, and at least I know she's as surprised as I am.

"GBS." He points to his belly. "Gastric Bypass Support. It meets Monday, Wednesday, and Friday. Mom and my sisters are making me go. But you guys can still hang at my place and use the kitchen. I'll be back home before you're finished."

GBS group three nights a week.

Well, whatever. Football took more time than that.

Only, I wasn't jealous of football.

Why do I feel jealous of time Burke's going to spend at group meetings?

With other people like him, losing weight fast. Proba-bly girls. Probably a lot more girls than boys, judging by male versus female stats on weight-loss surgery.

Bring those curves down to a manageable level, Jamie...yeah. My teeth click together as I remember that comment. *And you're worrying about curves and weight loss and Burke with other girls while you're busy wishing you could go hang with Heath on a late night "for the newspaper."*

You're so going to hell, Jamie Carcaterra.

Our parents finally make their exit from Principal Edmonds's lair. Heath's father drifts silently down the hall just like Heath did, and I can't help watching him, can't help thinking about Heath and wondering more about his life. I really don't know a lot about the boy, wonky taste in music and old-fashioned graphic design skills aside.

Bits and pieces, like the stuff we talked about that night under the drafting table.

Everything about Heath seems as liquid and hard to grasp as the way he moves. Just...flowing right through my fingers and slipping away.

As the Westins and my folks say hello to Freddie and NoNo, Burke asks me if he can borrow a few bucks. He looks toward the end of the hallway, to the vending machines.

"I don't have any money, sorry." I pat his shoulder. It's the truth, but I don't think I'd loan it to him even if I was flush.

Burke looks disappointed, but shifts quickly to a muscle pose. "You'll get good pictures for my final feature, right?"

Freddie glances in our direction and groans. NoNo laughs.

I sigh. "Yes, Mr. America. We'll get some major buff shots."

"Ones that really show how much I've lost?" Burke sounds anxious—like actually worried. Hall lights reflect off his bald head, and his entire body seems slick and shiny. "Because sometimes it doesn't show on film unless the angle's exactly right."

"It won't be hard." I pull his arm down out of his magazine model pose and hold onto it, then make myself kiss him on the cheek. His skin is soft and stubbly all at the same time. "Your weight loss is so obvious now. People will see it."

Burke seems satisfied. I feel him relax, and I turn him loose as Mom beckons for me to come with her.

"Later," he says, and plants one on my lips.

Somehow, I pucker back enough to make it pass for a reaction, then fake a smile.

NoNo's oblivious, like Burke.

Freddie isn't.

She's staring at me, her eyebrows doing funny–knitty movements.

"Gotta go," I say out loud. *Leave it alone*, I beg her with my eyes.

She does.

But she won't be leaving it alone for long.

FEATURE SPREAD
for publication Friday, November 2

Fat Girl
Fat Boy Chronicles: The End
JAMIE D. CARCATERRA

[insert photo spread here]

Drum roll, please.

May I introduce the new, improved Used-to-Be-Fat Boy?

He needs a new name. What say we go with Muscle Boy? Sooner or later we might get down to Slim or Stick or some other scrawny nickname, but for now, just appreciate the sculpting.

[insert muscle shot here]

In forty-five days, Muscle Boy has dropped an astounding fifty-five pounds.

He's infection free, his wounds are healing, and he can eat about a half-cup of food at a time. It has to be pureed or applesaucelike, no major chunks, but he's gettin' it down. He's also walking and starting back with light strength training, and going on some *major* shopping sprees. Best we can estimate, he's changing clothing size about once every week to two weeks.

Muscle Boy's on his way to a support group meeting, but he's graciously answering a few questions by telephone even as I write.

So far, is the surgery everything you expected?
Yes, it is. I know the weight loss will slow down. It's already slowing down some, but I hope everyone can see the results, and I hope those results keep coming. One day, I'll weigh "normal" for my height and, baby, will I *ever* be ripped then.

You suffered through some serious complications, hovered near death, and endured severe pain, not to mention infections and a longer-than-expected hospital stay. Would you do it again?
Absolutely. No question.

Why?
Because it's my one big shot at never being fat again.

Worst moment?
The first time I frothed stuff all over the place. I'm getting better at controlling it now, though.

Best moment?
Every time I lose an *X* in my clothing sizes.
Pretty soon, no *X* at all—yeah, baby!

As you get thin, what things are you looking forward to the most?
Flying on an airplane—you know, fitting in the seats. And fitting in seats at movies, and buying clothes from regular stores and having them look good on me. I want to go parasailing and bungee jumping, and maybe run track, if I can get fast enough.

Will you play football again?
I don't know. There's not much research on contact sports after bariatric surgery. Put that in the we'll-see column.

Any regrets?
Nope. Not one.

Would you recommend this surgery to other guys your age?
Hey, now, that's a tough one. Yes and no. If being thin and buff feels important to them, very important, then yes. If it's no big deal, then no. It takes some major dedication, or at least it has so far.

What's your opinion of Barbara Gwennet's report on this column and our Fat Boy spotlight?

That chick can eat my old, unwashed size 7X undershorts. Without ketchup. I'll save them out of the Goodwill donation bag. Hey, Barb—come on over and chow down, baby!

Because of recent nonprint media hype, insanity, and inanity, this will be our last chronicle of Muscle Boy's progress. If you want to know more, you'll just have to ask him yourself. Please direct complaints to Barbara Gwennet at WKPX.

CHAPTER
FIFTEEN

"Get undressed. Gowns are in the cabinet." The nurse points at a white bench with double doors on the bottom. "Get up on the table when you're finished."

She smiles, then leaves and closes the door behind her.

I stare at the closed door and wish I could grow wings and fly away. I so need a day off from *The Wiz* and homework and scholarship angst, and instead I'm doing *this*?

Every year, a couple of weeks before Thanksgiving. Mom and her health maintenance schedules.

I've never been to this doctor's office before, because Dad's company changed insurance carriers last year, and I had to swap doctors. So far, I hate this place worse than our last clinic, which is saying a lot. Our previous doctor's office was grimy and busy and loud, and I never saw the same doctor or nurse practitioner or physician's assistant twice, and they *always* bitched about my weight. Every single time.

This clinic's high-end and spiffy, with salmon carpeting, textured paint, and health and wellness posters covering the walls. Each one says something more stupid than the last. My least favorite is a shot of a giant man in a piano-sized coffin with the slogan OBESITY KILLS.

The chairs in the waiting room all had arms, so I had to stand in front of dead piano-coffin-man while everybody stared at me, and my back's hurting, and I hated getting weighed in the hallway in front of everybody. That stunk worse than OBESITY KILLS. Especially the part where the nurse slid the bottom weight all the way to three hundred pounds before she even started moving the top weight. At least she didn't shout the number out loud, but she might as well have, so many people walked by.

Then they took blood and of course couldn't find the vein the first time. Poke, prod, wiggle. Poke, poke.

I'm sorry, it's just a little harder with big people.

Yeah. I know.

More padding. More fat between the needle and the vein.

Would it kill doctors to get training for their nurses and techs so they could handle fat people better? Would it put them in the poorhouse to buy different-sized needles for different-sized people?

I rub the bandage in the bend of my arm. Probably be bruised for a month.

A dull, washed-out sensation spreads through me as I start to take off my clothes so I can put on an exam gown.

Now I strip naked, alone in the new-car-smelling room, and turn five shades of red because I hate being naked anywhere for any reason. I always feel like somebody can see me, even when I know they can't. As fast as

I can, I fold my clothes over one of the chairs and fish in the cabinet for the biggest gown I can find.

Great.

They're all the same size.

Regular. Standard.

Whatever.

One size fits all.

Except me.

I take out two gowns, put one arm in each, but my arms don't really fit. I can't pull them up enough to wear them, or even fake wearing them.

Hot all over, hoping nobody comes to the door, I give up on the gowns, toss them in the dirty clothes bin, and search the other cabinets until I find a sheet. It'll have to do. I am so not sitting naked in the exam room, or letting my ass and boobs hang out of gowns that don't fit even when I use two of them.

When I step on the exam table's bottom platform, the whole thing tips forward. I half-fall, half-lunge to sit, and it crashes back down. I squish hard into the little padded tabletop and tear the paper cover as I move. It takes some thought and a lot of swearing, but I drag myself upright and scoot back far enough to keep the table from flipping again.

The whole setup feels too small beneath me, like it's going to teeter and plop on its side, but I'm pretty sure it won't. Nothing new here. It's the same everywhere I've ever been.

They don't make medical clinics for Fat Girls.

After all my hurrying, I get to sit for a while, then a

longer while. Cold, then hot. Sweating, then shivering. Staring at this set of health-message posters. One of them shows a baby's head superimposed on a big fat man's body, with the words, THE EATING HABITS YOU TEACH YOUR CHILDREN LAST A LIFETIME. Another shows how arteries harden and the effects of high cholesterol on the liver.

I have to pee, but I am totally not wandering down the hall wrapped in a sheet. For a few seconds I see myself with a baby's head on top of my big fat body. That's probably what the staff would see if sheet-me took off to piss.

By the time I hear commotion in the hallway, my eyes are floating, and I'm ready to bite somebody.

The doctor, a guy named Meacham, knocks once and zips into the room, towing his nurse. They stare at the sheet.

Say something, I dare him with my eyes, but he doesn't take the bait. Neither does the nurse. She's all red hair and big smiles, while Meacham reminds me a lot of Mr. Dunstein, the way he's small and thin with big eyes that look even bigger behind huge glasses. Nervous and twitchy, too. It wouldn't surprise me if he starts spouting stage directions or commentary on dialogue and presentation.

Instead, he says, "I'll need the big cuff," to the nurse, who whisks out, leaving the door open. She comes back a few seconds later with the large blood pressure cuff, and Meacham wraps it around my arm. He pumps once, takes it off, and sends her back out for the "thigh cuff."

Okay, first time I've needed the next size up, but at least they have one. Sucker's huge. And it *hurts* when it squeezes. The urge to bite somebody gets stronger.

Once the doctor finally gets my blood pressure reading,

he seems surprised it's normal. "One eighteen over seventy-eight. Good."

About a minute later, a tech rushes in and drops off my initial blood work, then takes off, slamming the door in her wake.

Meacham studies the numbers and looks surprised again.

"Well," he says. "All the values are within range. Normal. That's amazing, all things considered."

"I'm pretty healthy," I say, ignoring the all-things-considered comment.

"You're young." Meacham gazes at me over the rims of his big glasses. "This free pass won't last forever, not at your weight."

Well, that didn't take long.

I so wish I could grow fangs. Maybe if I could sprout fangs and claws, I could teach people how it feels to sit trapped and helpless while somebody pokes holes in your skin *and* your feelings.

Dr. Meacham sits on his doctor stool, takes a PDA out of his pocket, and punches buttons as he talks. "What weight-loss programs have you tried?"

I pull my sheet tight around me. Couldn't we at least start with what grade are you in? What school do you attend? Hobbies? Even exercise habits?

But no. Straight to the weight.

Not for the first time in a doctor's office, I think I should just keep all my diet failures in a diary, bring my own gowns, and save money for a portable exam table that actually fits me. Today, though, I'm Fat Girl with fangs, so I quote research studies. "In my experience, diets don't work. They result in yo-yo body fat and weight gain greater than pounds lost."

More punching on the PDA. "So you're not interested in weight loss."

"That's *not* what I said." When I look over at the nurse, her smile freezes to petrified-fossil stillness. "I've tried low-cal, low-carb, Weight Watchers, and three different plans from different doctors in the last four years."

Meachem looks up. "Did you stick to any of them?"

My cheeks heat. "Yes."

The doctor doesn't even slow down, and he's punching on his PDA again. "How long?"

I shrug. "I'm not sure. A few months each. I went to Weight Watchers for almost a year, but it didn't do much good."

"I find that difficult to believe, Ms. Carcaterra." Down goes the PDA. Up come Meacham's eyes, only this time, his gaze is sharper, and lots less businesslike. "If you had truly complied with any of those plans, you would have lost weight."

"Look, I've *tried.*" I clench my fist, but make myself let it go. "I want to be normal. I want to be thin. Nothing works for me."

Christ, why am I getting upset with this dork? This whole scene is so old.

"Then you haven't tried hard enough. It's all about motivation, restraint, and nutrition, Ms. Carcaterra." Over-glasses-rims stare. "We have nutritionists and behavioral medicine specialists on staff. Consultations are free for the first two visits." He jabs the PDA, then turns his attention back to me. "I'll set you up."

He doesn't even give me the chance to refuse. I'm so hot now he could perk coffee on my shoulders. Meacham can see how red I am. He probably knows I'm upset, but he doesn't seem to care.

"We also have ample information on bariatric procedures for young people." He beckons, and the nurse produces a stack of pamphlets from her pocket.

She holds them toward me, but I shake my head. "Our insurance doesn't cover weight–loss surgery. We already checked."

Meacham frowns. "I'll see about appealing that. Your body mass index is over fifty percent, in the highest risk category. Sometimes companies will make exceptions for cases with medical urgency."

Medical urgency? Oh for God's sake. I'm not bleeding out on the damned floor. If I could turn the sheet into a blanket, roll myself up in it, and bounce away down the tiled hallway, I'd do it.

"Don't get your hopes up," I tell Meacham. "I'm not a cancer kid or anything."

This time I get an evil stare over the glasses rims. "Obesity is as serious as cancer, Ms. Carcaterra. If you changed your mind–set, you might have better results with weight control programs. Do your parents take this seriously?"

"Yes—" I start, but he cuts me off.

"If they do indeed understand the severity of your condition, they might look into loans or second mortgages to cover the surgery you need. I'll discuss that with them." Punch, punch, punch on the PDA.

My mouth falls open.

Mortgage—as in the house? Put our house at risk to get my gut stapled? Is he *insane*?

He gestures to the table. "Lie back, please. Carefully."

What, like I'll break the friggin' equipment?

I'd rather kick Meacham in the nuts, but I do my best to settle back on the little table. Feels like I'll fall off, but I don't, and it's hard to breathe. When he puts his hands on my belly, he looks disgusted, and I so wish I could puke on him. If he pushes too long or too hard, I just might.

The nurse hovers as the doctor scoots the sheet around, and presses on my stomach some more.

"Of course I can't appreciate the major organs with this bulk," he says more to himself than to me. "No gross abnormalities."

Except the fat. Go ahead. Say it. Not much different from bulk, *right?*

"Since you're not sexually active, we'll omit the Pap smear for now." Shove, poke, push, glare. "I probably couldn't get it anyhow. You'll need to see a gynecologist for that. They have better techniques for getting difficult smears."

I say nothing, even when he squishes my full bladder. Bastard wants to assume Fat Girls aren't sexually active— because of course who would *ever* want a Fat Girl—let him. Who gives a damn?

When Meacham finishes pushing on my stomach, he does a breast exam, and wants to know if anything hurts.

I answer with, "No." Even if I was near going into shock I'd lie, because he'd just say I'm in pain because I'm fat.

Why don't you try harder?

Why don't you do something about yourself?

Poor girl.

Foolish, lazy fat girl.

My bladder aches. My skin turns strawberry red and every inch of me goes hot and sweaty and sticky. Seriously, I'm going to puke, but I choke it back, because they'll probably make me stay for more tests if I blow chunks on the floor.

I finally lose it and glare at the man as I struggle up on his stupid little table. "If I threw up right this second, would you say the fat caused me to vomit?"

"Very possibly." He doesn't look up from the PDA. "Obesity seriously raises the risk for gastroesophageal reflux disease. Vomiting is frequent in patients with that condition."

My fingers dig into my sheet-covered legs. "Do skinny people get gastroeso—whatever?"

He still doesn't look up. "Of course they do, but that's beside the point."

So, if I piss on the floor, it's because I'm fat, and not because I have to pee and you pushed on my bladder?

That question would probably make him look up, and throw me out, and upset Mom. So I say, "A doctor a few years back told my mom I had cramps because of my weight. I had dysentery, and it didn't get treated until I almost died from dehydration."

Meacham sighs. "Ms. Carcaterra, as long as you're this

overweight, any doctor will have difficulty examining you." He keeps his attention on his PDA, punching away. "If you'd like another physician at this practice, I can arrange that, but I assure you, they'll share my opinions about your obesity."

Another doctor?

Oh, thank you so much.

I just want Meacham and his PDA away from me, out of the room, and the redheaded nurse with him. I want out of the sheet, into my clothes, and away from this place. Even if it does make Mom unhappy, I'm not coming back unless a body part rots off. Even then, I'll give serious thought to amputating it myself.

When Meacham finally does leave, I cry, and hate him and hate that I'm crying and stuff my sheet way far down in the dirty clothes bin, underneath all the gowns that would never fit me.

It takes a few minutes of splashing water on my face for me to get a grip, get my attitude strapped back into place, get dressed, go to the bathroom, and get the hell out of plastic-stink hell.

Mom's waiting for me in the lobby like nothing's wrong, so I go with that.

Nothing's wrong.

I smile at her and she pays our co-pay, and out we go to the car, then hit the road toward the Pick-Sack and then to Burke's to help Freddie and NoNo with the fliers.

"Did you like Dr. Meacham?" Mom asks as we head into a convenience store for a snack. "He seems like a nice man."

I shrug. "He's a doctor. They're all about the same."

My phone rings. I glance at the display as Mom heads toward the soft drink coolers.

It's Burke.

My heart thumps, then squeezes. The thought of talking to him feels like better medicine than any clinic could prescribe for me. Even if he's smaller now, he's been there, been in that doctor's office, under the sheet, hearing the fat lectures.

"Hello?" I smile as I answer.

"Hey, baby," Burke says, sounding so much like his old self I can see him like he used to be, kicked back in his leather recliner, all big and handsome and happy. "Where are you?"

"The Pick-Sack. We just got through at the doctor's, and—"

"Pick-Sack? Great! I'll be home before you guys leave, so will you *pleee-ease* hook me up with a candy bar? You know what I like."

My hand clenches around the phone.

I flash on wearing that sheet in Meacham's office, and pulling it tighter and tighter and tighter until the sheet and my fat strangles me to death, and I fall off his little table and make a mess on his ultraclean floor.

All my happiness at Burke's call starts draining away. "Listen, I was just at the doctor's office like I said, and—"

"Everything okay? You sick?" Nice of him to ask, even if he doesn't sound worried at all. I hear noises in the background, like he's probably watching television.

My foot taps against the store's streaked tile. "No, I'm not sick, but the doctor was a bastard."

Long pause.

Nothing.

Like... Burke's not really listening to me at all.

"You remember that, right?" I try again, a little louder. "Going to the doctor, and how they act because you're fat."

"Yeah, I remember—but that's gonna be no big deal for me now, is it?" Burke laughs and goes back to paying attention to whatever he's watching on the tube.

I grip the phone hard enough to crack it down the center.

"Jamie?" Mom calls from the back of the store. "Want one of those candy bar brownies you like?"

"Did she say candy bar brownie?" Burke's paying full attention now, practically moaning into the telephone.

Oh, hell.

"Get two," I tell Mom.

To Burke, I say, "Done. See you later, okay?"

And I hang up before he says anything else.

I can't quit thinking about Meacham and the thigh cuff and the sheet, and somehow Burke's brownie-moan blends into all that, and I just don't want to be in that store anymore. I don't want to talk to anyone, either. I just want to go home, but I can't ditch NoNo and the fliers, or Freddie will slay me.

Or say something about Heath.

Or say something about Heath to Burke.

To Mr. *It's gonna be no big deal for me now.* How nice for Burke.

My face is *so* hot.

How perfectly friggin' wonderful that Burke doesn't

have to worry about fat things anymore, like clothes that don't fit. Like reporters showing your belly on national television as an isn't–this–horrible example. Like bad doctor visits.

Like . . . me?

"Jamie?" Mom's at the register, and I'm standing in the middle of the store like a giant dillweed.

"Coming," I mumble, but I don't move.

Freddie wouldn't rat me out, would she?

But if she did, would it be that awful?

Right now, I'm thinking *no*.

And when Freddie asks me about Heath—and trust me, the subject *will* come up—what am I going to tell her?

Nothing.

Because there's nothing to tell.

Except that you're heading to the cave tonight, no matter what your parents say. Don't lie. You know you're going.

After the fliers. After Burke gets his damned oh–so–important candy bar. After everyone and everything else is taken care of, then it's *The Wire* and the cave . . .

"And Heath," I admit to no one.

A few minutes later, I follow Mom out of the store like a Fat Girl zombie. Every step, automatic. Every movement, mindless.

Maybe tomorrow I'll know what to say to Freddie.

The Wire

FEATURE SPREAD
for publication Friday, November 9

Fat Girl Speaking Latin

JAMIE D. CARCATERRA

This is an open letter to doctors who actually give a damn about Fat Girls getting healthier, and I'm writing this column right now, before the fire fades. So, yes, Dr. M., this Fat Girl's for you.

Dear Dr. M. and Similar Doctors Everywhere:
If you want to help me or any other Fat Girl follow this one simple rule I thought you all learned way back in medical school: *Primum non nocere.*

First, do no harm.

How do you harm me? Let me count the ways—and check your own medical journals, because the research backs me up. In fact, it would take a dozen or so pages to detail the injuries. Instead, I'm offering you a Do and Don't list, in hopes you'll get a clue.

DON'T assume all my health complaints stem from being fat. So I have stomach cramps. Do skinny people never have stomach cramps? What? They *do*? Well, what do you do for *them*?

DO give me a thorough, complete examination.

DON'T make my weight check, blood work, and blood pressure check an embarrassing theatrical production.

DO have equipment and supplies that fit my body, and weigh me privately.

DON'T lecture me or blame me or shame me. You'd think this one should be a no-brainer, but honestly, that crap doesn't help. It sets me up to avoid medical services not just now, but forever. I'd rather die of some puss-filled, snot-swilling, eye-bleeding infectious disease than go to a doctor's appointment. And I'm not alone.

DO ask if you can help with my weight instead of assuming I'm a blockhead. I know I'm fat. I'm not unconcerned or noncompliant or treatment-resistant. I probably know more about nutrition and weight-loss programs than you do. If you don't have new ideas or some real and lasting support to offer, just shut up and treat me.

DON'T use wonky health-message posters. Did you know that many or even most of your teen females will actually misinterpret those messages, feel worse about themselves, and become more likely to adopt psycho weight-loss "quick-fix" strategies? Check the research on that. I'm right.

DO rethink the scare tactics and gloom-and-doom messages. Talk to me about hope. Help me find hope. You'd do that for any other patient. Don't Fat Girls need hope, too?

Primum non nocere.
How hard is that?

CHAPTER
SIXTEEN

Lights blaze from Burke's house as Mom drops me off. I fold up the feature I just finished in the car, tuck it into my skirt pocket, then count vehicles. Burke's, Freddie's, Burke's dad's . . .

And great.

M & M are here.

Just this one evening, couldn't the vampires be off sucking blood from other victims?

I should introduce them to Dr. Meacham. They'd probably fall in love.

Gripping my brown bag from Pick-Sack like it's full of booze or grass or some other major illegal contraband, I ease up to the door and knock, not too hard, hoping it'll be Freddie or Burke or NoNo who hears me.

Of course, it isn't.

M & M answer at the same time, wearing black skirts, black jackets, and disapproving frowns. They eye me, then my bag.

I work up my best bright smile. "Is there a password?"

They glare at me.

Before I can start guessing words like *hex* or *witch* or *Nosferatu*, they let me in.

I slide past Mr. Westin and his television news, and find Freddie, NoNo, and Burke standing at the round kitchen table, with stacks of STOP GLOBAL WARMING fliers spread in every direction. NoNo's adding a splash of color to each page with an environmentally safe marker, and Freddie and Burke are folding the papers into three sec-tions. It's harder and harder for me to match old Burke with this new Burke and his stylish, athletic clothes. His muscles look a little slack and droopy, but that won't last. The bald head, though—that's hanging around. His hair just won't grow.

"Thank God," Freddie says. She leans back in her chair and kisses her fingers. "Another set of hands. I'm a damned paper-cut magnet."

"Don't draw negativity," NoNo cautions, and Freddie rolls her eyes at me.

I drop the paper bag with the illegal candy bar brownie on the table, give Burke a major look so I know he gets the point, settle into one of the big armless chairs, belly-up to the table, and start folding and stacking, too.

"No paper cuts," I say like a chant, smiling at NoNo. "Nimble fingers. Nimble fingers. Drawing the positive. Imagining the positive."

Like M & M failing to come into the kitchen. Like M & M turning into bats and going to hang from the attic rafters.

Hey, this positive thinking thing works.

253

M & M didn't follow me. Not sure about the whole bat thing, but at least they aren't in the kitchen.

Bald, fashion-plate, sort-of-saggy Burke shoots me a grin that says, *you're the best*.

I'm busy trying to figure out what's different about the kitchen—other than Burke. I finally realize it's the smell. No food, no spices. Like the kitchen hasn't been used in a month. Which it probably hasn't, if the Westins are supporting Burke and eating away from him so he doesn't feel too deprived by his pureed diet.

For a time, the bunch of us are quiet. Too quiet. It feels weird, like more than the food smells are missing from the kitchen. I hate this freaky disconnect, but I don't know how to fix it, so I just fold and fold and fold.

Then Burke announces, "I get to move to soft food tomorrow. Things I can chew."

Oh, *whee*. More weight-loss diet talk.

I fold my flier hard and zip my fingers down the crease. Why does everything have to be about *that* now? Any second now, he'll ask if we can tell how much he's lost, and we'll all have to say yes.

NoNo saves us with, "What do you want to eat the most?"

"Pizza," Burke says without blinking, "Nachos. Maybe a steak. But that stuff's a ways down the road. Gotta start small." His gaze drifts to the bag. I get another grin.

Yeah, well, one candy bar brownie is small for Burke. Before he got his gut stapled, he could put away five or six and *then* go for pizza.

"If I couldn't eat for a month," I say as I fold the next

flier, "I'd probably want popcorn. No, wait. Baked potato. Or some pasta."

"Meatloaf," Freddie says, and we all give her yuck-faces.

"I'd prefer pine nuts." NoNo dabs red and green onto the little flier drawing of the Earth. "Pine nuts in olive oil with roasted garlic over whole-wheat pasta—or maybe Shirataki noodles."

Burke, Freddie, and I pause.

"Okay," I press my hands against my stack of folded fliers. "I'm scared, because that actually sounded good."

"Shirataki noodles are made out of tofu," Freddie reminds me.

I shiver at the thought.

"Not all of them." NoNo paints another flier. "Some are just yam root. And they'd taste just like the garlic and olive oil, since they assume the character of the flavors you add."

Assume the character . . . ?

Freddie pinches her nose with two fingers. "Have you ever smelled those Shirataki things when you take them out of the bag? They're in this liquid, and it smells like rotten fish piss."

NoNo sighs. "They rinse very well, and they soften if you boil them for a few minutes. I'll make them for us one night."

"Ah . . . that's okay." Burke stands. "I'll take a pass on that one, 'kay?" He slides the brown bag toward him.

Nobody but me notices.

"Be back in a sec." And Burke's gone, taking the bag with him.

The silence seems to leave with him, too.

"You okay?" Freddie asks the minute Burke's out of sight. "I know you hate the doctor and all."

I manage to paper-cut my thumb, swear, and shake it off. "Yeah, it sucked, but thanks for asking."

"Burke won't always be so wrapped up in his own issues," NoNo says without glancing up from her fliers.

When I stare at her, Freddie says, "Don't look surprised. We've noticed. It gets on our nerves, too."

NoNo makes green and red dots on the paper. "I think it's natural, but the obsession with his size won't last."

"No, he'll be thin and obsessed about other stuff." I fold my next flier. "Like girls. Things he can do that I can't. Clothes he can wear that I'll never fit into. Tons and tons of other stuff."

"He's not like that," Freddie insists. "Burke's loyal. He's not a cheater."

Oh, thanks.

I hate myself, but I want to go to the cave even worse now.

Burke comes back from his private meeting with the candy bar brownie, pulls up a chair, and sits beside me.

I straighten up, like I've been caught doing something very, very wrong. But I can't help it. The whole flier-folding thing, being here with my friends and Burke, it should be a blast, but I'm tired and hungry, and everything feels out of place and to the left and just . . . not right. I don't know how to make it right. I want to leave. I want to go talk to Heath.

Because that feels right.

I'm still not believing he wants anything to do with

me romantically, but I've got to find out, or the thought's gonna torture me to death.

How can I be sitting in Burke's house right next to Burke and thinking about another guy? I want to slam my forehead against the table until my brain unscrambles, but I keep folding fliers for five minutes. Ten minutes.

We all fold fliers, and NoNo rattles on about different types of noodles and organic flours, and how bad pro-cessed wheat and sugar are for people. The stacks of fliers seem to stay the same size.

The clock's moving, but so, so slowly. Twenty minutes. Half an hour.

I'm going to crawl out of my skin.

Why did I even come over here?

Because I love Burke. I do. I don't want to make a mistake here.

But what's the mistake? Having a conversation with Heath about the nature of our relationship and how we need to be friends and co-workers can't be wrong.

That's not what you want to do.

Everyone's laughing about something.

I search Freddie's face and NoNo's, too, but I don't have a clue.

When I glance at Burke, he doesn't look right. He gives me a thumbs up, puts his hand on his belly, and belches.

For a second, I'm terrified he's about to froth all over NoNo's fliers, but he doesn't.

Freddie studies me. She studies Burke. NoNo studies her fliers.

The silence crashes back around us, except for Burke's breathing, which gets louder. He starts trying to fold fliers again, but stops. He rubs his chest, and I realize he's sweating and there's a vein throbbing along his neck and the side of his face.

I take his hand and feel the pound of his pulse.

"Burke?" Now I'm worried.

Is he allergic to candy bar brownies now? But that was half an hour ago, maybe longer.

How long do brownie allergies take?

Jesus. Did I kill him because I was sick of listening to him ask for sweets?

My stomach starts to hurt. Sympathy pain?

Burke belches again.

"You got gas?" Freddie asks.

Burke shakes his head. "Nah, just some cramps. It happens sometimes. Well, lots, but less than it used to when I first had the surgery."

I swear his stomach is getting bigger as I watch, but I have to be imagining that. He's sweating a ton now.

Burke's face contorts. He looks like he's trying to pass a load the size of Nebraska.

This, at least, get's NoNo's attention. "Something's… wrong." Her words come out in slow motion, like a bad movie.

Burke tries to wave her off, but yells in pain instead. He doubles forward, arms wrapped around his belly, and smacks his face down on the table.

Freddie jumps away from the table along with NoNo. I shove back my chair and stand.

Burke heaves once and turns loose a load of vomit, soaking two stacks of fliers at once.

"Mr. Westin!" Freddie screams.

"Help!" NoNo yells.

I can't scream or yell because I feel glued and frozen and stuck. Acid stink floats across the room, and some other stink, and I realize Burke has turned loose on both ends.

Oh. God.

The brownie killed him. It really did. Or blew out all his staples, or something. I've murdered Burke.

My stomach hurts and twists and Mr. Westin comes running in with M & M right behind him. They rush to Burke. Mr. Westin grabs the phone, but Burke's moaning and puking more and begging them not to call the ambulance, and confessing about the brownie.

"I'm dumping," he chokes. "Just dumping." And he pukes and poops some more.

Then everyone except Mr. Westin stares straight at me.

. . .

"Do you want him to be miserable?" Mona, the older of the Ms, lets her eyes bore into me like lasers.

"Of course not," I fire back, but I can't muster laser-eyes. I feel too awful. I want to crawl in a hole and never come out. I want to be anywhere but here, doing anything but this.

We're sitting in the Westin living room, Freddie, NoNo, and me on the couch, Mr. Westin in his armchair, and M & M on the loveseat across the room. The house still smells faintly of waste and air freshener.

Burke's upstairs in bed. He won't die, but he'll be

miserable for the rest of the night, maybe tomorrow, too, according to his dad.

Marlene, the meaner *M*, clasps her hands together as she glares at me, too. "Do you want Burke to be fat again, Jamie?"

Yes. No. Yes? Screw you!

Out loud, I say, "No." I shift against the couch arm and bang into Freddie, who grunts. "He just kept asking, and I got tired of saying no. I was—too tired today."

"He was asking NoNo and me, too," Freddie admits. "We were thinking about it. If Jamie hadn't brought him something, I probably would have, tomorrow or the next day."

NoNo nods.

"Damn that boy." Marlene shakes her head and leans back in her chair. "I can't believe he's been pestering all of you to sneak him sweets."

Before I can say anything, Mona jumps in. "You knew he'd have to try. You know how he is."

"Stubborn." Marlene actually seems sympathetic to Burke and to me. "I know you didn't hurt him on purpose, girl, but don't you do anything like this again."

"The boy hurt himself," Mr. Westin says. "It was his choice to make a fool move like cramming all that sugar down his throat. It's not Jamie's job or anyone else's to be his food police."

"Um, yeah," Freddie says.

NoNo's dead quiet, still in shock about her ruined fliers and all the body fluids. Probably just as well.

"I thought he wouldn't want food with a stomach so

little." Freddie directs her question at Mr. Westin. "What gives with all the begging for candy bars?"

"Part of his food cravings are here." Mr. Westin taps the side of his head. "Like an addict, he wants his drug."

This makes Freddie grunt again. "But if the surgery doesn't stop the food cravings, why have it? I mean, can't Burke stretch that little stomach pouch and end up back where he started?"

Mr. Westin nods. "He could if he tried. But dumping usually convinces people not to do that."

"What's dumping?" NoNo asks in a tiny, scared bird voice.

"Yeah, really." Freddie shivers. "I thought frothing was bad, but this—much worse. Like watching somebody die."

Marlene lets out a breath. "Burke's stomach pouch dumped brownie into his small intestine too fast. It can happen any time he eats too fast or too much. He'll get stomach pain, bloating, throw up, get the runs, that kind of thing. And his heart will beat fast, and he'll sweat and get dizzy—it'll get his attention."

"Kind of like a punishment," Mona says. "And it's not over. There's a second kind of problem, called 'late dumping,' too. Because he ate so much sugar, his glucose level will shoot way up, then crash back down. He won't be able to eat enough to offset it, so he'll be hypoglycemic—sleepy and probably exhausted from low blood sugar all the way through tomorrow."

"Because of a brownie."

Damn, I said that out loud.

M & M don't instantly fly in for the kill, so I keep

going, more out of nerves than anything else. "But he used to eat so *many* of those. How could one brownie do that much damage?"

"I'm sure Burke thought the same thing." Mr. Westin's smile seems gentle, patient, and Burke's sisters act calmer than usual, like they've been waiting for this, and they're relieved it finally happened.

Something about the whole situation feels way past twisted to me.

"Next time, when he tries to pressure you again—" Marlene begins, but I cut her off by holding up my hand.

"There won't be a next time." I shake my head. "No thank you."

NoNo makes a whispery–gurgly noise that might have been, "Yeah."

Freddie says, "Damn—uh, darn straight."

From upstairs, Burke calls, "*Da-ad.* Hey, Dad!"

Mr. Westin's up before I process what's happening. My thoughts seem to be working slower than the rest of the world's.

Marlene gestures toward the door. "You all should probably head out for the night."

NoNo virtually leaps to her feet. Freddie stands with more dignity. As I shove myself off the couch, both knees pop. My whole body hurts, like *I* dumped instead of Burke.

Marlene heads upstairs to help her father with Burke. Mona braves the newly scrubbed kitchen to retrieve the unruined stacks of fliers, loads us up, and sees us out.

I manage to pause on the front stoop and look at

Mona, so she can tell I'm serious. "Will you tell him I'm sorry? I had no idea. I really didn't know."

Mona's usually sharp, severe expression softens. She pats me on the shoulder. "I'll tell him—but you don't have to apologize. This is on Burke, one hundred percent. He needed this lesson."

The Wire

FEATURE SPREAD
for publication Friday, November 16

Fat Girl Flirting

JAMIE D. CARCATERRA

So many assumptions.

Here's one. If a Fat Girl manages to have a boyfriend, she needs the guy's attention to feel good about herself.

Truth is, feelings of well-being in fat people have more to do with strong family connections—like moms and dads and siblings—than with a love life. Which is a good thing, because sometimes love-life connections get way bungled up and impossible to fix.

Here's another. Fat Girls get depressed because they're fat.

Guess what? Big studies with thousands of kids show that the depression-fat connection works in reverse. Fat kids aren't necessarily more likely to be depressed, but depressed kids are likely to be fat. So depression might cause fat, but fat doesn't have to cause depression.

Surprised?

Here's another big one I faced recently. Fat Girls don't have sex (unless we're the town slut, because of course, we're fat, and how else would we get laid?).

News flash: That's not true, either.

Half of us Fat Girls are sexually active, just like our skinny friends. We just don't tell *you*. Or sometimes, anyone else. We have a harder time getting adequate female exams and proper birth control, and we suffer more side effects from virtually every available method—but baby, let me tell you, we're out there using the stuff anyway.

We. Love. Just. Like. Skinny. Girls.

We worry what our hair looks like when a guy flirts with us. We worry if our clothes are straight, or if we have dirt on our noses, or that our breath might smell bad. We stiffen up when his hands move toward our butt—but not too much, especially if we *want* his hands to move there.

Sometimes, we do want those hands to move.

Trust me on that.

Am I squicking you out?

Why? Because I'm talking about a) sex or b) Fat Girl sex?

If you answered *a,* I have some books for you to read. If you answered *b,* there's this doctor named Meacham who thinks Fat Girls don't have sex. You'd really like him. Stop me in the halls. I have his card.

CHAPTER
SEVENTEEN

I finish getting a week ahead on my column about half-way to Garwood High, and I tuck the scrawled-on paper in my pocket.

My hands are still shaking from Burke's dumping incident.

For a few more miles, I stay quiet, still too mad to speak.

We're almost to the front parking lot when my mouth goes dry. My head starts to pound. Every muscle in my body cranks so tight I feel like I'm going to snap in seven different places, and I just want to fill the backseat of Freddie's Toyota with endless screams.

"I've been right there every step with him." Heat and more heat floods my body. The seat belt starts to suffocate me. "I'm trying to do everything and finish applications and keep up with the play and the paper and homework and worrying about college and scholarships and he's making me watch him vanish inch by inch and pound by pound—and now he sets me up to be eaten by his sisters and hated by his entire family?"

"They don't hate you." Freddie's not yelling, but close. "He tried to get us to bring him stuff, too."

I bang my hand on the fliers. "You aren't his girl-friend!"

"Yeah, well, it seems like you don't want that job any-more!" Freddie slams on the breaks and we jerk to a stop in the Garwood High main drive.

For a few seconds, I sit there breathing, breathing, then rip off my seat belt and jerk open the car door. "Maybe I don't, okay? Does that mean we won't be friends any-more?"

"What?" Freddie looks truly wounded. She bites her bottom lip.

"Don't," NoNo says quietly. "Our friendship with you isn't all about you and Burke, but you can be an ass. Don't be an ass."

Freddie's got tears on her cheeks, and her expression says I stabbed her directly in the heart.

Give me a friggin' break.

Two thousand totally cruel things ram through my brain, but I look from NoNo to Freddie, from Freddie to NoNo, and I get the hell out of the Toyota before I can say anything else.

I slam the door.

Freddie squeals off.

I don't care.

Yes, I do.

But I'm turning away from the taillights and moving fast toward the buildings, into the dark, away from Burke and my friends and everything about my entire life. I want to be somebody else. Somewhere else. I want to be in the cave, doing layout and talking to Heath about stupid stuff like soccer and not-so-stupid stuff like scholarships. Anything but Burke, or bariatric surgery, or weight loss, or anything remotely related to frothing or dumping or any other *-ing anything.*

When I burst into the cave, Heath stands up from the layout table, takes one look at me, and drops his blade and T square.

"What's wrong. What is it?"

"Burke!"

"Jesus. Is he—?"

"Bariatric surgery!" I'm on a roll now. "That's what's wrong. Frothing. And *losing weight.* And doctors—and dumping! And Freddie. The national news—NoNo and deadlines and college and the National Feature Award!" I shake my head. Rub a hand across my forehead. Swallow an urge to keep ranting or start laughing like a lunatic baying at the full moon.

Heath's standing in front of me now, taking hold of my shoulders. "Look at me," he says.

I'm still making lists in my head. Heath's on the list. I'm about to tell him that when he says, "Look—at—me."

Deeper. More commanding. More direct.

I look at him.

Straight into those worried blue eyes.

"Breathe," he says.

I breathe.

Once. Twice. One more time for good measure.

Heath nods. "Better. Now stand still."

I stand still.

He leans down, pulls me against him, and presses his lips tight, tight, tight against mine.

. . .

. . .

. . .

He tastes *good.*

Like cinnamon and chocolate, probably from those lit-tle mints he pops when we're pulling a late night. I don't know where to put my hands, what to do with my arms, so I wrap myself around him.

Music plays softly in the background, some old song about the Only Living Boy in New York.

Heath's the only living boy in Garwood, as far as I'm concerned.

His lips feel like heaven, and his tongue is all rough and smooth at the same time, and he holds me like I'm tiny and fragile and perfect, like I'm the only living girl in his world.

Our bodies press together until there's no air between us. My heart pounds so hard I'm afraid it's going to leap right out of my chest.

I can't breathe, but I don't want to breathe and I don't ever, ever want this moment to end.

Heath breaks off the kiss but starts another without ever opening his eyes.

I squeeze my eyes shut tight, like if I open them again, I might break the spell.

My entire being tingles, head to toe, inside out and outside in. He strokes my face with one hand, then smoothes my hair as he kisses me deeper, even better. My skin catches fire everywhere he touches me.

A few seconds later, when his hands move around my body, I *don't* get stiff. I *don't* want him to stop. And I'm not thinking about features or manifestos or anything in the universe but Heath Montel.

His palms trace the curves of my hips for a few more kisses, then he stops, and eases back, and I still don't want to open my eyes.

"Jamie."

Not opening my eyes. Not doing it. Nope.

"Jamie. You can look at me."

"If I look, I might wake up."

When I open my eyes, he's smiling this lazy, happy smile. "If you're dreaming, then when you wake up, come find me and kiss me. Things'll turn out the same, I promise."

"How long have you wanted to kiss me?"

Heath shrugs and rubs my shoulders. "A while."

Typical Heath answer. Hard to pin down, impossible to grasp.

Now I'm wanting to ask why, but I don't. Can't. Scared to death to hear the answer, so I lean forward and kiss his cheeks instead. Smooth, but stubbly near the bottom. He stands still and holds me gently, but tighter when I kiss his neck, which has that delicious spice–aftershave scent.

"You always smell so good," I murmur as I pull back.

He gives me a raised–eyebrows sort of look. "You notice how I smell?"

Insta–red face, for me. "Um, yeah. It's a girl thing."

More with the raised eyebrows.

Redder and redder. Cripes, I'm acting like I'm thirteen. Breathe. Breathe.

"Okay, Jamie," Heath mutters into my ear, sending waves of happy–chills up and down my back. "How long have *you* wanted to kiss *me*?"

Thinking fast, I go for, "A while," and smile before he can argue.

More kissing.

A *lot* more kissing.

I get lost in Heath, in the way his mouth feels, and that spicy guy scent, and how his arms feel so perfect around me. I'm me, but I'm not me. I'm something else when he touches me, something more and brighter and happier. We move like we already know each other, no awkward bumping or stumbling, no miscues. Like we're laying out the perfect paper, with print, pictures, and columns.

How long have we been standing here?

Minutes?

Hours?

Do I care?

Except, the paper's not done.

Except, even though it's usually just Heath and me working on layout, there's a chance somebody could burst through the cave door.

Except, outside the cave, the world's still there, waiting.

And I'm supposed to do a thousand things.

And I'm supposed to have some best friends, only I pissed them off by being a bitch *again*.

And I'm supposed to have a boyfriend.

What was his name again?

Started with a *B* . . .

Do I care?

No.

I really, really don't.

Heath holds me tighter, and I hold him and I don't let go. The cave's an island now, and we're the only living people on it, and the whole world and all its deadlines and rightness and wrongness can go straight to hell.

Heath finds this place on my neck, this perfect spot. Even his breath makes me shiver, and he knows it, and he nips me there, and kisses, until I wriggle and beg for him to stop, then do it again.

It doesn't take me long to find that spot on his neck.

More kisses, and more, but we're slowing down a little. Not as desperate and fast. Not as rushed and scared.

God, like this might not be the only time. Like this might last?

I get tense.

Too much to think about. Too much reality.

"What's wrong?" he asks, because we are in sync, we're always in sync. I *do* know him, so much better than I realized, and he knows me. Heath knows my patterns, my rhythms, my reactions, almost better than I do.

When I look at him, I don't even have to speak, and I know he knows.

Nothing. This is perfect. Which makes absolutely everything wrong.

For a while, Heath holds me without kissing me.

I press my face against his shoulder and don't cry,

because I don't feel sobbing sad or half out of my mind. I feel like I'm floating, just drifting along in that ethereal way Heath drifts through everything. It's contagious, that vague, smoky existence of his. He's so visible, yet invisible, too. Hard to define. I wish I could be like him, that I wasn't so Jamie, so Fat Girl, so everything I've made myself be.

If I were like Heath, I could start myself over anytime I wanted to.

If I could start myself over right this second, I'd have broken up with Burke maybe last year, when I caught him making google-eyes at a visiting team's cheerleader. That would have been a good excuse. I at least would have kicked him to the curb when he lied about getting grounded instead of telling me he'd decided to have that monstrous surgery. Nobody would have blamed me for that.

Now—now I'll be the asshole, no matter what I do, or how I do it.

If I could start myself over, I wouldn't be an asshole. I'd be gentle and sweet like NoNo, and only half-visible like Heath, and maybe curvy like Freddie instead of Carcaterra-huge. That would be the ideal Jamie. Something more . . . moderate, softer, and easier to take.

"Should I be nicer?" I whisper.

Heath kisses the top of my head. "You're nice." Another kiss. "Most of the time."

"Thanks. I think."

Heath laughs. I like the way his laugh feels, so close and rumbly.

Why does none of my past feel real?

It's like Burke never existed, like I don't know my friends, or have any worries. My family, college—nothing. *Poof*, all gone.

This is completely, totally different from anything I've ever felt before.

Is Heath feeling the same way?

We need to talk. Only, if we talk, we can't kiss, and kissing is so fine.

In sync, yeah.

Heath kisses me again.

Then he says, "I guess we should talk, or something."

"Something."

More kissing.

After a few minutes of tongues and lips and hands moving everywhere, we finally sigh and sit down against the wall by the door. For a second or two, we don't say anything. Then, like somebody gave us a stage direction, we both get back up, walk over to the drafting table, and sit down against *that* wall, with the table like an umbrella over our heads.

The radio plays softly, and everything feels normal now that we're sitting shoulder to shoulder and leg to leg underneath the drafting table, where we belong.

This part of my past is real, the part where it smells like school cleanser and developer and glue and newspaper-in-progress. We pass a little time covering the basics—like the weather and all the college applications we've finished and mailed, which schools we hope to hear from, and that I got the Fat Girl portfolio submitted for the NFA on time.

Barely. And we wonder what the judges are thinking—and watching—so far.

Then I dare to tread on scarier ground. "Have you had a lot of girlfriends? And don't just shrug and say 'a few.'"

Heath freezes midshrug. When I glance at him, he's staring straight ahead and looking a little embarrassed. "Six or seven, I guess. I haven't been keeping records."

"Who?" I take his hand in mine and play with his fingers.

Heath names off a few girls from his freshman year, one from his sophomore year, then sheepishly admits to a brief fling with a Catholic girl from over at Father Ryan's down the road, mainly because he thought her uniform was sexy.

"She turned out to be a real bitch, though. Almost got me beaten half to death by some nun who caught us out by a Dumpster." Heath shakes his head. "My junior year, I grew a brain. Calmed down some."

Millions of questions churn through my mind, but the one I ask is, "How do you do it? Be handsome and liked by everybody, but stay so far off the gossip radar?"

This time, he does shrug. "Guess I just don't talk much about my life, so other people don't talk either."

I lean my head against the cinderblock wall. "I talk about mine too much, don't I? In the newspaper, no less."

"Not really." Heath squeezes my fingers. "I mean, you do talk about the obvious stuff, but the down-deep stuff you keep to yourself until it explodes. Like tonight."

"Freddie said the same thing."

"Freddie is a good friend."

I give him a look, then can't help kissing his cheek, which makes him grin. "Freddie's been bugging me about you," I say quietly, hoping my voice tickles his ear. "She knew something before I'd admit it, even to myself."

"Like I said, she's a good friend." He turns his head to look at me, and I could go swimming in those perfect blue eyes. "Will you tell her about tonight?"

Reality does a slide–click and shift, and some of my actual life elbows back into my brain. "Um, yeah. I will."

Like the second I leave here, even if it's four in the morning?

But she's mad.

But she'll go postal if I don't tell her something like this instantly.

"How many boyfriends have you had in high school?" Heath's voice intrudes on my worrying, snapping my attention back to him.

"Just Burke," I answer, only half–present. "And . . . and now . . ."

Do I say it?

"And now me." Heath sounds definite.

"Now you."

Why does that make my chest hurt?

"Let me guess." He toys with my fingers the way I played with his. "You and Burke, you're not officially broken up."

When I don't answer, I feel Heath sigh.

"I'm not about poaching another guy's girl, Jamie."

For the first time since I got to the cave, I go a little stiff. "I don't belong to Burke, you know. I'm not some guy's property."

"Okay, okay, claws in."

Claws?

What claws?

I'm a kitten.

Kittens have little-bitty claws.

"But you will talk to him?"

"I'll talk to him." God, that feels huge. "But Freddie first."

"Freddie first, whatever, that's a girlfriend code or something, I know. But Burke has to be next."

When I look at Heath, he's serious. "A guy code thing," he says. "I don't want to end up having to throw down with a dude who just had surgery."

Leave it to Heath to be all honorable. Bizarre.

"You won't have to do that. I'll take care of it."

And even as I'm kissing Heath again, I'm wondering what in the living hell I'm going to say to Burke Westin.

FEATURE SPREAD

for publication Monday, November 19,

Pre-Thanksgiving Special Edition

Fat Girl Choosing, Again

JAMIE D. CARCATERRA

Choices.

Did I make the choice to be fat?

Is it possible for a baby, a very young child, a little girl, to choose a lifetime of obesity, and all that entails?

Do I consciously, every day of my life, choose to eat in ways that keep me fat?

A few months ago, I would have said no.

Now I'll say, I don't know.

I don't think I do, but I'm learning that making a choice can be subtle. That sometimes I decide things and don't even know I've decided them until I'm face-to-face with the consequences.

I didn't choose to have a national media explosion centered on me and the column I write, but I *did* choose to write the column, and put it in print, and never shy away from my own opinions just because they might be controversial.

I didn't choose for Barbara Gwennet to make me look like a total buttface—some of that was her choice, to boost her own press and ratings—but I *did* choose to talk to more reporters even though that local witch of a news anchor taught me the risks.

Are people responsible for events when they make a choice knowing that danger, pain, damage, or disaster is a *possible* outcome?

The law says yes. What do you say?

I say I don't know. I'm not sure.

Choices make ripples that never stop. Choices make ripples that can stir up the entire ocean. The sucky part is, I don't always know when I'm choosing, and I don't always see that tidal wave of consequences towering over me.

The only thing I can think to do is become more aware of choosing, and quit bitching and moaning when some ripple I set in motion nearly drowns me. I need to learn to swim better. I need to learn to swim faster. I also need to learn to look back and catch myself in the secret, subtle act of choice making.

Maybe fat is a choice.

Maybe it isn't.

Maybe if I swim long enough and hard enough, maybe if I watch the water around me closely enough, I'll figure that out.

CHAPTER
EIGHTEEN

"Oh, no you did *not*." Freddie laughs as I fold up the column I finished just before she and NoNo got to my house this evening—putting me two ahead and clear for the upcoming holiday—*yes*. "You're kidding, right? Last week? You're kidding. I know you are. Why didn't you tell us *sooner*? But seriously, you're kidding."

When I don't tell her I'm kidding, Freddie looks mad. Then worried. Freaked out. Then she covers her mouth and laughs again. Then she rolls around on my bedroom floor like a crazy woman. "You really did it. You made out with Heath Montel! I knew it. I *knew* it."

NoNo—hey, she's my friend, too, so I had to tell her ... no, wait, I chose to tell her—just sits at the foot of my bed and shakes her head and turns scarlet-purple-red. Dye free, of course.

The smell of Mom's homemade pizza drifts through the house, making my stomach roar. I shift on the bed and lean against my headboard. I know if I eat a single bite of that pepperoni delight, I'll turn green. Too nervous. Too much to think about.

"Sorry, sorry." Freddie tries to get a grip. "God, this is going to be so complicated. Burke will flip the hell out."

"It'll be like divorce," NoNo says. "We'll have to split up holidays. Share weekends. Reconfigure family gatherings." She sighs.

Freddie wants to be furious and all parental, but she's too busy laughing again. "What can I say?" she shrugs. "Gotta love romance. Even straight romance."

Thank God it's only a couple of weeks before Thanksgiving break and we don't have much homework, because Freddie has a thousand questions. She bounces all around the room and wants a thousand details, from how Heath smelled to what he said to whether or not the word *love* actually got used.

That last one makes me take a deep breath, because I've told Burke I love him *so* many times. He's told me the same thing.

Am I really ready to throw that out the window? Am I ready to admit I don't love Burke? I guess it's possible to say *I love you* so many times it's automatic. Like, *Can you tell I'm losing weight?* And, *Yes, absolutely.*

Heath and I didn't use that word, *love.*

Does that mean something?

I close my eyes and bang my head back against the headboard. *Oh, God, don't start doing this, obsessing over every little detail.*

But I do.

And I keep coming back to words I've written, about how Fat Girls don't play the lead or get the guy. About how we're not supposed to be popular, how we're supposed to be pathetic, sad wallflowers.

I was poking fun at those myths. So, what the hell? Do I believe them myself, at least a little bit?

"You're not sharing," Freddie says, sounding grouchy. "You're doing that thing again, where you keep the real stuff to yourself."

I open my eyes. "I am not."

Hands on hips now, with a major Freddie-glare. "You are, too. You *always* do it."

Before I can argue again, NoNo puts my deepest fears into words with, "You know, Heath has more courage than I thought."

Freddie quits bouncing. She scrubs her hands against her jeans and slowly sits on my floor where she can see both of us.

My body temperature shoots up and down about three times as I try out different meanings for NoNo's comment. Finally, I give up. "Explain, please?"

NoNo huddles in her oversized hemp sweater, then straightens as she says, "I've always seen him as a little shy. Sort of . . . absent and undefined. Maybe too much of a coward to stick up for his beliefs."

Okay, that meaning's all too clear. "What—if he's going to date Fat Girl, he's got to be brave?"

NoNo gazes at me without blinking or smiling. "Yes."

Freddie tenses, like she's scared I'm about to blow, and

I think about it. Think about it some more. My stomach stirs around and turns a little flip.

Is that why Heath didn't say he loved me?

Because he doesn't know if he's got the guts to go public with Fat Girl?

But he said he was my next boyfriend . . . sort of. Right?

An evil, evil part of my brain urges me not to talk to Burke until I know for sure Heath will be there for me.

What is wrong with you?

NoNo's unwavering gaze makes me want to slap her, but I really, really want to slap myself.

"If I had a magic wand," NoNo says slowly, "and I could wave it and make you thin, who would you be, Jamie? What would you believe in?"

Now *that* slaps me.

Everything inside me jerks sideways.

I wrap my arms around my midsection and choke back a lot of fast, harsh remarks. Then I realize I have absolutely no idea what to say to NoNo.

But I don't want to admit that.

I don't want to say out loud that I'm not sure I want to be thin, or "lose weight," or whatever trendy phrase anyone would like to choose. Being Fat Girl *is* who I am. It's my shtick.

Right?

To take on size-ism and fat discrimination, to demand my right to be as big as I want to be.

I'm Fat Girl.

If I wasn't Fat Girl, *who would I be?*

Holding myself tighter, I feel the fat, really feel it, the

totality of it, the weight of it. Like a lining between me and the rest of universe. A buffer zone where pain stops . . . and bullshit begins?

It defines me.

Do I *let* it define me?

It must be possible for brains to fry, because mine's sizzling.

The longer I don't yell at NoNo, the more it heats and cooks, but I can't yell at her. I won't. I choose not to.

Nobody speaks for a few minutes.

Freddie breaks the silence, her nervous energy lashing the air as sharply as her words. "Okay, that's like so too deep for me, NoNo. It's nearly vacation, for God's sake."

NoNo swallows. She looks like she might back down, but when she catches my eye, she says, "I just want to know how much of Fat Girl is really Jamie."

I can't answer that either. I think I get it, but I'm not totally sure. Like Freddie says, NoNo's diving deep, shooting under all my safe places, heading into areas I so don't like to examine.

Is Fat Girl just another role, like Evillene in *The Wiz*? Another "fat part" I play with flare and drama?

Could I scrub Fat Girl off like green glitter?

NoNo's not finished. "Do you really believe the things you write about?" She leans forward and rests her chin on her knobby knees, all the while looking straight at me. "Because if you believe in your causes, sooner or later you have to take risks for them. You have to behave like you believe. Maybe that's what you're doing with Heath. Finally choosing to take a real risk."

If I pull back any farther from her, I'll stuff the headboard and myself through the wall into my parents' room.

Choice.

There's that damned word again.

And what about all the times I've chosen by not choosing? All the times I've gone sliding along through my life and everyone else's, whining about how I can't change anything—from other people's attitudes to my own body?

I bitch about things, but what do I ever *really* work to change, like NoNo does?

"NoNo...I run my big fat mouth about my big fat beliefs, then turn around and act like a coward."

Freddie's mouth moves, but no sound comes out. NoNo's look says she agrees, but she's not sure if I'm going to scream at her or not.

"Sometimes I hate you," I whisper. "Sometimes I rag on you because I know you see *everything*."

NoNo looks a little sad when she smiles. "That's okay. Sometimes I hate me too—but I never hate you."

Bitch.

Tears form in my eyes. "I know."

Freddie gulps air. "No hating. It's like, nearly Thanksgiving. There will be no hating in my presence."

My frying brain keeps right on popping. *Who do you really hate, Jamie?* I glance down at myself, in all my fat, strange, different—beautiful?—glory.

Come on. Dare you to tell the truth on that one.

My door rattles.

We all jump and stare as somebody knocks.

It's Mom. I can tell by the soft taps.

"Come in," I mumble.

Mom pushes open the door, letting in a cloud of pep-peroni and fresh-baked, hot pizza crust. She glances around the room. I can tell she notices something's going on, but she doesn't ask. She just pushes forward with what she came to do.

Like me?

"This was in the mail." She holds out a brown enve-lope. Her expression's tense.

When I take the envelope, I see the NFA stamp in the corner.

Maybe it's the heavy conversation, or the fried brain, or holiday fog, but I can't make sense out of getting an envelope from the NFA now. It's too early for the an-nouncement. Still two or three weeks until we're sup-posed to know anything.

"Maybe they picked you already!" Freddie jumps up, breathless.

NoNo looks like Mom, nervous and concerned.

Numb, cool dread spreads through me as I hold the envelope. It's heavy. Like it's stuffed with papers.

Or a portfolio.

Whatever this is, it's not good.

"It's early," I manage to say before I read, with everyone in a half-circle behind me, looking over my shoulder:

Dear Ms. Carcaterra:

Thank you for your entry into the National Feature Award scholarship competition.

As our guidelines state, the NFA targets outstanding journalism promoting the public well-being. While your column is both educational and enlightening about the beliefs and experiences of a subset of our population, and your writing is certainly fresh and engaging, our committee does not believe the content fulfills the primary criteria of promoting public well-being. As such, your entry is disqualified.

We're returning your materials herewith enclosed, and wish you good fortune in pursuing your collegiate career.

Sincerely,
Thomas Sanderson, PhD
Chairman
NFA Search Committee

"Oh." Mom puts a hand on my arm. "Honey."

NoNo turns away and shakes her head. "Unbelievable. Talk about cowards. I bet they can't handle all this national PR heat."

"It's Barbara Gwennet's fault!" Freddie's voice booms, and her face flares bloodred. She snatches the letter out of my hands and shakes it about a foot away from my face. "No way we let this stand. You're on the phone in two seconds with this Sanderson bastard, and you're on a plane to meet with this committee tomorrow!"

"I can get a lawyer," Mom offers. She gives my arm a squeeze. That suddenly hopeful look she can get tears at my insides. "Dad's employee assistance program offers legal advice."

"There's the ACLU," NoNo adds.

My head swims. I should be crying. Gasping. Hollering louder than Freddie, or getting civil liberties phone numbers from NoNo.

I should do something. Feel something. But I just feel tired.

What the hell? Strap on the big guns. Get ready for the big battle.

Because this would be a battle worth fighting—if I believe in it. And I believe in it.

Right?

Out loud, I say, "I don't know."

"What?" Freddie, Mom, and NoNo answer at the same time.

"You always want the truth. The real stuff. Well, that's it." I meet Freddie's eyes and make myself not look away. "*I don't know.*"

Freddie thinks I'm kidding. She's still red. She's still furious. "Oh, no way. Fat Girl always knows the best way to stick it to this kind of asshole." She makes stabbing, twisting motions in the air. "Fat Girl always knows what to say."

Still no anger. Still just tired. That's the truth.

"Fat Girl always knows what to say, but I don't. I don't know what I want. I don't know if I want to fight other people. NoNo's right. I don't know if I'm a coward or an activist or something in between. *I don't know.*"

Maybe I need time to think. Maybe I need time to rest.

Maybe I need to figure out if fighting scholarship people is a risk I want to take.

But I do know one thing for sure, one risk I do need to take. One I *must* take, if I believe in this whole honesty thing, if I have any beliefs of my very own to be true to.

And I have to take this risk right now, no more delays, no more putting it off, no matter how I feel.

I turn away from all the stares and scramble to find a piece of paper and pen, knowing I'm about to get three columns ahead—and scared to death of what I'm planning to write...and do.

When I'm ready, I turn back to hopeful Mom and furious Freddie and stunned, quiet NoNo and say, "I need to go to Burke's."

The Wire

FEATURE SPREAD
for publication Friday, November 30,
Post-Thanksgiving special edition,
if I am still alive

Fat Girl Confessing

JAMIE D. CARCATERRA

I'm writing this confession in Freddie's Toyota, on my way to make another confession. And honestly, I'm not sure which admission will be harder.

My confession to all of you is as follows:

After all my ranting, mouth running, and stand taking, after all my costume-wearing attitude and dramatic stage presentations, after all the times I've acted like I know more than every last one of you (about everything), I might just be a coward with no real clue about what I want or what I know. That has nothing to do with me being fat, by the way, and everything to do with me being an idiot. Sometimes I really, really *can* be an idiot.

As for the other confession:

That's absolutely none of your business.

CHAPTER
NINETEEN

Early Thursday night, Burke sits in his leather recliner with his hands folded in his lap. He's nervous. He knows something's way wrong, and it's killing me, and I don't know how to get started.

His big bedroom looks like something out of a *Technology Today* magazine, and his dozens of machines and gadgets keep distracting me. Sometimes his computer whirs and clicks. His modem blinks. His neon clock flickers. Everything smells like leather and plastic and guy. Everything smells like Burke, and I'm sitting in his rolling desk chair, and I'd rather look at anything but him and his nervous expression and his totally transformed body.

I cannot begin to fathom how much he's changed. Like a new guy. Like a totally different guy. He's nearing sixty pounds lost, working out with the football team again, walking every day, starting to run—he's turning into a major god, no kidding. And he will achieve his dream of being buff and fabulous when he walks across the stage at graduation, I have no doubt.

"I admire you," I admit, looking down at my own hands for a little relief. "I've been jealous in so many ways, because you had this opportunity and I didn't, but the bottom line is, you believed bariatric surgery was right for you and you went for it. You've battled through horrible things I don't think I could ever face, and you're winning. You're really doing it."

"I'm, uh, sorry about the whole candy bar brownie mess." He gets a hopeful look like Mom does when she's grasping for answers, trying to help, and it kills me a little more. "Literally. I mean, the literal mess, and the mess of bugging you to bring it to me, Jamie." When I glance up at him, he's staring at a spot on the floor somewhere between us. "My dad really jumped my shit about that. He was right, too. It wasn't fair, what I did."

I'm an ass. I'm an ass. I'm an ass . . .

"Hey, I *do* understand." My tone's softer than I mean for it to be. I don't want to lead him on, but I can't help but be nice about this at least. "If anybody gets eating stuff that's not good for me, I do. And I get wanting to eat it anyway. Needing to eat it."

Burke's head comes up. He looks at me funny, kind of like he's seeing me new or different, or for the first time. "Whoa. Okay."

His reaction surprises me. "What? What whoa?"

"Whoa because—I don't know." Burke sits back in his recliner. "I've just never heard you say anything like that."

"Anything that honest, you mean?" I'm relaxing, even though I know I don't need to. Even though I'm here to say tough things, it's still Burke. I still like talking to him.

God, am I doing the right thing?

Burke shakes his head and grins. "You're always honest, Jamie. You tell it like it is. Just look at Fat Girl."

"Fat Girl's loud, but not necessarily honest. I need to be honest now." I scoot forward in the chair and try to get ready.

Burke's expression goes way past tense. He starts to say something, but I hold up both hands, take a deep breath, and leap into that lovely tidal wave of consequences I wrote about. "You're one of the most wonderful guys—wonderful people—I've ever met, but I—I don't feel the same way anymore. About you."

He reacts like my tidal wave hit him instead of me, bending in the middle, going still, then fighting up again to the edge of his seat. "Is it because I'm thinner?"

"Maybe. Maybe I can't handle all your changes." I scrub my hands across my cheeks. "Maybe I secretly feel like crap about myself, and I got so afraid you'd leave me that I left first. I'm not sure, Burke."

"Jamie, come on. We can get through this, baby. You can—"

"I like somebody else." Deep breath. *Deep breath.* "Heath Montel. Last week, I kissed him. It was wrong to do that before I talked to you. Chickenshit, in fact. And for doing it that way, ass-backwards and cowardly, I'm really, really sorry."

For a long time, forever, too, too, long, Burke doesn't say anything at all. He just gapes at me while the fans in his computer run and his modem lights blink and his neon clock flickers. I feel like everything I've eaten all week's about to dump right out of me, way worse than Burke's candy bar brownie incident.

He shakes his head, slowly this time. Closes his eyes. Looks like he's going to cry—absolutely ripping my heart straight out of my chest. When his eyes snap open, his expression turns blank for a second, then hard.

"I can't believe you're doing this to me now." His voice is way too quiet. "After everything I've been going through. What happened to *I love you, baby*? What happened to *I'll be right here*?"

It's tough to breathe now, but I manage. "I really don't know. If I did, I'd tell you." .

Burke shoves himself out of his chair and stalks away from me, toward his bed. "That's just bullshit. Bullshit!"

I abandon the whole I–want–to–be–your–friend part of the talk, because it's obvious he's not going to go there. From the look on his face, he might go totally into orbit if I say the wrong thing.

I guess everything I'm saying is the wrong thing to him.

Burke wheels on me. If he weren't standing across the room, if I didn't know him so well, I'd be scared of the rage on his face. "You're one selfish bitch, you know that, Jamie?"

Me, selfish? I didn't decide to change the life of everyone around me to get my gut stapled and get skinny so I could look *better! Hello? Me? Me?*

But I think about Freddie and NoNo and Fat Girl, about the choices I made to keep talking to Heath and getting closer to him.

Deep breath.

"Yes. I know I can be a selfish bitch. In lots of ways, you're right."

Burke's not sure what to do with this. He glares at me, probably to be sure I'm not making fun of him.

When he sees I'm not, he yells, "Why didn't you just call me? Write me a letter? Why did you even come here to pile all this shit on me?"

Wasn't expecting that question.

But I do at least have an answer. "Because I owed you the truth . . . and the chance to tell me what a selfish bitch I am. Because I owed you an apology."

An entire minute of silence from Burke.

He's seething.

I know he's really hurting, but this is how guys do hurting, right?

I'm an ass. I'm such an ass. God I hope I'm doing the right thing.

Outside in the hall, I hear voices. Burke's parents, talking to one of his sisters. They're probably wondering what's happening.

Burke spins around and slams his fist about two feet into the drywall over his bed. Plaster crumbles. The dull thud of the punch resonates all over my body.

That's my cue to get up and move toward the door, but Burke turns back to me so fast I stop.

"You told me the truth and apologized," he says in a spooky-quiet voice. "Now get out."

For a few long seconds I'm facing Burke, and I can see him again, the sweet-faced, round, happy guy I enjoyed for so long. The safe guy.

This new Burke, the hurt one, the angry one, maybe he won't last long. Maybe he'll charge farther and farther into his new life of being thin, his support groups, rediscovering sports, and come out the other side able to forgive me and be my friend.

Knock on the door.

"Burke?" his dad calls. "Jamie? Please open the door."

I'm only too happy to grab the knob, turn the lock, and yank the door open.

Burke's entire family is waiting in the hall, even his mom, who's showered and polished and dressed for her night shift.

Everything inside me aches. I'm losing Burke's mom and dad, too, aren't I? Even his vampire sisters. They look like twins again, hands over their mouths, worried eyes staring from me to Burke to the hole in the wall over his bed.

Burke's dad sizes up the situation in a hurry. He nods to me as I edge out of the doorway into the hall, then holds up a hand to stop M & M and Mrs. Westin from heading into the room. "I've got this," he says in a don't-argue voice. Then he strides inside Burke's room and shuts the door.

I face Mrs. Westin and the vampire sisters, and all I can say is, "I'm sorry."

It's all I can do not to close my eyes in anticipation of the big furious-female-hiss-and-claw attack.

But Mrs. Westin only sighs and pats my cheek and nods. "Be good, baby. It'll be okay." Another pat. "Things pass."

Her eyes shift to Burke's door.

My eyes fill with tears.

Mona's shaking her head, looking just as sad as her mother, and I completely don't know what to do with that.

Marlene seems to be in shock. Without warning, she launches herself forward and hugs me so tight I almost wheeze from the force. "You take care of yourself, you hear?"

Stunned, I almost forget to hug her back. When I do, I realize she's crying, and I start blubbering, and feel like a bigger idiot than ever in my whole life.

"Let us hear from you." Marlene pulls back. Before she lets me go, she wipes her face with her sleeve, and then she wipes mine.

Too much.

Too much.

I'm going to die of being-an-assness. Gotta go. Now.

"I can . . . uh . . . let myself out, okay?" Pathetic, sniveling smile, but it's the best I can do.

Mona gives me a curt nod.

After one last look at Burke's remaining ladies, I take off down the stairs and get myself out.

.   .   .

When I get to Freddie's Toyota, I swear Freddie and NoNo are completely blue from holding their breath the entire time I was in the Westin house. Freddie's black hair is plastered against her sweaty face, and NoNo's red spikes look like she's smeared them down fifty times. The heater's blasting away, and I almost choke on the holiday cinnamon–pinecone scent flowing from the air freshener hanging from Freddie's rearview mirror.

They don't speak when I slam the door, or while I'm still sobbing like a fool and fastening my seat belt.

Freddie speaks first with, "I better get out of here before he sees my car and executes me for being a traitor."

About a mile down the road, NoNo reaches across the backseat and puts her hand on my knee. "Was it hell?"

I nod.

She pats my leg.

Freddie says, "Okay, we've decided. Christmas Eve with you, Christmas Day with Burke, and Thanksgiving we're ignoring both of you and hanging out with our own families. Will that work?"

"Yeah." I sob again.

Divorce.

"This won't last," NoNo says, sounding more hopeful than I feel. "Sooner or later, we'll all be okay together."

Another mile down the road, she adds a nervous, "Right?"

Fat Girl
As Yet Untitled

JAMIE D. CARCATERRA

Let's start over.

Hi.

I'm Jamie Carcaterra. I'm about to turn eighteen. I'm a writer and an actress, even though I don't know what to call this feature anymore, and I just refused to play the role of Ursula the Sea Witch in this spring's *Little Mermaid.* It's Princess Ariel or bust, by God.

I'm a decent student, and I want to go to college even though calculus *sucks*, my ACT composite's a bit wobbly, and my advanced biology grade could be better.

I'm Freddie's and NoNo's friend, and Heath's girlfriend. I'm a daughter. I might be an activist, but I'm not sure I've found my cause. I also might be a big-ass weenie, too, but I'm working on that.

I don't have a lot of money, but I do have

a lot of plans, and a lot of dreams. One of those dreams involves Burke Westin forgiving me one day, so we can be friends, and so we don't have to share custody of Freddie and NoNo.

Oh, yeah. One other thing.

I happen to be fat.

Being fat bugs me some, but it's not my whole life, and I refuse to let anyone define me that way anymore—especially myself.

I'm about to try something new, called honesty. And, according to Freddie, "sharing." I got blown off by the National Feature Award people because they thought my manifesto about living fat in a skinny world wasn't in the public interest, that it only addressed the concerns of a small "subset of our population." When I talked to them on the telephone, they said they worried my column "supported and promoted unhealthy behavior in today's teens."

I think that's bull.

I think it's discriminatory and wrong. I think they freaked out because some fat-biased news reports put public pressure on them, and I think they need to get a clue.

My mom got a lawyer through my dad's employee assistance program, and the NFA people have granted me a hearing. Dad and I fly to New York City a few days before

Christmas. I probably won't get to stay in the competition, and even if I do, I probably won't win. There's always junior college and work study and alternative college funding. I'm looking into all that. But what the NFA did was wrong, and I refuse to let it stand.

Here's the thing.

For fat people, traveling, especially traveling by airplane, sucks. I'm scared about slogging through the airport, where the hallways look ten miles long and I know my knees and back will kill me, and I'll sweat, and maybe smell awful by the time I get where I'm going. I don't fit well in public toilets. I completely don't fit in airplane seats, and I have to use a seat-belt extender, which usually gets handed to me in some very public, embarrassing fashion. I've only flown once in my life, and the airline was horrible to my family and tried not to let us get on the plane unless we bought extra seats. We could barely afford one seat for each of us, much less two. How insane is that?

The trays don't fit over my belly. I have no room for my legs. I'm miserable the whole trip. Then once I get to New York City, there'll be a lot of walking and meeting people and having to make an impression. My clothes are pathetic. I never feel like I look good in anything. I mean, I know all girls are like that, but for me it's worse because of the weight.

Like I said, I'm scared. I'm dreading all the little things. That's part of the real, deep truth about being fat. Being scared. Being tired before battles even start. Dreading the weight of the weight.

But I can do this. I will do this.

That's all.

Thanks for listening.

CHAPTER
TWENTY

Heath's lips still taste as good as they did that first kiss. He hugs me tight, and I hug him back with all I've got. I love how his body feels against mine, I love the way he touches me, firm, but also soft and gentle, in all the right ways and places.

My dad coughs.

Oh yeah.

Real world.

Hello.

From the corner of my eye, I see Mom smack Dad's shoulder.

Beside him, NoNo taps her foot and nudges Freddie, who says, "For God's sake, hurry up. It's almost your turn."

The space around me slowly comes back into focus, from the airport shops to the polished tile floor to the long line of impatient-looking people snaking behind us.

Dad has our photo IDs and tickets ready for the security person to examine, and he's already taking off his shoes to put them in the little basket to be x-rayed.

Heath's blue eyes comfort me, cheer me up, calm me down.

We've had our talk, Heath and I, about the whole guts–to–love–a–fat–girl issue.

I don't know if he's got what it takes to tolerate the stares and digs and teasing over the long haul. He's been pretty honest that he doesn't know, either—but we both think it's totally worth the risk of finding out.

For now, it's not an issue, and I'm refusing to worry about it anymore.

"You look ready," he says as he turns me loose.

I smile at him, because he always makes me smile. "I'm ready to teach some NFA judges a thing or two about promoting public well–being."

Freddie pokes at my carry–on backpack until I let Heath go.

"You got the whole portfolio, right?" She jabs the back-pack again.

"Yes, Freddie."

NoNo's turn. She taps the pack, too. "And the signed petition?"

"Got it, NoNo."

Then I almost tear up at the thought of the petition, signed by most of the students and parents from Gar-wood High School, and a lot of people from town, too.

The petition officially protests the NFA's decision, out-lines the ways *Fat Girl Manifesto* educated my community and illuminated the struggles of a *lot* of people—who strongly dislike being referred to as a *subset of our popula-tion*.

Lots of people wrote their weight beside their signature.

Almost as good as all of that, I'm wearing a custom-sewn hip blue business suit commissioned by Burke's mom, who dropped by the send-off party at the school this morning with these clothes and two other outfits.

I should have paid more attention to those columns you wrote before Burke's surgery, Mrs. Westin said. *We do know all the good tailors, and none of our folks are going to the big city looking like a ragamuffin—or a piece of old-lady fruit.*

She even jerked me aside for half an hour and did my nails.

In bright pink.

Mr. Westin and Burke didn't come. Burke's fine, according to Mrs. Westin, but he needs more time.

A lot of time, according to M & M, who don't seem so carnivorous now that I'm not dating their brother.

At least Burke's speaking to Freddie and NoNo. Barely, but enough that they haven't killed me yet. They even cheered when Principal Edmonds presented Dad and me with two big surprises right before we left for the airport.

Apparently, Principal Edmonds and Mr. Dunstein organized another petition, as well as a collection. Dad's carrying a stern note to deliver to the airline headquarters in New York about their size policies, with over five hundred signatures—also with weights inscribed next to names. In addition, Dad and I have two seats each, courtesy of the Garwood High Parent-Teacher Association.

Heath gives me one more kiss before Dad jerks me through security with him.

As I'm stripping off my shoes and stuffing my carry-on into the bin for x-raying, I glance back at my cheerleaders. They're standing by the coffee shop, just outside the roped-off security section, waving like nutjobs.

I wave back.

For once, I don't feel tired and scared. I don't feel like I've lost before I ever start the fight.

Maybe that's honesty at work. Maybe it's good friends. Maybe it's Heath, or being more aware of my choices.

Maybe it's all of those things.

I don't know, because believe it or not, universe, I *don't* know everything—but I'm choosing to be okay with that today.

ACKNOWLEDGMENTS

Many thanks to Jen Sexton, who helped me with details to make this piece as real and accurate as possible.

I don't know what I'd do without Debbie Federici, my champion critique partner, who reads every word just after it's written and bugs me to finish what I start. Without you, my words would fall flat. Thanks also to Christine Taylor-Butler and Tara Donn, who gave me honest initial opinions—fast.

My agent, Erin Murphy, deserves points for patience and perseverance, especially when I suddenly write unexpected books.

Endless appreciation to my editor Victoria Wells-Arms, who tackled this piece in record time, with big fat enthusiasm that helped every big fat minute. I appreciate her and everyone at Bloomsbury more than I can say.

Read on for a peek at *Exposed*

Looking for love
in all the wrong
chat rooms . . .

EXPOSED

susan vaught

Chan has her life pretty well put together—good friends,
good family, good grades—but she risks losing everything
when she falls in love with a boy who isn't quite the
perfection he appears to be . . .

MONDAY, OCTOBER 13

"It's all a total fantasy," Devin Macy says as we shove our way down the crowded school hallway, making the long trek to the gym after last bell.

Devin's my best friend, and that's what she thinks about Internet relationships. She's not much on fantasy—or relationships. Not because she's not beautiful. She's completely gorgeous, like supermodel unbelievably pretty, but she's way Baptist. Which is fine. But kind of strict about stuff like fantasies and serious boyfriends.

I'm not sure I believe in real-life boyfriends, not since the whole Adam-P nightmare last year. Adam Pierpont's a quarterback, not a Baptist. He's not my friend at all anymore; he wouldn't know a fantasy if it busted him in the nose, and he might not even be human.

I squeeze my stack of books against my chest to keep them from flying everywhere and get close enough to Devin to say, "I don't want to get into anything real with a guy."

She manages to laugh at me even though fifteen people bang against us with backpacks or books in a span of less than five seconds.

"Not exactly," I add. "Well, sort of. Maybe?"

Devin laughs again and doesn't even bother looking at me as we leave one building and jam our way into the next one.

"Okay, not a flesh-and-blood boyfriend, but is it a huge crime to want a nice guy in my life without all the complications?" I elbow past a couple of sophomores near a water fountain. "Somebody I can be close to. Somebody I can talk to who'll say sweet stuff to me and be there when I need him and tell me everything about his life and his mind and his heart."

I can't help a big, huge sigh, but I so shouldn't be thinking about any of this right now. And I definitely shouldn't be thinking about it here at school in the hallway before practice, right beside Devin, who has asked me everything about why I'm thinking about finding a guy online—including whether or not I'm planning to sign up with an online dating service.

I'm not.

I promise.

Really!

Though that *would* be an idea. . . .

"I'd like it if you had a special guy again." Devin sounds a little faraway and distracted, even though she's having to talk really loud when our heads aren't right together. "It'd be nice to see you happy that way."

Her expression says the rest—that we both know I'm never going to find a boyfriend here at West Estoria High School. Even if I did find someone I liked, he wouldn't have anything to do with me. Not after the Adam-P mess.

Thinking about all of that makes us both go quiet as we walk.

Devin whips through guys like disposable tissues, so it's not like she doesn't want a guy, too, in spite of her religious beliefs. She's looking for that feeling just as hard as I am, only she doesn't have my problem or my reputation, so she has more options.

It's been a *year* for me.

It would be so nice to have somebody again. A guy I can ask anything, tell anything to, do anything with, and not have to worry, ever. Except about Mom (uptight, even though she's a Democrat). And Dad (not uptight, even when he should be). And my little sister, Lauren, bursting in on my private conversations because she can't sleep. (If Lauren were black, I'd think she was secretly Devin's sister and not mine. She's high maintenance and gorgeous, too, even though she's only eight.)

Thinking about trying online dating and maybe getting caught by somebody in my family makes my heart beat fast.

What will *he* be like when I find him?

Imagining *him* makes me tingly, and I never get to feel that way except when I'm planning how I'll talk to *him* or living in that place in my head where only *he'll* be able to take me.

So, some of it will be fantasy, yeah. But some of it will be real, too.

And we won't get serious for a long time, and it won't really be *serious* even if we do, at least not in my opinion.

I shake my head and try to focus on here, now, on real life and the next hallway and Devin. There must be two hundred things I need to be doing instead of daydreaming about online guys. Like plotting a new strategy to help my dad lose weight or figuring a better way to help my little sister get over freaking out all the time. Oh, and finding an aspirin before twirling practice because we've got to dance today, and dancing makes my back hurt, never mind my brain.

I just wish any of that seemed important.

People are still bashing against us as we make it to the last building before the gym. It's god-awful hot, and the air smells like sweat and mold.

Devin stays close, briefly changing subjects, chattering about the English paper we just got assigned and all the outlines and rough drafts we have to turn in before the final product, how we're dividing up the workload, how we're going to get our *other* work done—and I couldn't care less about that, either.

It's *him* in my head.

All *him*.

Whatever *he'll* be, whoever *he'll* be.

I know it might be a totally screwy idea, but the weird thing is, I'm not sure that bothers me. It's not like I'll ever see my soon-to-be dream guy in person no matter how bad I end up wanting to. So, I could fall in love with him, no strings, no complications, no problems. Unless I get caught, of course.

"Skank!" yells a girl I used to like. Ellis Brennan. Blond. Senior majorette. Thinks she's better than the rest of the universe.

She's banging Adam now, so I should feel sorry for her.

Ellis and her friends act like I stink as they mince past without touching me, like I'm poisonous. Add that to the couldn't-care-less list, along with the half of the school that thinks Ellis is exactly right about me.

Devin ignores the witch-monster and her minions because she's good at that, and we've both had a year of practice.

"So are you going to try this tonight?" Devin asks as we finally get out of the main school building and reach the gym door. "Finding a guy online?"

Her question welds me to the door handle, fingers on the warm metal. Two seconds flat and I'm already there in my head, *tonight*.

"It might not be such an awful idea." Devin's worry

and excitement cuts beneath the class-change clatter. "The pickings around here are way slim. Totally slim." She clutches her books and bounces up on her toes like a little kid, stretching her long, dancer legs as she waits for me to open the door. "So, how are you going to do it? If you've been thinking about it all this time, you've got to have a plan."

"No plan." I'm smiling like a total freak and sort of lying, and not getting the door open no matter how hard I try. "I'll just put myself out there and hunt around a little."

Devin grins until she's all teeth. "I'll bust you when you start scribbling love poems all over your class work."

"Yeah, well, at least I don't draw hearts. With flowers. *Shaded* flowers."

She blows me off with, "You'll have to give me all the details every step of the way, or I tell the Bear something awful, like you ate six cupcakes last night."

The Bear is Alexa Baratynsky, our twirling coach. Russian. Short. Wicked. Does *not* approve of cupcakes.

I yank at the door, and it bangs open against the outside wall. "I did not eat six cupcakes!" I grab it before it can swing back and smash me in the face. "Only two. Well, maybe three. And a half."

Devin's laughing. At almost six feet tall and totally slender and graceful, she has to be the most perfect majorette ever, no matter how many cupcakes she can stuff down her throat in one sitting. She'd never tell the Bear about our food binges, either. That would be like blas-phemy or sacrilege, or one of those other heinous-betrayal words.

"Brat!" I shout over the roar of people jamming the gym hallway as we head toward the locker room.

"I want all the dirt!" she yells back. "When are you going to start? *Tell me.*"

If I could steal a magic lamp and rub out a genie, my three wishes would be *sooo* simple—after I tried the whole infinite-wishes trick and endowed myself with wealth, brilliance, and the ability to write poetry like Emily Dickinson, of course.

Wish one: let me look like Devin and dance like her, too.

Wish two: make my dad healthy, my mom patient and understanding, and my little sister all relaxed and happy.

Wish three: find a really cute, really sweet, totally perfect guy to talk to online so I can have all the fun and absolutely *none* of the real-life hassle.

"When are you going to start?" Devin repeats, twice as loud to make sure I answer her.

"Okay, okay." I lean toward her as we stop outside the locker room door and whisper the magic word.

Tonight.

Jersey Hatch doesn't know why
his best friend hates him.

He doesn't know how to keep random words
from flying out of his mouth.

And he doesn't know why he tried to shoot his own head off.

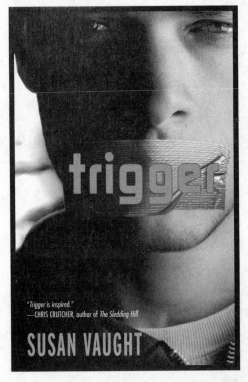

"*Trigger* is inspired."
—CHRIS CRUTCHER, author of *The Sledding Hill*

SUSAN VAUGHT

★ "Both engrossing and excruciating. . . . An original and meaningful
work that provokes thought about action, consequence,
redemption, and renewal." —*Booklist*, starred review

www.susanvaught.com
www.bloomsburyusa.com

BLOOMSBURY

CHECK OUT SOMETHING NEW, DIFFERENT, AND TOTALLY ENGROSSING FROM SUSAN VAUGHT AND J B REDMOND

A murderer shoves a prince to his "death."
An assassin legally kidnaps a terrified boy.
A ruling lord orders an atrocity so devastating it will
change the course of history.

SO BEGINS THIS EPIC FANTASY FULL OF DANGER,
ADVENTURE, ROMANCE, AND INTRIGUE!

www.susanvaught.com
www.bloomsburyusa.com

BLOOMSBURY

SUSAN VAUGHT is the highly acclaimed author of *Stormwitch*, *Trigger*, *Exposed*, the Oathbreaker saga, and a number of books for adults. She is a practicing neuropsychologist and lives with her family in Kentucky.

www.susanvaught.com